Windows of My Heart
LOVE CAN BE MESSY

MERCY

BOOK TWO

JAN REA JOHNSON

FARMHOUSE
PUBLISHING

Copyright © 2023 by Jan Johnson

www.jan-johnson.com

All rights reserved. No part of this publication may be reproduced, distributed or transmitted in any form or by any means, including photocopying, recording, or other electronic or mechanical methods, without the prior written permission of the publisher, except in the case of brief quotations embodied in critical reviews and certain other noncommercial uses permitted by copyright law

Windows of My Heart

Published 2023

Farmhouse Publication

94436 Mustonen Rd

Astoria, Oregon 97103

ISBN:979-8-9863725-5-6

E-ISBN: 979-8-9863725-4-9

This is a work of fiction. All of the characters, organizations, and events portrayed in this book are either products of the author's imagination or are used fictitiously.

Acknowledgments

This story would not have been possible without the constant advice from nurse Sidney Johnson and her coworkers who made themselves available to me to spur ideas and medical corrections. Not to mention the additions of humor along the way, input on plot ideas and fictitious patient stories.

Windows of My Heart
Book 2 of The Mercy Series
Written by Jan Rea Johnson

This is a work of fiction. All characters, organizations, and events portrayed in this book are either products of the author's imagination or are used fictitiously.

For Sidney

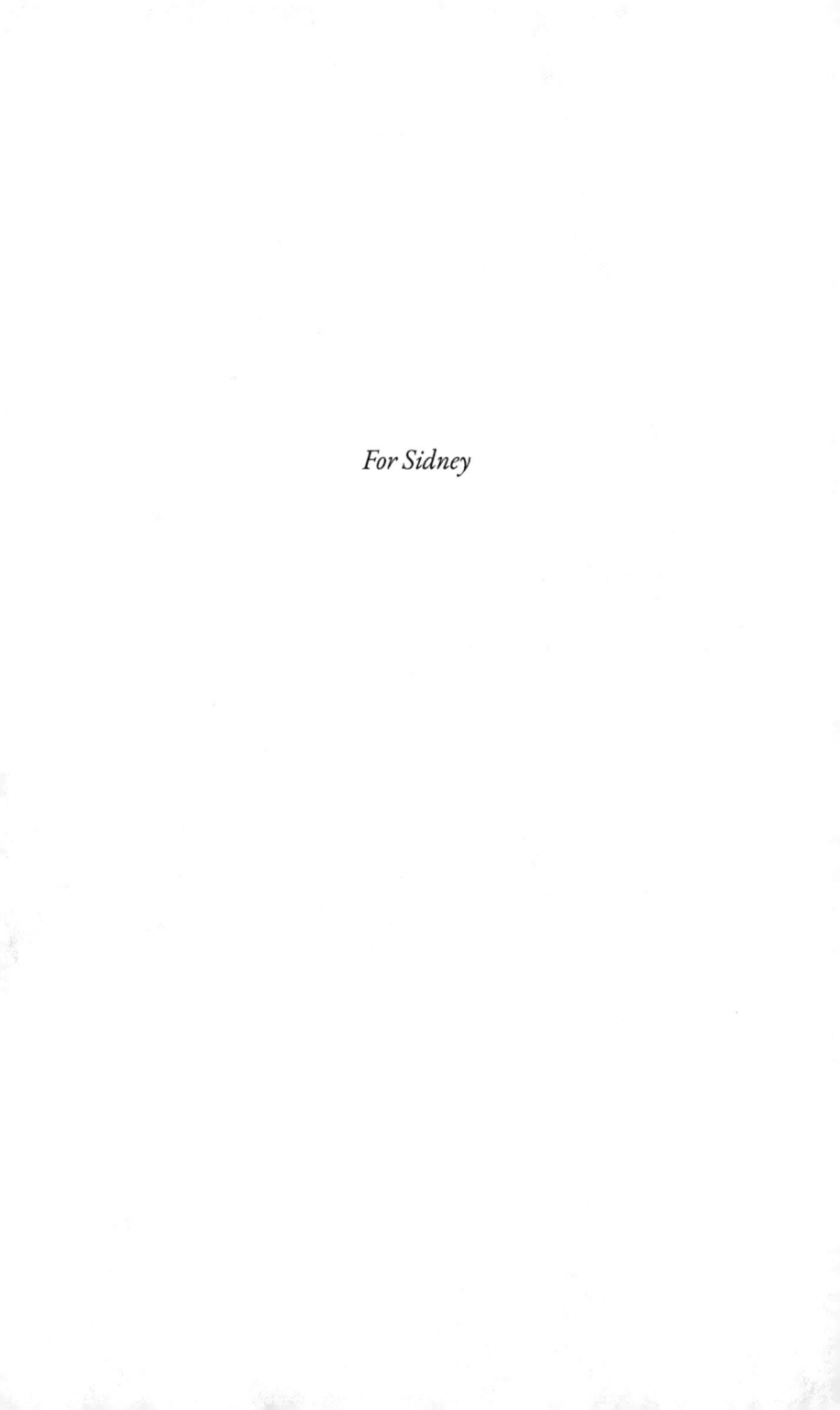

Chapter One

Tina Halverson squinted as she glanced at the bright light illuminating the operating room. A trickle of sweat slid under her scrubs. How could she let this level of anxiety choke her? This wasn't who she was. She was strong. A leader. An optimist. A fixer. Yet seeing this lifeless woman lying under the blue gown having been cut and sewn to remove all traces of cancer undid her. Her gloved hands started for the reassurance of her locket, a gift from her mom on her fifth birthday.

Maybe one day she'd be able to let go of that talisman. Let go of the need for an ever-present memory of her mom.

Today wasn't that day. Today she could only focus on the daughter she'd seen in the patient's room earlier who would live with unbearable loss if this surgery wasn't successful. A daughter like she had been.

Kaitlyn Monroe stood across from Tina, gloved hands covered in blood.

"Tina, are you okay? You look a little pale." Kaitlyn, her bestie since forever had been there when cancer had taken her mother's life.

"Yeah, I think I need to step out."

Tina peeled off her gloves and hurried out to the hall. She leaned against the wall and felt herself sliding to the floor. Her hands reached up and cradled her bent head. She willed herself to hold back the tears. Hearing footsteps, Tina glanced to see a pair of men's Nikes standing in front of her.

"Tina, give me your hands." Daniel Wright grasped her hands and pulled her up.

Tina's slack body fell into his arms.

"Rough surgery?"

She gave a slight nod.

"Just breathe." He ran his hand over her back. She gave a hiccuping breath and nodded. He moved his hands to her shoulders and looked into her eyes.

"Looks like you could use a tissue."

He grabbed one from the nurse's station. Tina took it and wiped her eyes. A deep breath escaped her lips.

"Okay. I've got this. Thanks friend." Tina gave him a faint smile.

"You sure?" Daniel asked.

She shook the tension from her shoulders and hands.

"Yep. I need to get back in there and finish up."

♥ ♥ ♥

How had things reversed? She had always been the one to help Kaitlyn through her ups and downs. Now she was the one who needed the hugs and words of encouragement, warm brownies covered with ice cream in a mug, and late-night Fixer upper reruns.

Tina threw her scrubs on the floor and stepped into the steaming shower.

"Oh mom." She sighed. "Why did you have to leave me? There were a lot more things we were supposed to be able to do together."

Tina scrubbed shampoo through her hair.

"I didn't realize how hard working in surgery would be. But mom, I can't tell you how relieved I was to tell the patient's daughter that we got all the cancer. At least there's hope for *them*."

The hot water cascaded over her, loosening her tight neck muscles, and washing the stress of the day down the drain. Still, she had a hard time shaking off the pain she knew followed some families home.

She toweled off and slipped into her leggings and tank top.

"Oh, you're home!" Kaitlyn slid the glass door to the patio shut. "Come over here. You need to look at this."

Kaitlyn patted the spot beside her on her red couch.

"Sit yourself down here. I thought you might want to relive some of the good times." She laid open a memory book over both of their legs.

Photos of her mom reached out to her; the moments as real as when they actually happened.

"Aw, look how cute you were when you were a baby."

"Yeah, wasn't I? That was when Max was three. Look how good he looked then. Healthy."

Kaitlyn flipped the page. "See, I always did like brownies."

"And you haven't changed one bit—chocolate batter all over you mouth." Tina smiled.

"Remember when we went to Cannon Beach? That had to have been spring break when we were in kindergarten. I was so excited mom and dad let you come with us!"

It had been mom's favorite place to vacation. Tina couldn't

remember how many times they had gone there, but it was the only beach she had clear memories of.

"I was so jealous that you got to wear a two-piece swimsuit. My mom had me in that one piece." Kaitlyn said.

"A little too small—look at it hiking up your butt," Tina snorted.

"Yeah, well look at your outie belly button!"

Tina bumped Kaitlyn's shoulder, then froze when Kaitlyn turned the page.

Max must have been around eight. Tina remembered how he had fallen into the tide pool. She clung to her mom's leg as Max began flailing around.

Kaitlyn glanced at her. "You okay?"

"Yeah. Just remembered that was the first day he'd had a seizure."

Her dad had rescued Max from the water. The same dad that had never rescued *her*. Not from the sadness of losing her brother. Not from the grief of losing her mom. She shook the thoughts away.

Tina turned to a photo of her snuggled on her mom's lap reading the book *I'll Love You Forever*.

"Our favorite book!" Kaitlyn began singing softly and Tina joined in.

"I'll love you forever, I'll like you for always, as long as you're with me my baby you'll be."

Tina blinked back tears.

Kaitlyn slid her arm around Tina's shoulders. "I loved her too, you know."

A knock at the door and Luke made his way in.

"Hey, you guys hungry? I brought pizza." Luke juggled the box and a grocery bag.

Tina set the album down and slid off the couch.

"Oh, hi!"

The rich aroma of pepperoni and melted cheese floated through the air.

"What's in the bag?"

Kaitlyn gave Luke a kiss. She took the bag and pulled out a bouquet of flowers. Luke set a bottle of cider and a plate of brownies on the table.

"Kaitlyn texted and said you might need a pick-me-up tonight. Hope I chose the right flowers."

If only Luke had a twin brother. His killer brown eyes, dark hair, deep voice...

Tina ran her fingers through her copper hair, pushing strands from her face.

"They're beautiful. Was it just a guess that I love freesia? And brownies?"

Tina opened the freezer door.

"I think I have some vanilla ice cream."

Kaitlyn pulled out her colorful fiestaware dishes and set them on the table. Kaitlyn and Luke hadn't talked of much else besides their upcoming wedding. How was she going to live without her best friend? She'd never be able to find a roommate who knew her through and through like Kaitlyn.

"And milk? Gotta have milk." Kaitlyn said.

"We've been looking at houses," Luke said. He took a piece of pizza, long strings of melted mozzarella connecting it to the whole. He pinched his fingers around it and separated it before he stuck it in his mouth.

"Have you found anything you like?" Tina asked. Her stomach tightened.

"Yeah, there's one a few blocks from here. It would be perfect. We could be neighbors." Luke said.

"And one day when you find the love of your life and have kids, they can play with our kids and we can have family barbecues and babysit for each other and..." Kaitlyn chimed in.

Tina held up her hand. "Woah there, sister. Slow down. There's plenty of time. My eggs haven't expired quite yet. One thing at a time. Let's get through the wedding first!"

She smiled. These guys. They were always there for her. Always had been. Always would be.

It was true. She did want the love of her life. But having kids? She would make sure that never happened. The chance of having a child with batten disease was too high.

Tina startled at the sound of her cell phone.

"Dad? What's up?" Tina held her finger up and walked into the living room.

"Yeah. Mmhm. Okay. I'll be right over."

"Sorry. It was my dad. He needs me to come over. He's having computer problems and needs a millennial to help him out. He said something about not knowing how to ex out of something—classic dinosaur."

She shook her head. "I'll catch you later." She grabbed a brownie and headed out the door.

Chapter Two

Tina pulled out of the drive, being careful to watch for the neighbor's cat. No need for an emergency vet run at this time of night. Her mother, as sweet as she was, had had a nasty habit of turning the family pets into roadkill. Gruesome, but the memory made her smile.

The setting sun cast an orange and pink glow through the clouds. Spring made her hopeful—longer days and more sunshine. She could get out in the garden and pull some weeds. Maybe put in a few red geraniums. Her mom's favorite.

She took her time driving the five miles to her dad's. It wasn't like she didn't care about him. It was just that, well, you'd think that by now he could figure out some of this computer stuff by himself. He had a master's degree for Pete's sake. He was no dummy.

After Max died, her mom and dad sold their craftsman bungalow with the large backyard and moved into a smaller, two story-house, one of those that mirrored every neighbor's. Every fourth house had been painted the same color. Theirs was cream with beige trim sandwiched between a rotation of burnt umber, puke green and canary yellow. Fortunately, theirs was near the corner, so growing up, she never had to remember which one was hers.

Having a lot of families in the neighborhood meant she always had kids to play with. With no yard to run around—she and her friends played tag in the street. But Tina never got over the homey feel of the first house with its oak moldings and stone fireplace.

The upkeep in the craftsman had been labor intensive. She guessed her mom and dad didn't have it in them to expend that much energy after Max died. And of course, when she got cancer, taking care of a yard was the last thing on their minds. This new neighborhood had a homeowners a association, so they never had to mow their yard which was the size of a postage stamp. It took longer to start the mower than to actually mow.

Tina swerved her car around the little roundabout, hoping her dad had pulled far enough into the driveway that she could fit her little teal Fiat behind it. But no, his Highlander was parked smack dab in the middle of the drive which could easily have fit her tiny Fiat had he only been considerate enough to pull all the way in. Finding nowhere to park along the street, she circled the block, hoping there'd be at least one small space she could maneuver into.

Tina saw her dad watching out the window for her as she passed. He waved his long arms as she drove by the first time. Maybe he could have gotten a clue as to why she had to keep going? She finally found a spot two blocks away. Grateful it wasn't raining she slammed her car door and made her way to his front door.

Mark Halverson never locked his door. He would rather someone just walk in and take what they wanted than to break a window or jimmy the door. She walked in where her dad, dressed in a polo shirt and cords was anxiously waiting.

"Hey Tina."

He signed a breath of relief. You'd have thought she was an ambulance there to rescue him from some great catastrophe.

"Hey back. You don't think you could have parked closer to the garage so I could have pulled in behind you?"

She redid her sloppy bun, transferring her frustration into her hands.

"Oh, yeah, I guess I could have. I wasn't thinking."

Clearly.

"Thanks for coming over, Tina. You know how I am—I think I know how to do something on that dang thing, and the next thing I know I've hit the wrong key or something and messed everything up."

He placed one arm behind his back and grasped his wrist.

"Okay. Let me take a look."

She followed him through the living room and into the study. Her dad and mom had set up a coffee table in the corner of the living room with a photo of Max, his last Lego creation, and his favorite shirt—the one with Jeff Gordon, the race car driver, carefully laid out. After her mom died, he had placed her ashes in a sea green urn and set them next to Max's which were enclosed in a wooden box with his favorite race car painted on the top. Was there ever going to be a time when the pinpricks of anxiety didn't hit her when she saw Max's shrine? Her dad just needed to move on. He probably didn't even look at them anymore— their photos were covered with dust.

"All I did was log on and try to get into my spreadsheet. I was trying to get the taxes done for the foundation. This is so frustrating!"

His hand raked his full head of red tinged hair and landed on the back of his neck.

Tina sat at the swivel chair and wiggled the mouse. The desktop had a photo of Max sitting in his wheelchair, a crooked smile on his face. *Just get this done. Don't get your panties in a bunch.*

"Where do you file your spreadsheet?" Tina asked.

"I'm not sure. I think it's in the Batten Foundation folder."

Tina clicked on the icon. A long list of files came up.

"You know you can name your files, right? Like if this is your tax sheet, you would name it Tax Sheet and the year. Then it would be easy to find." She sucked her lips in.

"Honey, can you show me how to do that again?"

He looked over her shoulder and sighed. She decided to go directly to the program and try to find the file from there.

"Watch. All you have to do is click open and it will show you what you were last working on."

She clicked and voila, there it was.

"Now, watch how I click save and give it a name. I have to tell it which file folder to go in. Maybe you should just write down all the steps here, so you'll remember."

Tina took a deep breath and handed him a notepad. She knew as soon as she got in the car, he'd be calling her again, hoping she could help him out of the next mess over the phone. Why couldn't her mom still be around to help him with this stuff? She had never wanted to fill that gap.

If Tina were smart, she'd link his computer to hers and then she could help him from her cozy house, comfy pjs, moose slippers, and a glass of wine.

Tina looked over the steps he had written and gave him a patronizing pat on the back.

"Okay, you good?"

"I think so. I'll let you know." *No doubt.* She let herself out.

A simple thank you would have been nice. But what did she expect? She couldn't remember the last time he had thanked her. Why would things be any different this time?

Chapter Three

Tina stood in the hall on her floor at Mercy Hospital, scanning the surgery board to see where she would scrub in. Dr. Philip Roberts, head of surgery, stood behind her.

"I'm going to need you to help me out with this coronary artery bypass. It's for a seventy-five-year-old woman."

"Yes, of course."

"You scheduled in here too?" Peter said.

"Yeah, I only choose surgeries with the cute docs."

Tina gave an exaggerated wink. She glanced at Dr. Roberts.

"Can you tie my gown, Peter?"

"Turn around. What have we got going on this morning?"

"Dorothy Smith had felt pains in her chest. Her boyfriend stopped by and immediately brought her in."

"Her boyfriend?" Peter raised his eyebrows as he placed his surgery cap, covered with John Deere tractors, on his head.

"What?" Tina shoulder bumped him. "You don't have to be young to have a boyfriend. Grandmas need love too, ya know."

"Just sayin'." He smirked. "And thank you so much for that

mental image, I'll never look at an old person the same way again."

Peter was like a brother to her. Peter, Daniel and Kaitlyn had started working at Mercy together. She'd been there for Peter when he'd been in his motorcycle accident.

They'd both had to learn to navigate the city. Peter had been raised on a farm and had won awards in FFA for tractor driving and pig showmanship. Riding the Max and finding great eateries were not his forte. But take him to the zoo? That was another matter. The kid could spot a well-bred zebu from a mile away. She once found him instructing toddlers about the proper way to dock a tail on a lamb at the petting zoo before the zookeepers staged an intervention.

"Okay team, let's get a move on."

Doc Roberts held his gloved hands up, keeping them sterile and ready to roll. The nurses, attending physician, and anesthetist gave him their attention. Tina stood next to the tray of shiny, sterile tools.

"Our patient came in complaining of pains in her chest, the back of her jaw and arms, classic symptoms of a heart attack. Peter, I'll need you to keep track of her blood pressure. Everyone ready?" He glanced around.

Tina sent up a little prayer and turned to Peter.

"We can't mess this up. Michael, Dorothy's boyfriend is devastated. He's going to fall apart if this doesn't turn out right."

"Oh, that must have been who was pacing the halls when I came in."

Tina had been used to patching people up after surgeries and keeping infections at bay. But this. She couldn't think of anything better. She still winced when the surgeon made the first incision but seeing the intricacies and perfection of the organs always amazed her. She was constantly in awe of what the Creator of the Universe had designed.

Doc Roberts looked at her.

"Tina, you ready?" His hazel eyes locked with hers.

"Yes sir." She turned her eyes to the instrument tray.

"Okay, hand me the scalpel."

Tina grimaced as he made the first incision.

"You okay?" Peter said.

"Yeah, it's just that it's hard not to feel it. Every incision makes me wince."

They watched Dr. Roberts deftly make his way through the first layers, then she handed him the small hand saw to cut through the sternum. She checked the monitor to make sure Dorothy's heart rate was okay, then handed Dr. Roberts the retractors.

"It's so amazing to have a window on a beating heart," Tina said.

She watched it pulsing as she held the suction in place. She was in awe of this heart that held life. So much was wrapped up in this one little organ. Not only was it key to keeping a person alive but held love, the necessary ingredient to make one whole. She watched Dr. Roberts expertly proceed to repair that vital organ.

···

"Are you going hiking with us this weekend? Daniel wanted to go on the Marquam Nature Trail," Peter said.

He carefully pulled off his gloves by first rolling down the cuff an inch and pulling it off, enclosing the exposed side. He placed the used glove in his remaining gloved hand. Next, he slipped two fingers under the other glove and pulled it over, removing the glove with the other one tucked inside and tossed it in the garbage.

"Just you and Daniel? And why didn't I get the memo before this?" Tina glanced over her shoulder at him as she scrubbed her hands. "You guys don't love me anymore?"

Peter shrugged, pulled back and held his hands out in his don't-blame-me look.

"Hmm—Kaitlyn was supposed to tell you." Peter said. "She's been so wrapped up in her fiancé she probably forgot. Anyway, Saturday at ten. Meeting at the base of the trail."

Tina made a concerted effort to shrug it off. She shouldn't get upset about a little thing like this. It wasn't like they intentionally left her out. They were all best friends, for pity's sake. What was wrong with her?

♥ ♥ ♥

Tina pulled back the curtains and peeked out her kitchen window as she poured grounds into her coffee pot. It was going to be a beautiful day for a hike. She loved her work schedule— three twelve-hour days and four days off. A hike would rejuvenate her. She placed some bacon in a pan and scrambled some eggs— two servings. Kaitlyn should be up soon. Maybe Tina could fit in a run before the hike. It was still early.

She put a lid on the bacon and cut up some strawberries. Her phone pinged a reminder. She had to stop by her dad's foundation at nine and drop off some papers for him. So much for the run.

Kaitlyn's footsteps plodded down the stairs dressed in her elephant pajamas.

"Well good morning." Tina fingered Kaitlyn's hair. "How do you get your hair to stay so curly? Perfect ringlets."

Kaitlyn tossed her head to accentuate her curls.

"Just lucky, I guess. Mmm—you made breakfast? For me, I hope."

"Of course." Tina dished up the eggs and bacon onto a yellow plate. "Does Luke cook? Is he going to make you breakfast?"

"You might have to give him lessons. Or, I'll just have to make my way over here to be spoiled."

She took a bite.

"We're supposed to be at the trail by ten. I was going to go for a run but remembered I have to stop by my dad's foundation." Tina frowned.

"Why do you always get grumpy about stopping by there?" Kaitlyn asked.

"I don't know. I just don't want to be a part of it. It's his and my mom's thing and I guess I can't ever wrap myself up in it with the same passion as dad has."

"Maybe you just don't want to be reminded about your brother dying," Kaitlyn said.

"Maybe." Tina grabbed a tangerine from the dish and started ripping the rind off, letting the peelings fall haphazardly on her plate. "I don't know."

♥ ♥ ♥

It was a thirty-minute drive to her dad's office. Forty if there was traffic. Luckily, it was Saturday and people were sleeping in. She pulled onto Hwy 217 south and headed to Lake Oswego. Taking the exit into a commercial area, she smiled at landscaped apple and peach trees in full bloom—pinks and whites. Petals were beginning to drift down like snow. Azaleas were starting to show their colors- bright pinks and peach bordered sidewalks. Tina imagined how she would paint that. Splashes of watercolor on the page.

Tina took the overpass and pulled into Trader Joe's. She picked up some organic apples and granola bars for the hike. Maybe she was just making an excuse to drag her feet. Why was it that she was so averse to helping her dad with the foundation? Everyone liked and looked up to him. "You're so lucky to have a dad like him. He's so passionate and generous," they'd say. She wished she could see him that way. The Batten Foundation was doing well—really well. And it made her dad happy and feel useful-—like he was making a difference in the world. Wasn't that the ultimate goal in life? She felt like she was doing that with her nursing. She didn't need to join his endeavor to feel worthy. Did she?

Tina parked her car and grabbed the file folder. The Batten Foundation – *Finding the Cure* was written on the plate glass window. A picture of a young boy, based on her brother Max, was etched below it. She pushed open the glass door and entered.

"Hey Tina," Spencer said.

The receptionist wore a headset and looked up from jotting notes on a pad.

"Hey back! Is my dad in?"

"Yeah, he's in his office. Good to see you!" He pointed his chin in that direction.

Tina walked down the hall. The walls were covered with posters— Donate Now, Find a Cure. Join us in the Fight. Join the Fun Run! Smiling kids. Hopeful looks on parents' faces.

Tina reached her dad's office. A tall, handsome guy wearing cargo pants and a company t-shirt stood in the doorway. Nate

Bronson. She stopped short. No sense going in when her dad and his right-hand man were in a discussion.

"...about the new findings of the research. They're really getting close to a cure."

That was Nate with his deep voice. It was good her dad had hired him. He was an expert for medical research, there was no doubt about that. Batten disease was terrible, and not well known. And having a good researcher on hand was imperative if there was ever a chance to save families from the grief hers had gone through.

"How soon do you think it will be before we can give everyone the good news?"

"It's close, but it will still take clinical trials which may take a year or two." Her dad sighed.

"Nate, you're doing a fine job. I am so grateful to have you on the team. Keep up the momentum!"

Nate nodded and turned, bumping into Tina. Her folder flew to the floor scattering papers everywhere.

"Oh, I didn't see you," Nate said and walked off.

Jerk. He couldn't help me pick up this mess? He may be a brainiac but geesh, a little lacking in social skills.

"Is that you, Tina?"

"It's me, dad."

Tina frowned and straightened the pile before putting it back in the folder.

"Well come on in."

Did he not just see what happened? "How are ya?"

"Okay, I guess. Here's your folder—I went through and edited the documents. Hopefully they're in the right order."

"Just set them on the desk. Isn't Nate the best? You heard him say he's close to a cure, right? Do you know what that would mean..."

"Gotta go," Tina interrupted. "I'm meeting the guys at the park for a hike."

She walked out before he could lure her into any other projects.

♥ ♥ ♥

Tina got into her car, put her head on the steering wheel and sighed. *Lord, you gotta help me. I do not know why I get so darn frustrated when I'm around my dad. He certainly has all the time in the world for Nate.* She lifted her open hands, visualizing releasing her dad to Him. She pressed start and backed out of the parking spot.

Traffic was light and she reached her destination in no time. She turned off on Marquam Road and pulled into the park. Daniel's pickup was parked next to Kaitlyn's Prius. They stood next to their cars deep in conversation. She eased into the spot next to Daniel's.

"Hey, I thought you'd never make it. The sun's going to go down before we even get started!" Daniel said.

Tina punched him in the arm. "It's not even noon, you goon." She laughed.

Kaitlyn grabbed Luke's hand, gave him a quick kiss, and started for the trail. Miya, Daniel's girlfriend linked arms with him and followed, her head barely reaching Daniel's shoulder. Peter glanced at Tina.

"Well? I guess it's just you and me babe."

He grabbed her pinky with his and they trailed after.

"Aren't they cute? All lovey- dovey and all. We're the only ones left, ya know," Tina said.

Peter nodded. "I'm sure there will be someone wonderful

sooner or later. I mean—you and me? We could make quite a team." He gave an exaggerated wink.

"Ah, yeah. Maybe not." Tina unlinked pinkies.

Tina breathed in the fresh scent of the giant hemlocks and firs. A hike always restored her soul. Small bright green buds were forming on the ends of the branches. Trilliums were in bloom; their three white petals reminded her of happy faces. Ferns and sorrel lined the path. Blue jays and nut finches sang, filling the woods with chatter.

They hiked over the wooden planked bridge and further up the trail.

"We need to get online and pick out bridesmaid dresses," Kaitlyn said, breaking the silence. She had turned to face the others.

"Can you just pick a color and let us choose our own dresses?" Miya said. "It's always hard to come to a style consensus."

"That would be fine with me," Tina said, "if it's okay with you, Kaitlyn."

Kaitlyn stopped and put her index finger on her cheek and looked up through the tall trees.

"Yeah, I guess that would be all right. I'm just getting so excited. Only six more months!" She did a happy dance, and a squeal escaped her lips.

Luke put his arm around her and grinned.

"I'll make it easy on you guys—dark grey suit with pink shirts and polka dot ties."

Kaitlyn pulled away with a look of mock horror.

"You wouldn't!"

Daniel laughed. "Yeah, I can see it now. The girls can wear polka dot swing dresses."

"And little accordion pleat bows in their hair," Peter said.

"That would be cool—and black dance shoes? I'm loving it," Miya said.

"And we could get those guys, what's their group's name? That played at the hospital banquet?" Dan said.

"Oh, yeah, the Bent Shingles. The ones made up of staff at Mercy. Good choice!" Miya said. Her dark eyes sparkled.

Kaitlyn crossed her arms and stomped up the trail. They laughed. She put her hands on her hips, turned and glared at them. Daniel laughed.

"We're just joshing you. You know you love us. "

"I do like the Bent Shingles. I might ask them to play," Kaitlyn conceded.

They trudged to the trail's end at the top of the hill. It opened up to a splendid view of Mt. Hood and the city below. The towering buildings of Mercy Hospital stood out boldly. Tina always felt good surrounded by these friends. Maybe they were enough. She didn't need a guy in her life. She grabbed Kaitlyn's hands, twirled, and fell down laughing.

Chapter Four

Kaitlyn's little terrier Bentley looked at Tina with pleading eyes, his whole-body wagging, expecting to go for a run with her. After all, she was putting on her running shoes.

"Sorry, little buddy. You've got to stay here. Your legs are too small to keep up with me."

She stepped outside. A soft breeze blew red tendrils from her face. It was a little cool, but perfect for short sleeves. Her run would warm her up.

She jogged past Mrs. Wilson's house. Her hydrangeas were budding blue and purple. Kaitlyn thought they were old lady flowers, but Tina liked them—you could cut and dry them. Their individual flower petals were fun to press, too. You could make cards or bookmarks. So many possibilities. She should stop by and check on Mrs. Wilson. See if she needed anything. It appeared she lived alone. Tina seldom saw other cars there or anyone that appeared to have been her husband.

Children's laughter caught her attention as she rounded the corner by the park. A boy of about six was pushing a girl with curly red hair. His sister, maybe? A memory of Max pushing her on a swing in this same park. She had loved her big brother. He was fun and caring. He never acted like she was a bother.

When did things switch? When did she become his big sister? It must have been around when she was seven or eight and he was about ten. That's when he had moved from being mobile to a wheelchair. His muscles had deteriorated to where he couldn't walk, and his neck wasn't strong enough to hold his head up. His vision had failed.

Looking back, her mom must have been exhausted. Tina had tried to fill in the gaps to help her out. Tina had held Max's books close to his eyes. She had helped him dress, slipping his head through his shirt, then carefully maneuvering one hand through a sleeve and then another. Sometimes one arm would get stuck and instead of getting frustrated, they would get the giggles, trying to stop. One would take a breath and then the other would burst out laughing again.

She could always make him laugh by singing silly songs or doing crazy dances—anything to cheer him up. If he were particularly down, she'd turn on the TV to a race car channel. Engrossed, he'd forget about his disabilities.

She had to admit she missed his sweet spirit. She missed him more than she would like to admit. And maybe it wasn't just him as a brother. More like the anguish of missing out on the big brother she should have had. One that would have watched out for her, protected her. Maybe even found a boyfriend for her. Someone he could tease her about. Or have been there with her to watch their mom go through chemo.

Tina's running shoes hit the sidewalk in a measured cadence. Sweat and tears stung her eyes as she rounded the corner back to her house. She leaned over, her hands braced on her knees. Her chest was heavy, and her cheeks wet. She shook her head and wiped the tears with the palms of her hands. Kaitlyn didn't need to see her cry. Not now, when she was so happy about her wedding. She paced back and forth several times to walk it off.

When Tina opened the door, she breathed in the tantalizing fragrance of fresh waffles and bacon.

"Strawberries? You've got enough for me in there, right?" Tina put on pleading eyes.

"Who do you think I am? Delores? 'Food is only for patients, not for stupid nurses.'"

Kaitlyn squared up her shoulders and puffed out her chest in her best impression of their former terrorizing charge nurse. She laughed.

"Of course, I do!"

Tina smiled and ran upstairs to take a shower and change. When she returned, plates were set out and beautifully displayed with whip cream, strawberries, and chocolate syrup drizzled over the waffles. Kaitlyn had even cut some Gerbera daisies, Tina's favorite, and put them in a vase.

"Okay, mighty wedding consultant," Kaitlyn said, "You have to help me get all these wedding details in order. I am totally overwhelmed with all this!" She spread out her hands.

"Oh, I see... the waffles were a bribe. " Tina laughed. "Of course. What have you figured out already?"

"Should I go with the polka dots ties, do ya think?" Kaitlyn's lips curved in a half smile.

"It would be kinda cute. But what do you want your look to be? Really formal? Or add some unique flavor?"

"Some formal. Some unique, I guess," Kaitlyn said. She took a bite of her waffle.

"What if we all wear the themed scrubs your mom makes for us— what should the theme be?" Tina said.

Kaitlyn playfully punched her arm.

"Okay, let's get serious. Have you tried on wedding dresses yet?"

Mock horror crossed Kaitlyn's face. "Why in the world would I go dress shopping without you?"

"I don't know. You've been gone so much."

Tina swirled her waffle bite in the syrup.

"Grab a piece of paper and let's start a list."

Kaitlyn wrote *Wedding Plans* across the top.

"Date?" Tina asked.

"Thanksgiving. Then we'll always have time off to celebrate our anniversary."

"Place?"

"My church with Pastor Mike."

"Groomsmen and bridesmaids?"

"You, of course. And Maggie. And Miya. And let's see, for groomsmen? Daniel and Peter. And Luke will want his brother Ryan," Kaitlyn said.

"Next, invitations."

"You. You're going to design them for me. You're such a talented artist."

"Yeah, I could manage that," Tina said.

She had always loved drawing and painting, and people praised her work.

"Flowers? Do you want to visit that lady with the flower stand that Luke talks about? You know, the one he bikes by?"

"Oh, yeah. That would be good."

"Photographer?"

"We can ask everybody to take photos on their phones and give them to us. I don't want to spend a lot on that."

Tina glanced up. "I guess that's about it. Wedding planning wrapped up with a red bow."

Kaitlyn got up and wrapped her arms around her.

"I don't know what I'd do without you. You're so perfect at putting everything in order and making life simple."

"That's me. The fix-it gal."

Tina wished everything were that simple. Why couldn't she put her feelings about her dad in a nice tidy list and be able to fix it? Maybe some things were impossible.

Tina went upstairs to her workroom and searched through craft papers. What should she use for Kaitlyn's invites? She said she wanted a mix of formal and unique.

Tina decided on watercolors. She picked up a cup and filled it with water. Pulling out a broad brush, she dipped it and created broad strokes across the sheet. Then she squirted small amounts of watercolors from tubes into her palette. She held the brush against her chin and her eyes roamed to the ceiling. She suddenly nodded. "Got it!"

Filling her brush with red, she swiped across the top of the page. She dabbed some yellow and swirled it across the top, forming a sunset. Next, some purples and touch of blue to create a ridge with a trail. At the base of the trail, she dotted white and yellows with green stems for wildflowers. Once it had dried, she chose grey to paint a boulder against which she sketched in two bicycles. Tina stretched and stood. She'd wait until it dried to pencil in Luke on his knee, presenting Kaitlyn with her ring.

It had taken a botched relationship to finally bring Kaitlyn to the perfect match with Luke. Was there hope for Tina? She hadn't even gone on a date. How could she be twenty-seven and not gone on a date? Something must be drastically wrong. You'd think there'd be some guy who absolutely adored red curly hair and green eyes. Tina had considered standing on a street corner with a sign, "Single, will bake for love." Or maybe an ad in the local paper, "Red hair, green eyes, nurse, personality like you wouldn't believe, can bake brownies. Only serious offers need apply." She sighed. Bentley looked up from laying at her feet and wagged his tail.

"Come here, boy."

She ran her hands through his wiry hair and scratched his ears. Tina's eyes flicked to the door as she heard it close as she watched Kaitlyn leave.

"It's going to be pretty quiet around here when Kaitlyn gets married."

Chapter Five

Nate pulled up to the parking lot of the Batten Disease Foundation and parked his silver Lamborghini, careful to choose a spot away from other cars, and trees that would drop leaves or pollen on the shiny exterior.

He was anxious to get to work on a cure for CLN3. Being a researcher was what he was meant to be. He remembered when he was small, maybe six, and had found a dead bird. It hadn't been enough that it was dead. He had to investigate, not satisfied until he found out the reason it had died. He couldn't remember a time when he hadn't wanted to find out how everything worked. It was never enough to find an easy answer. He wanted to dig deep. He was at his best when he was pushing the boundaries of human scientific knowledge.

When Mark Halverson had invited Nate to join the team, he jumped at the chance. Only one in one million people had batten disease. This was a challenge he could dive into. Some guys had sports. He had research.

"Hey Nate," Spencer said. He looked up from his computer. "How was your weekend?"

"Okay. The usual. I went on a ten-mile run and watched some documentaries. You?"

"Went to a concert with my wife. A much-needed date night."

Nate nodded and headed to his desk. Having a wife was something he couldn't foresee happening. It was rare for him to even have a date, yet alone have a lasting relationship. It wasn't that he never thought about girls. He did. A lot. But...

Nate opened a large file folder on his desk. He preferred to print things off rather than read on his screen all day. He sat back in his comfortable padded office chair and flipped through the pages. He was particularly intrigued with the studies on small molecule therapy. It involved the patient's own cells to assess the restoration of abnormal proteins. Nate had begun the process of studying children with batten— families who were passionate about helping find a cure. He was sure, given enough time, he could be one of the leading researchers to end this terrible disease. He tried hard to distance himself from watching the lives of these children and hearing their stories so he could focus on the cure. But then again, seeing them made him want to work harder. No one should have to endure this curse. He couldn't imagine how hard it must have been for Mark and Tina.

"Nate," Mark said as he knocked on the doorframe. "Do you have a minute?"

Not really. I hate interruptions. It throws my thought process off.

"Sure. What's up?" Nate willed himself not to look annoyed.

"I've been thinking of asking Tina to come in and volunteer on her days off. Is there anything you would need her to do?"

Nate looked at the ceiling. "Can't really think of anything. What I'm doing has to be done by me."

"Okay, just thought I'd ask."

Nate's pulse quickened. About that. Thinking about girls. Especially about that red, curly-haired one. He knew he should have helped her pick up the papers when he bumped into her the other day, but he was so flustered by her that he thought it would be better to just keep walking. Stupid. He shook his head and forced himself to delve back into his work.

Monday evenings Nate visited his mom. It had been this way since he graduated high school. Nate pulled into the Chinese restaurant and picked up his order of take-out.

He always felt uncomfortable driving up in his Lamborghini. The trailer court she lived in wasn't one to win an award. Her trailer was falling apart—one side was dented, as if something had run into it. Peeling duct tape was holding the window in place. One corner of the awning sagged; the metal support was rusted out. A carpet of trash surrounded overfilled cans.

When Nate had been in middle school, he and Loretta had moved into a trailer. Despite the decline of their new living conditions, moving was the best thing that had happened to them. If his dad had stuck around, Nate was sure it would lead to a murder conviction. He often fantasized strangling Alvin or shooting him in the back.

His dad, the man who was supposed to love him, wouldn't be home five minutes before he started finding fault. It didn't matter how Nate had tried to please him by picking up his toys or curbing the appropriate rat-a-tat sounds of his GI Joes or roar of the engines of his toy cars. Nate saw the quaking of his mom's hands and quivering lips as Alvin called him worthless, kicking him in the stomach, or locking him in the closet.

He had once locked Nate outside overnight to "teach him a lesson". There was the time when he was taking a bath and his dad had gotten angry because he had spilled some water on the floor. His rough hands had dunked Nate's head under water until he was sure he would drown. When Nate came up spluttering, Alvin sneered, ugly laughter filled the room.

At school, Nate would make sure his sweatshirt sleeves were pulled down to cover the cigarette burns his father had inflicted on him. Once, when he had to dress down for P.E., his teacher had called him aside, asking how he had gotten the bruise on his wrist. Nate had looked down, biting his lower lip, taking a deep breath.

"If you tell, you'll get sent away forever and you'll never see your mom again."

His father's threat echoed in his mind, clouding all rational thought. What if they did send him to foster care. Who would be there for his mom?

♥ ♥ ♥

Nate pulled into the cement driveway and parked under the corrugated tin roof. Parking in the street was a risk. Someone was sure to mess with his car. Mitzy, his mom's Pekinese was barking enough to raise the dead. He grabbed the bag of Chinese and opened the front door.

"Mitzy, be quiet. It's just Nate," Loretta said.

She picked her up and started petting the dog's smooth, groomed hair.

"You're okay. Just settle down."

The rhinestone dog collar sparkled in the light, contrasting with his mom's ruffled camp shirt and pajama pants.

"Hey mom." Nate pecked her cheek and went inside. He set the bag on the kitchen counter and took out a couple of chipped plates and mismatched silverware.

"Smells good. Sweet n sour chicken? There's some iced tea in the fridge. Or some beer. Help yourself."

She coughed and took a drag on her cigarette.

Nate sat on the cracked vinyl chair. Maybe he should bring some duct tape next time. The peeling wallpaper on the kitchen walls— brown and gold images of teapots and cups, chickens sitting in baskets and plates of cheese wedges held years of stains from cigarette smoke. It matched the brown and gold flecked shag carpet. He remembered how excited his mom was when Nate had gifted her with a gold recliner for Mother's Day, before they had to move. He had saved for months, turning in his dad's beer cans.

He poured a glass of iced tea and dished up rice and chow mein. His mom picked out pieces of chicken and fed them to Mitzy who was sitting on her lap.

Nathan made a point of putting blinders on when he came to visit. Otherwise, he would find himself criticizing everything. He chose to love his mom for who she was. She would never stop chain smoking. She was satisfied with her trailer and old furniture and surroundings.

If he had offered to buy her a new house and fill it with the best furnishings, she wouldn't be happy. He knew that. Somehow, she was satisfied with the RCA boxed big screen TV. She'd gotten it at a garage sale in the '90's and spent her time watching old reruns of Golden Girls and Wheel of Fortune. Come to think of it, Wheel of Fortune was probably the most educational show she ever watched.

"How have you been feeling, mom?"

Nate looked at the bags under her eyes. He wondered if his Monday dinners were the only food she ate all week. She couldn't have weighed more than a loaf of bread. Her button-down camp shirt hung on her frame like the clothes on a scarecrow.

She coughed. "I'm okay. My arthritis is bothering me. But that's nothing new."

"When's the last time you went in for a checkup?"

"I don't need no doctor to tell me nothing. I ain't got no insurance. I'm fine." She coughed again.

"You still have two more years to qualify for Medicaid?"

"I guess. How are you? Enough of this talk."

She took a bite of chicken and fed a bite to Mitzy who licked the sweet and sour sauce from her fingers.

"I'm fine. Still working on a cure for batten disease. We get closer every day, but it's not soon enough for my taste."

Loretta put her hand on Nate's.

"I'm so proud of you son. Choosing to help people. I wisht your dad could have recognized the gold he had in you."

Nate wished the same. He couldn't ever recall when his dad had praised him or given him credit for anything. He got up and cleared the dishes. Washed and dried them.

"Watch a little TV with me before you go?" Loretta asked.

"Sure." Nate was ready to leave this smoke-filled place but looked for somewhere to sit that didn't have dog hair. He chose the vinyl lounge and pulled out the leg rest. He put his hands behind his head and settled in for a game of Jeopardy.

"What is the only country that borders both the Caspian Sea and the Persian Gulf?"

"Iran!" Loretta called out. Luke looked at her. How would she know that?

"The beach version of this has been an Olympic sport since 1996."

"Volleyball!" Nate said.

He fist pumped. At least he got one right. He looked at his watch and slid out of the chair.

"Hate to cut this short, mom, but I gotta go to work tomorrow." He walked over and kissed her cheek. She held her hand out to him.

"I love you, son. You're a good boy."

"I love you too, mom."

Chapter Six

Tina and Daniel stood in the hospital room of Salman and Zahid. Fifteen-year-old Salman was the picture of health, while Zahid kept wincing, holding his side. Salman looked at Zahid. His dark eyebrows formed into a vee over his black eyes.

"It won't be long now. Hold on a bit longer," Salman said.

"We'll get him fixed up before you know it. How are you feeling, Salman? This is a brave and noble thing you are doing for your little brother," Daniel said.

"I'm fine. I would do anything for my brother. I just want him to get better." His eyes held a pleading look.

"Not everyone is ready to give up a kidney, even for a brother. " Tina said. "I'm going to take your vitals and we'll get you two into surgery."

Daniel moved towards Zahid's bed and adjusted the blood pressure cuff.

"You're not looking too good, pal. Let's get you fixed up and ready to go. Dr. Roberts is the best and we'll have you back playing basketball in no time."

Zahid gave a faint nod.

Transport wheeled them to the operating room with Daniel and Tina following.

"Would you give a kidney for a family member?" Daniel asked.

"I only have my dad. Maybe. I don't know. I guess," Tina said.

She wondered if she would have donated something to her brother if it could have cured him. She began to scrub in, rubbing the soap a little too vigorously. It was as if she could wash away all thoughts of Max.

"You'd give one to me, though, right?"

Tina side-eyed him. "Maybe to Kaitlyn if she needed it. I'm not sure I'd want to always know you had one of my body parts in you."

"Some friend you are."

"I'm there for you. Mostly." Tina laughed.

♥ ♥ ♥

Tina rolled her shoulders, exhausted. The surgery had gone well, but it was taxing, keeping two humans on machines and monitoring every move. Her eyes lit up as she walked into the break room. It was full of treats for Nurse's Appreciation Week. Tina couldn't decide what to fill her plate with—mini cupcakes, scones, apple fritters, chocolate candies or blueberry pie.

"This is when it's worth being a nurse," Kaitlyn said.

"I'm feeling appreciated, that's for sure."

Tina decided on a blueberry scone. And a chocolate muffin. Then took some celery and carrots to balance it out.

"Did I tell you my dad called last night and wants me to come volunteer at the foundation on a regular basis?" Tina said.

"What did you tell him?"

"I said I'd think about it. I'm not sure I want to give up a day a week."

"What does he want you to do?" Kaitlyn asked. She filled her cup with coffee and breathed in the nutty aroma.

"I'm not sure. Filing maybe. Whatever." Tina shrugged her shoulders and took a bite of her scone.

"It might be good dad time," Kaitlyn ventured.

Tina looked at her pointedly. "The surgery went well," Tina said, changing the subject. "Those two boys were troopers."

"Yeah, their dad's face could have split apart with that wide grin. They must be good parents to have raised kids like that."

"I know, right?"

"I think you should volunteer," Kaitlyn said.

She snuck her hand out and grabbed the muffin off Tina's plate.

"Where?" Kaitlyn watched Tina as she took a bite of her scone, a mischievous grin playing on her lips.

"With your dad, silly."

"Hey! That's mine!"

She grabbed what was left of her muffin, crumbs exploding onto the table. Kaitlyn started giggling and pulled off some paper towels to wipe the crumbs.

"It would be good for you," she said. "I'm sure there is plenty for you to do. Non profits always need volunteers. You, of all people, would be an encouragement to siblings with batten disease."

Tina took a bite of her scone and stared vacantly. Was she ready to spend dedicated time with her dad? What was it that made her freeze every time she thought about it? It was a great foundation and many families were being helped and supported. It would have made all the difference if her parents had had the type of support these families have.

Kaitlyn took the scone out of Tina's limp hand. "Breathe. Out, two, three, four. In, two, three, four."

Kaitlyn made a square in the air for each number.

"It's gonna be okay."

Tina steered her little Fiat into the parking lot, looking for the farthest space possible. She liked to get some exercise in, even if it was just a few extra steps to her destination. She pulled in next to a silver Lamborghini. The teal of her car created a nice color contrast to the silver. She'd remember that pairing to use on her next painting.

She straightened her deep green blouse over her jeans, squared her shoulders and forced a smile. That's what Kaitlyn would do when facing an uncomfortable situation. If it worked for Kaitlyn, it could certainly work for her.

Spencer greeted her with a wave as she walked in the door. He was a perfect fit for a receptionist—always had a ready smile surrounded by a full brown beard, and his close shaved hair and comb over made her look twice.

"Hi Spencer. New tattoo?"

"Hey Tina. Yeah. Got my baby girl's name with a rose. You like it?"

Tina examined it. "Yep, she's gonna love it when she's old enough to know what it is." *Lucky girl to have a dad who shows his love.*

"Is my dad in his office?"

Spencer nodded. Tina forced a smile and walked down the hall. She peeked through Mark's open door.

"Hey dad."

"Tina. So, you made time for your old man, did you? Glad you're here. We've got so much to do and so few people to do it."

He motioned to the lounge chair across from his desk.

"What do you have in mind for me?" Tina sat stiffly and tightened her lips.

"Could you help with the mailing today? Stuff envelopes? Get them to the post office?"

"Sure. Just head me in the right direction."

Mark's phone rang. He held it to his ear and nodded towards the work room.

Spencer was putting newsletters through the folding machine. Piles of envelopes sat in boxes with sheets of address labels beside them. Tina started peeling them off and placing them on the envelopes. Spencer placed a stack of letters on the table beside her. She picked one up. A photo of a family and daughter with batten disease. She sat in a wheelchair, her head titled to one side, a crooked smile and eyes clouded. A balloon was tied to her arm rest. The rest of the family had a cheery smile. Make that a brave smile. She knew what it was like. You could try to smile, but there was always a cloud over you. Always a monkey on your back weighing you down.

"It's hard, isn't it?" Spencer said. "I can't really imagine. If I found out my baby girl had that..." Tina shook her head.

"Yeah, but you get through it." *Somehow.*

Nate walked in and filled a cup of coffee. Tina could feel his eyes on her. She looked up and he quickly glanced away. He walked out without a word.

"Does he ever talk to anyone?" Tina asked.

"Yeah, sometimes. He's focused. But he's a good guy."

"He seems to be my dad's golden boy," she said. She put another label on an envelope.

"Probably because he's hoping Nate's the key to a cure. And finding that cure propels Nate."

Tina heard a family enter the counseling room next door to the work room. The walls really needed to be sound proofed because she could hear every word of their conversation. She would talk to her dad about fixing that.

The conversation began with cheerful introductions, but quickly moved on to pain points.

"Finding out about his condition was devastating—knowing your child is going to die."

That must be the dad.

"To find out he will be losing his eyesight, losing his faculties and losing muscle control. A parent wants to do anything they can to try to save them. When you know their days are numbered you want to appreciate every day—make every moment count."

A woman's voice.

Tina set the envelopes in a stack and walked out, drawn to the counseling room. She peeked her head into the open door and raised her eyebrows. A picture window looked out on a manicured lawn edged with pink blooming camellias and red geraniums. The parents were seated on soft upholstered chairs, a coffee table in between, an open box of tissues sitting on it. Amanda, the counselor sat with her legs crossed, her ankles showing under her cropped skinny jeans.

"Is it okay if I join you?"

"Yes of course."

Amanda gathered her long jet-black hair in her hand and twisted it into a rope. She reached back and tied it into a knot. She introduced Tina to the couple and motioned to a chair.

"Brenda, Tom. Tina is our director's daughter. She was raised with her older brother who had batten ."

"Really? What was that like for you, as a sibling?" Tom asked.

What was that like? She had adored her big brother. But she had gotten lost in the crowd. She remembered hiding under the table, arms wrapped around her knees, listening to her parents fight about what direction to take with him. She heard her dad stomp out of the house and her mom throw her coffee cup on the floor and run to her room. Tina had crawled out from under the table, picked up the broken pieces and mopped the floor. She had stood outside of her mom's bedroom, listening to her cry, and had wanted to crawl into bed with her and hold her hand. Instead, she found Max and cuddled with him.

"There were some hard times," Tina said. "How are your other children reacting?"

"They seem to be doing alright. Brian, the oldest, gets a little moody sometimes. But maybe that's because he's a middle schooler," Brenda said.

"I would suggest you make sure you give each of your children the attention they need. It's easy to get wrapped up in the cares of your son, but a pat on the back, a smile, a hug go a long way for the siblings," Tina said. "Good luck to you. I've got to get back to work. It was nice to meet you."

Brenda and Tom both nodded. Tina could see how her dad was so wrapped up in this cause. A word here, a word there. It might be the very thing that family needed. She at least hoped she had raised the level of awareness for the parents. Maybe God had a reason for putting her in this family. And just maybe it was to give words of counsel and encouragement.

Chapter Seven

Nate sat cross legged on his contemporary white couch, guitar in hand. The high walls of the vaulted ceiling reflected the morning sun streaming in from the floor to ceiling picture window. In one corner, an enormous plasma TV hung on the wall. An Eames lounge chair and ottoman sat across from him. Just in case anyone ever came over, which wasn't likely, they would have a place to sit. A four-foot painting hung on the wall, under golden wooden beams. Bright colors collided in bold strokes against a white background.

He plucked chords to Moon Shadow and sang along. The guitar had become a comfort to him growing up, the soothing sounds reaching into his soul. His mom had found one at a garage sale and bought it for his twelfth birthday. He could never figure out how she was always attuned to what he wanted.

In middle school, geeky and unsure how to navigate in a world of hormonal preteens, Nate had stood during break, mesmerized, outside the door of the music room listening to the teacher playing his guitar. Mr. Baker glanced up to see

Nate's intent eyes watching him. He ran his hand down his reddish beard and motioned him in. Nate cautiously stepped just inside the door.

"You're not in any of my music classes, are you son?"

"No. That sure was beautiful."

Mr. Baker smiled. "I started playing when I was about your age. Would you like to learn how to play?"

"I don't have a guitar. I'm not sure if I could learn even if I had one."

Mr. Baker looked at him intently. "All it takes is desire and you can learn anything. Come by tomorrow, same time. I've got an extra you can learn on." Nate's lips turned up into a wide grin.

That's all it took for him to realize what feeling in love with something was. There was just something about picking or strumming the chords that resonated with him. He would spend hours lost in learning technique and chords. Not satisfied to only know E, A and G he quickly soaked up anything Mr. Baker introduced to him.

He had been careful to avoid letting his dad know. He could hear his dad's voice in his head telling him he was nothing but a sissy. This was when he was glad his dad didn't come home each night until late. When Nate had finished practicing, he would carefully hide his guitar under the far side of his bed.

Tch tch sounds came from the large cage in Nate's living room.

"Hey Chuck. You like my music? You do, don't you."

Nate set down his guitar and opened the cage.

"Come on." He took a handful of nuggets and held open his hand. "There, now I've got you."

He pulled out the chinchilla and let him eat out of his hand. He cuddled him under his chin for a brief moment before

Chuck had had enough and jumped to the floor. Nate chuckled as he watched him run around exploring every nook and cranny.

He wondered what Tina would think of him. Not that she'd ever get the chance to meet him. Nate couldn't help looking at her in the work room. Her curly carrot colored hair and green eyes. Thoughts of her kept swirling around in his head. There was something about her that made him want to protect her. From what? He wasn't sure. He just had a sense that something wasn't right—like she was holding back from life.

He, of all people, knew about holding back. He wasn't sure that was such a good thing. Meaningful relationships had always been hard for him. Like the time when he tried to strike up a friendship with Mandy in high school. It took all his courage to ask to sit with her at lunch. He'd watched her for weeks either sitting alone or with a friend. Stomach swirling, he finally took the leap.

It hadn't been as bad as he thought. Her sweet smile was welcoming. They talked about the basketball game, and different teachers. Her brown eyes sparkled, luring him into more conversation. Everything seemed to be going well for a few months, until she asked about his family.

That was a subject he didn't want to discuss with anyone and for sure, he would be mortified if she found out about his addicted dad and the constant abuse. She accused him of not caring enough to share all of his life with her. He would have loved to, but that was a part of his heart he just couldn't give away.

Nate grabbed Chuck as he was running by and gave a last stroke on his head. He returned him to his cage where he happily ran up the little staircase to his perch.

Nate turned as his phone rang. He picked it up from the coffee table and looked at the screen. Spencer. *Why would he be calling?*

"Hello?"

"Hey. Christy and I were wondering if you had plans tonight. We were going to barbecue ribs and thought you might join us."

Plans? What plans would I have, other than going to the gym?

"Uh, yeah. That would be great. Home cooked food? I'm in."

"Okay, see you at six."

Nate drove to the end of the cul-de-sac and pulled into the driveway of the modest home. He glanced at the clock. Right on time. He grabbed the gallon of sweet tea and pita chips. He wouldn't have felt right coming empty handed. Delicious smells of barbecue swirled around him. The lawn was freshly mowed. A large planter held a variety of pansies, petunias and marigolds. The front door opened, and Spencer greeted him, his baby strapped onto a front pack.

"Hey!" He patted Nate's shoulder. "Good to see you, man."

The baby twisted her head up at Nate and grinned.

"We've got company, Elizabeth. That's right baby girl. Give my friend Nate a big smile," Spencer said.

"She's pretty cute," Nate said. A radiant smile filled his face. "Where should I put these?"

He followed Spencer to the back yard where a picnic table was set with paper plates.

"Nate—Christy. Christy—Nate."

She looks rather good for just having had a baby.

"Hey. Nice to meet you Christy. Thanks for the invite. I haven't had a home cooked meal in a while."

"You don't cook? You look like you'd be all right in the kitchen." Christy cocked an eyebrow.

"I'm not bad. But it's just me. I have to admit I call Uber Eats more often than I should."

He sat on the edge of the picnic table.

"Do you want me to help with anything?"

"There are some glasses in the cupboard. And you could get the fruit salad from the fridge."

Spencer followed him in. "Do you want to help me out of this contraption? Little 'Liz is getting a bit fussy."

Nate undid the straps and watched Spencer take Elizabeth out. She blew bubbles and giggled as he rubbed his head on her belly. *What would it be like—that relationship with a little human being?* Nate couldn't help but smile.

"You look like you were made to be a dad," he said.

"I'm loving it, that's for sure. I never ever thought it would be this fun. But you see this little tiny kid and her eyes look just like her mama's with long lashes and dimples. And you think, wow, we did this! We made this little bit of adorableness."

He pulled Elizabeth out of the pack and kissed her on the cheek.

"With a little bit of God's help." He conceded. "You want to hold her?"

Nate nodded and the next thing he knew, Elizabeth was in his arms.

"You're a natural," Spencer said. "I wasn't sure if you knew how to hold a baby." His eyebrows raised.

"She's so tiny."

He held her under her armpits and balanced her legs on his stomach. She started dancing up and down.

"I should have brought my guitar. I could have played you some dancin' music."

"Hidden talents, I see," Spencer said.

Christy came in. "I see you have a new friend there, little 'Lizzie."

As soon as Elizabeth heard her mom's voice she turned and held her arms out to her.

"You have a gal in your life?" Christy said. Elizabeth nestled her head into her shoulder.

"Nope. I'm not the marrying kind." Nate said and looked down.

"Get jilted?" Spencer said.

"No. I just had a really hard time watching my dad knock my mom around. He's a drug addict. I don't want to take a chance on repeating that."

"What your dad was doesn't have to define you," Spencer said.

Nate scuffed his shoe.

"You could give your past over to the ultimate Dad who loves you more than any earthly father and has your life in His hands."

Nate looked at him and tilted his head. *What did he mean by that?*

"My home life wasn't all that hot either. It took me a few years of working through resentment and feeling abandoned. Then my sweet Christy came along and introduced me to the Big Guy in the Sky."

He smiled and wrapped his arm around her waist. She smiled up at him.

He wasn't going to preach at him, was he?

"Yeah, I tried that stuff. It's not really for me," Nate said.

That "Big Guy" and I haven't exactly been on good terms.
Spencer gave a slight tilt of his head and tightened his lips.
"Come on. I think the ribs are done," Christy said. She handed her husband the tongs. "Let's head outside and chow down."

Chapter Eight

Tina took a last look in the mirror, ran her fingers through her hair, fluffed it up and grabbed her keys and bag.

"Kaitlyn," she called up the stairs. "You ready to go?"

Kaitlyn bounded down wearing her scrubs with the matryoshka dolls printed on them. Tina often heard Kaitlyn's patients comment how the smiles on the wooden dolls somehow made them happier. Tina was sure their joy was because of Kaitlyn's compassion and comforting words, no matter what she wore.

"Let me grab my mocha," she said.

Traffic was heavy at seven. Seemed like everyone was headed to work. Tina glanced at the joggers, wishing she were right there with them. Not that she didn't like going to work. She did. But running always freed her mind and body.

"How's it going with the foundation? You're going again Thursday?"

"Okay, I guess. I just do odd jobs—whatever needs to be done. The other day a family was counseling. They had a little girl and her older brother had batten. It reminded me of us. The girl kept hiding under the coffee table, peeking out hoping to get her dad's attention. She would reach out and flick his pants leg. The dad would pull back. Then she untied his shoes. I think she was feeling left out and just wanted attention."

"I remember when you were in first grade. You used to hide under furniture. You'd get frustrated about something and then hide under a desk or behind a wall until someone found you. Mrs. Patterson would depend on me to find you whenever you went missing." Kaitlyn laughed.

"You always knew where to look. Remember that time when I tore up little pieces of paper and left a trail, like Hansel and Gretel, hoping someone would follow it and find me?"

Kaitlyn turned to face her. "I do remember that. I think it was during choice time and all the kids were playing and a whole lot of chaos was going on."

"You were always there for me. I don't know if I've ever told you how much I appreciated that."

Tina started to choke up and she brushed the moisture forming on her lashes.

Kaitlyn leaned over and put her head on Tina's shoulder. "Awwww...."

Her car swerved, narrowly missing the curb and Kaitlyn pulled back, leading to an eruption of giggles.

※ ♥ ♥

"What do you think we have on the schedule today?"

Peter said. He walked down the hall flanked by Daniel, Kaitlyn, and Tina.

"It's always a surprise, isn't it," Tina said.

"Yes, it is," Daniel agreed.

"It might be that little old guy who came in the other day. He took a turn for the worse. Congestive heart failure."

Peter shook his head. Tina flicked her gaze at him, recalling the many trips to the hospital when Peter had accompanied his grandpa for the same thing. She squeezed his shoulder.

"Did you see the little girl who had eaten a bunch of buttons? I guess she was sitting on the floor with her mom while she was sewing and got hungry." Daniel said. He choked out a laugh.

"Unbelievable! How old was she?" Tina said.

"Two. You'd think after she ate one, she wouldn't want anymore. Maybe they were colorful like skittles!" Daniel said.

"Did she require surgery?" Peter asked.

"No. After they did the x-ray, they decided to let her poop them out." Daniel laughed.

"Somehow I can picture you doing that as a little kid, Peter." Kaitlyn nudged him.

"Couldn't have happened. My mom didn't sew and there weren't random buttons laying around."

"Yeah, but you might have eaten goat pellets thinking they were Sugar Daddies." Daniel chuckled.

The team gathered in the operating room where a teen girl lay on the table. Her long brunette hair lay on her pillow and trailed down the front of her t-shirt. Tina looked directly into her green eyes, as if she could connect with the girl's obvious pain. For Tina, her patients were a call to fix them. She felt certain she could send this patient home restored—like a white board being cleaned ready for the next story.

"Hey Bridgett," Tina said.

"Hi."

"What do you have going on here?"

"We were out target shooting," she said. "I heard a loud

bang and looked down and squirts of blood were pumping out of my thigh."

"You and who?" Daniel said.

"My family. It was my mom, younger sister, and brother. We were with some friends."

"Who shot you?" Kaitlyn asked. Her eyes widened.

"She didn't mean to. I was kneeling down aiming a thirty aught six and she was holding a pistol. I think she was trying to load it and it went off."

"How old is she?" Peter asked.

"She's nine." Bridgett winced in pain.

"And she was shooting a pistol?" Peter shook his head.

"Can we just get on with this?" Bridgett asked.

"May I take a look?" Tina said.

Bridgett nodded.

"It looks like we're going to have to cut your pants off to get to the wound."

Bridgett gasped. "My designer jeans? Do you know how much I had to pay for these?"

"I'm sorry. They already have holes in them from the bullet," Tina said. "And aren't holes in your jeans kind of a thing?"

Peter handed her some surgical scissors and Tina began to cut the denim.

"Where did the bullet end up?" Daniel asked.

"I'm not sure. My lower leg hurts like heck, though," Bridgett said.

Blood had seeped through her lower left pant leg and through her upper right thigh.

"Am I going to be able to walk again?" Bridgett asked. Her lips trembled.

"We'll get you fixed up good as new," Tina said.

She exchanged looks with Kaitlyn who handed her sterile gauze and butadiene to cleanse the area.

"We're going to give you a shot of Lidocaine to numb it. This will sting a little." Tina held the syringe up and flicked it to remove any bubbles.

Bridgett clenched her fists and bit into her lower lip.

"Do you want to lay back? We can adjust the table."

Bridgett nodded.

Dr. Roberts strode in and glanced over the chart.

"Gunshot wound?" Heads nodded. "Let's see if we can get this young lady back on her feet."

Tina stepped back. "Were you robbing a bank?" His eyebrow raised.

Bridgett crossed her arms, clearly not in the mood for banter. Tina handed Dr. Roberts a probe and he started poking around.

"Ouch," Bridgett said.

Tina looked at doc. Bridgett wasn't supposed to be feeling anything.

"Give this little gal another round of Lidocaine. Can't have her squirming around."

Tina made a small poke. Doc lanced Bridgett's lower leg where the bullet had lodged. He dug his gloved finger into the hole and searched around until he found what he was looking for.

"Did you want to keep the bullet?" Doc asked, holding it up.

"I could do that?" she asked. Her eyes widened.

"Of course. A little souvenir to show your friends."

"Or you could use it to hold against your sister, maybe as a bribe to do dishes or anything else to make her guilty," Daniel said. He laughed.

"You could make it into a necklace." Peter said.

"Time to sew you up. You are one lucky little gal. That bullet could have hit your femur and shattered it. Instead, it just went straight through."

"Must have been God looking out for you," Tina said. "A shattered bone would have had you in reconstructive surgery and crutches for much longer."

"Let's bandage her up. Daniel, see to her meds. Kaitlyn, call transport. Bridgett, you'll be free to go in a few minutes."

Tina followed the wheelchair to the waiting room where Bridgett's brother lay on his back on the floor tossing a small ball up and down. Her mother paced the floor. Tina couldn't help but notice there was no dad on the scene. Maybe he was at work. She'd give him the benefit of the doubt. A younger girl came running up to Bridgett, tears streaming down her face.

"Are you okay? I was so worried. I'm really really sorry."

She grabbed Bridgett's hand. Bridgett took her own hands and cupped her sister's face in them.

"It's okay. I'll be okay. You're just going to have to do my chores for at least a month. And no complaining!"

Tina smiled. Just like her helping Max. The difference was that this little sister would live with guilt.

"What kind of mom would take her nine-year-old daughter target shooting?" Tina said.

"They obviously didn't have a clue about how to shoot guns," Daniel said. They continued down the hall.

"Must not be farmers," Peter said. "Farm kids learn to shoot when they're in first grade."

"And where was the dad in all this? Were they divorced?" Peter said.

"Don't know, but he didn't appear to be giving Bridgett the support she should have had," Tina said. *Just like someone else I know.*

Kaitlyn linked elbows with Tina. "Come on, let's see if there's any treats in the staff room."

Peter looked at Daniel. "Race you. We can't let those girls get them all!"

Chapter Nine

Nate scrolled through the Oregonian taking an occasional sip of his morning coffee. He stopped on an article with the headline, *New Cure Found for Huntington's Disease*. He took note of the researchers and immediately found a web page of their studies. Adrenaline coursed through his veins, riveted by these findings.

Huntington's is a neurological disease that results from a problem gene received from one of the parents. It affects the central part of the brain that is responsible for thinking, movement, and emotion. This leads to problems with concentration, memory and reasoning, and motor problems.

This is so similar, he thought. By the time he had broken away and checked the time, it was already ten. *Dang, I'm really late.* He called Mark to apologize and let him know he was on his way. Chugging the rest of his coffee, he grabbed an apple. Chuck gave a squeak and Nate threw him a few dandelion treats before he headed to his car.

He frowned as he noticed a mar on his car door and wiped it with his finger. Realizing it was only a little dirt, he let out a sigh of relief. *Time to wash and polish.* There was a detail shop near work. But he would rather handle it himself. He didn't trust anyone with his baby. He slipped in and pulled out onto the street.

He couldn't let go of what he had just read. What if this could be the key to a cure? He'd contact these researchers the minute he walked in the door. What were their methods? How did they come to a breakthrough?

Nate was so absorbed he almost ran a red light. Sobering, he pulled his thoughts back to the world as he swung into the foundation lot and parked. The sun filtered through the towering maple. He smiled, not exactly sure why that picture made him happy. Maybe the strength of the sun weaving its way through the leaves so that the veins were illuminated? The way he hoped this new information could shed light on his research.

He sped to the door and pushed it open.

"Good morning Nate. Or should I say good afternoon? You're a tad late, aren't you?" Spencer said. He cocked his eye.

Tina was sitting on the edge of his desk, relaxed, travel mug in her hand.

"Yeah, I got caught up in an article. Did you know they found a cure for Huntington's disease?"

Nate's words bubbled forth like a gushing fountain.

"That's awesome, dude," Spencer said. They shared a high five. "Do you think there might be a link?"

"Yes! I'm going to contact the researchers now." He took a few steps towards his office.

"Do you want us to pray for the outcome?" Tina asked.

Nate stopped in his tracks and slowly turned. Tina set her thermos on the desk and looked him in the eye as she slid to her feet.

"Uh."

Nate looked at Spencer and down at his feet.

"Great idea," Spencer stood and gave a quick nod.

"Yeah, I guess. If you think that would help."

Nate felt doubtful. Why would God care about what Nate was doing? That is, if there even was a God.

Tina rubbed her hands together.

"Okay God. Since you're the Guy who knows all things, you know about all these kiddos with batten disease. You know how hard Nate has been working on this cure. Give him wisdom and knowledge."

Spencer chimed in an amen.

"You've got this dude," he said as he slapped his back.

Nate gave a little nod, took a few steps towards his office, and looked back over his shoulder. *Did they really think prayer would do anything? There were never any results he could see from his constant prayers that his dad would stop meth.* He shook his head and headed to his office.

A small giggle escaped Tina's lips. "What is this guy's story? He's so serious all the time. He looked like he thought we were some type of virus going to attack him. "

Spencer smiled. "He came over for dinner the other night. Christy and I wanted to see if we could coax him out of his house."

"How was he? I mean, did he talk? Or loosen up any?" Tina asked.

"He was okay. He's really good with the baby."

Spencer lowered his voice.

"He said he didn't ever want to have kids though cuz he doesn't want to be like his abusive father."

"Hmm."

Abused? No kids? Maybe we have one thing in common.

"Does he have a thing against God?"

"Maybe. It happens. People think their dad is a representation of God," Spencer shrugged.

"I guess you'll have your work cut out for you, then, straightening him out." Tina paused. *That's not me, though, right? I don't think of God as being like my dad.*

Spencer answered the phone. Tina gave a little wave and walked down the hall. She settled on the cushioned couch in the entryway and watched a family with a young girl as they played with fidget spinners. She pulled out her drawing pad and pencils and leaned back on the arm of the couch. She bent her legs and placed her pad on them. Her eyes traveled to the corner of the ceiling; her pencil poised on her lower lip. She watched the girl a few more minutes and sketched in a few curves, eyes, and nose. She was so intent she didn't hear her dad come up behind her.

"What are you working on? That's really good," he said. "When did you learn to draw so well?"

Tina looked up at him like he was crazy. *I've been drawing since forever. It's like you don't even know me.*

"I've always drawn, dad."

"Well, you're very good at it, sweetheart. Your lines are so realistic. The detail in the eyes."

He looked at the girl, now reading with her mom.

"Really nice."

Tina looked up at him. *Was this an actual compliment?*

"Say, what would you think of drawing several kids that we could turn into greeting cards? We could sell them or give them as gifts to our donors. What do you think?"

"Um. I guess I could do that. It might take me a little time," she said. *I might even drag it out. He just wants to use my talents for his gain.*

"It's okay. Maybe by the end of this month? Then we could get them to the printer?"

Nate came bounding in, reminding Tina of an exuberant Labrador.

"Mark! I just spoke with David Chang who is one of the researchers at the Huntington Disease Center. They've found a cure! Do you know what's more? He really thinks he could share their process and information and it might be remarkably similar to batten."

Nate paced back and forth.

"I just can't believe it. This is the breakthrough we've needed."

He flicked his gaze at Tina.

Watching his animated hands made Tina smile. She was tempted to imitate them. But then that would be distracting. She didn't want to draw attention away from him.

Mark slapped him on the shoulder. "That is genuinely great news. How long do you think it will take to come to our cure?"

"Soon, I hope. We've got to get a cure for these kids. Seeing those grieving parents. It gets to me. Anyway, I can't really say exactly how long. But we're getting close. Okay, gotta get back to work."

He whistled as he strode down the hall to his office.

Mark's eyes followed him.

"That's quite a guy we've got here. Do you think you might be interested in him? He's single. You're single. He's cute. You're cute." He held his hands out questioningly.

"Don't push your luck."

It's true, Nate is cute— when he smiles. But he's got a few social skills to work on before I would ever consider being seen in public with him. Tina shook her head and continued her drawing. Besides, giving her dad anything to gloat about was not on her to do list. If anything were to happen between her and Nate it would have to be her doing, not her dad's meddling.

Chapter Ten

Tina reached down and scratched Bentley between the ears as she entered the house from her morning run.

"Hey pooch, how ya doing? You like this don't you?"

Bentley's tail wagged so hard it swung his whole body back and forth.

Tina pulled off her running shoes and poured a glass of water. "Kaitlyn?"

"In here," said Kaitlyn.

Tina followed her voice.

Kaitlyn lay snugged up on the couch with a book. She looked over the top. "We still going dress shopping today?"

"Yeah, I was just about to ask you about that. I want to make a batch of cookies first. I thought afterwards I'd stop by Mrs. Wilson's and check in on her."

"The lady down the street?"

"Yeah, I pass her house all the time when I jog. She's either in her garden or getting her mail. It just seems like she might be lonely."

"Okay, that will give me enough time to read another chapter." Kaitlyn's eyes twinkled above her book.

Tina took a quick shower and got started baking. Every time she ran, she thought of stopping by to see Mrs. Wilson, but something always got in the way. She wondered how long she had lived alone. Had her husband died? Did she have any kids? Did they live nearby? She never saw anyone parked at her house or signs of visitors. She thought of how lonely her grandma had been when her grandpa had died. Maybe she could put a smile on this woman's face.

Kaitlyn walked in as Tina pulled out a tray of cookies. Kaitlyn reached for a warm chocolate chip cookie and took a bite.

"Cookies." She took a deep breath and closed her eyes.

"Silly girl," Tina said. She poured Kaitlyn a glass of milk and added a napkin. "Help yourself," she said. Tina filled a plate up to take to Mrs. Wilson's later.

"Which store do you want to go to?" Tina asked.

"The bridal store on 10th. My mom and Maggie will meet us there. I even thought about going to Goodwill or a thrift store. Sometimes there's some pretty nice dresses there and for a third the price."

"You'd go to a thrift store? For your wedding dress?"

"Why not? The dress was only worn once." Kaitlyn looked at Tina like that would be a perfectly logical thing to do.

"I guess. Maybe. Huh. Well, let's go," Tina said. She shrugged her shoulders. Sometimes you had to wonder about that girl.

A few minutes later they arrived at Hannah's Bridal Boutique. Kaitlyn's mom and sister were already there, waiting. Tina watched Kaitlyn run to Maggie and her mom's arms, giving them a group hug. Tina's throat constricted and she wrapped her arms tightly around herself, wishing it was her mom giving her a hug. *Shake it off, Tina. This is Kaitlyn's big day.*

The sign was done in an elegant font. Mannequins wearing flowing dresses adorned the windows. A floral arch surrounded the front door where a clerk met and welcomed them in.

Kaitlyn met Tina's eyes. Kaitlyn held in all her excitement, her shoulders tense. Eyes wide. And then she twirled, arms out, a broad smile filling her face. The dresses were beautiful. Absolutely gorgeous. Tina would have to remember this place if she ever got engaged. Silly thought, that. She might have to remember it for a long time.

Tina watched the clerk slide her hands down the sides of her skinny jeans. Her grey ankle boots glided over the floor as she led them to a lounge. A long gold necklace jangled in the front of her lacy white top.

"Let's come in here where we can sit and talk," she said. Her perfectly plucked eyebrows hovered over her false eyelashes and purple eye shadow. She motioned for Kaitlyn and Tina to sit in the teal cushioned chair. "Tell me what your dream wedding is going to be like," she said. A soft beige lipstick covered her perfectly formed lips.

Kaitlyn looked at Tina. "I want to get married in my church. I want a white flowing dress with a bit of a train. Not satin. Maybe a little beadwork or lace."

"She wants something modest," her mom said.

Kaitlyn nodded. Tina knew that, although Kaitlyn had something to show off, she would be mortified wearing a dress that accented her cleavage.

"Well, let's get started then."

The clerk guided them to a room filled with racks and racks of white dresses. A hall led to several dressing rooms with covered benches and three-way mirrors.

As Kaitlyn tried them on, Tina tried to picture herself

wearing a beautiful dress like that. She and Kaitlyn had played dress up for hours when they were small. Kaitlyn was sure she would marry someone tall and handsome and kind. Well, that dream came true. Tina had always figured she'd be the one who kissed a frog that turned into a prince. A quiet giggle escaped as Nate entered her mind. Who knew? Maybe there was a prince hidden in there somewhere.

"What about this one? Do you like it?" Kaitlyn twirled and the thin, lacy overlay spread out in a full arc. It fit her perfectly, accentuating her figure in just the right places.

Tina imagined Luke in a grey tux and flashy tie, a goofy grin on his face as Kaitlyn walked towards him down the aisle.

A pang of loneliness crept in, thoughts of what it would be like when Kaitlyn and Luke moved to their new house. No one to cook her waffles. Or stay up late watching sappy romances.

"I love it," Tina choked and swallowed. She put on a smile and said, "You look absolutely beautiful. Luke will have no doubt that he's marrying the right girl."

Kaitlyn beamed.

Tina dropped Kaitlyn off at the house, grabbed a plate of cookies and walked down the sidewalk to Mrs. Wilson's house. She rang the doorbell. Why was she feeling nervous? This sweet old lady wasn't going to bite her. What if Mrs. Wilson didn't like chocolate chip? Of course, she will. Who doesn't like chocolate chip? She argued with herself. A bad sign.

The screen door opened. Mrs. Wilson greeted her, dressed in a pair of flowered rayon comfy pants and a white knit shirt.

"Now who do we have here?"

"Hi, I'm Tina, your neighbor. I live in the yellow house on the next block." Tina pointed towards it with her chin and held out the cookies. "I made these for you."

Tina felt like she was in second grade when she and Kaitlyn had dropped bouquets on front porches for May Day. Only then, they ran off and hid in the bushes, watching people answer their doorbells, hoping to see their smiles.

"For me? How thoughtful. Would you like to come in?"

"I'd love to."

Mrs. Wilson ushered her into her living room. A flowered couch rested next to the wall. A Duncan Phyfe coffee table sat in the middle flanked by two Victorian style armchairs. A crystal vase had been carefully set in the middle on a doily filled with red and yellow chrysanthemums and contrasting bluebells.

"Sit down. Do you like coffee or tea? I have both."

"Coffee sounds good. Just black, thank you."

Tina looked at the paintings on the wall. Portraits that could have been in a museum. A bronze statue of a ballerina was poised on an end table. A photo of Mrs. Wilson wrapped in the arms of a man. Must be her husband. He looked like he adored her.

"Here you are, dear." Mrs. Wilson handed her a porcelain cup and saucer, covered in delicate flowers, their red petals delicately painted.

Tina breathed in the aroma, a satisfied look on her face. What was it about coffee that made everything right?

"Oh, I've forgotten my manners. I haven't even told you my name. I'm Martha Wilson."

Tina held out her hand. "I'm so glad to meet you." She smiled.

"I've seen you out running. You are really fit. I used to run up until a few years ago when I had a hip replacement," Martha said.

"Thank you. I love to run. It puts me in my happy place. It's a good time to think and pray," Tina said.

Martha held out the plate of cookies to her and set some napkins on the table. "Tell me about yourself. What do you do, what are your hopes and dreams, what are you passionate about?"

Tina set her cup down. "Well, let's see. I'm a nurse at Mercy Hospital. This is my second year. I'm fortunate to work with three of my pals. One of them is my roommate Kaitlyn. We have plenty of fun together."

"Which floor do you work on? I used to be a nurse."

"I'm in surgery. I'm really learning a lot." *A lot they never taught her in clinicals. That would be an understatement.*

"I wonder if you were there when my sweet Robert had his heart surgery."

"I'm not sure. When was it?"

"Oh, he had surgery a year before he died and that was five years ago. So, I guess you weren't there yet. You were probably still in school. Silly me."

"I'm so sorry. Have you been alone since then? Is that his picture?" Tina nodded towards it.

"Yes. But I've adjusted. Tell me more about you," Martha said.

Tina took another sip of coffee. She had been hoping to learn more about Martha and not so much revealing herself. "I love to draw. I think I'm fairly good. I'm working on some drawings for my dad's foundation—they'll be gift cards for the donors."

"Oh, I'd love to see them. Are they pencil? Pen? Watercolor?"

Tina chuckled. "You're an art connoisseur I see. They're pen and ink and colored pencil."

"What's the name of the foundation? I'd love to support them —even if it's just to get some of your drawings!"

Tina smiled and thought how nice it was to be appreciated. "The Batten Foundation. My older brother had Batten. My dad is obsessed with working with families and trying to find a cure." Tina looked at the floor. A twinge of anxiety flew through her stomach.

"You don't sound too thrilled," Martha said.

Tina looked up. "I don't know. I mean, I guess I should be. It gives my dad something to do. He's pretty driven. He started it with my mom before she died."

"You lost your brother and your mom? That doesn't seem fair," she said.

"Exactly what I think. Then I get embarrassed that I would think that. I mean, I know God has a plan for my life, but it's hard to trust that all the time. Sometimes, I find myself angry at Him."

Martha reached her hand over and patted Tina's. "God's got big shoulders. You might not believe this, but I've had times when I was mad at God too."

"That's hard to believe. You seem so together," Tina said.

"Things haven't always gone the way I thought they should, and I was sure I must know better than God what was best for my life." She ran her finger around the rim of her saucer. "But I'll tell you, in retrospect, there's always been something that's come into place that I never expected. If my Robert hadn't lost his job years ago, we would never have moved here to this lovely neighborhood with caring people."

Tina nodded. Could He have something good in mind for her? She finished her cookie and carefully wrapping the crumbs in her napkin. Martha took her cup and napkin to the kitchen.

"Tell me a little about your mom," Martha said, returning.

Tina paused. "She was beautiful. I've always been glad to have her red hair. She was so kind. My friends always told me they wished they had her for a mom. She'd throw the best birthday parties and let me have sleep overs. She was the mom that went to all our school functions and helped with the parent club. At least until Max got so bad. Then she dropped everything to take care of him."

Martha set down her cup. "How long after Max died did your mom pass away?"

"Max died when I was nine and he was twelve. Mom got cancer when I was sixteen."

"Aww honey, that had to be hard." Martha patted her knee. "You would have been in high school. That should have been a time to go to games and dances and join clubs."

"It was hard. But you have to move on, right?" Had she been sharing too much? She didn't even really know this woman. "Speaking of which, I should get going."

"So soon?" Martha stood up. "It's been a real pleasure. I don't get many visitors. Come by anytime. And Tina, I'm sure your mom would be so immensely proud of you." She put her arm around Tina and gave a squeeze.

Tina smiled. "I will."

Tina shut the screen door and stepped out onto the sidewalk. Had she moved on? She accused her dad of being stuck, but maybe she was too.

Boys were tossing a football and cheered when a good throw resulted in a catch. A Dalmatian tugged at his leash urging his man down the sidewalk toward something that must have piqued its curiosity. A teen couple sat side by side on porch steps, laughing and teasing.

Tina smiled. She loved this neighborhood. Loved feeling a part of it. Even more so now that she had spent some time with

Martha. Tina had thought she was going to bring a smile to Martha's face. Instead, it had been Martha that had brought perspective to Tina's life. Funny how that happened. Made a girl realize that maybe someone bigger than her was in charge of her life.

Chapter Eleven

Tina climbed the stairs to her room. The weather had been unusually warm and she needed to change into something cooler. She reached into her drawer and paused when her fingers wrapped around a matchbox car. Max's. She had taken it from his shrine, the one her dad had created in his home. Tina had given him the model of his favorite race car driver on his last birthday.

She ran her thumb over the hood, lost in thought. Her dad had looked all over for that car when he and her mom set up the shrine. Even now, she felt guilty she hadn't said anything. Was it wrong that she wanted something of her own to remember him by? Something important to him. Her mom would have understood. Maybe one day she'd sneak and put it on the shrine. Or not. She slid it carefully back in her drawer.

Tina slipped on a pair of shorts and checked herself in the mirror.

"How was your visit?" Kaitlyn peeked over her shoulder. She sat on the bed and crossed her legs, patting the spot next to her.

Tina fluffed a pillow and joined her.

"It was great. She's such a cute little lady. She has twinkly eyes and you know those little lines old people get when they smile?" She drew her finger next to her eye. "Yeah, that's her."

Kaitlyn nodded. "Did she love your cookies?"

"What's not to love?" Tina laughed, remembering the ease with which she shared her heart with a complete stranger. "No, she served me coffee in these cute porcelain cups and saucers, you know, the ones with flowers painted on them and gold rims."

"I wanna go next time," Kaitlyn said. "What'd you talk about?"

"Just stuff. She asked what I did. I told her I was a nurse. Her husband, Robert, had a heart attack and surgery at Mercy. It was way before our time, though. Anyway, we just talked about all sorts of stuff." Tina stood and dumped clean clothes out of a basket onto the bed. She folded a shirt.

Kaitlyn gave Tina a long look. "You're not telling me everything."

Tina glanced at her. "We talked about, you know, just stuff. One thing led to another and I told her about Max and mom." Tina folded a sock over the other and tossed it in the pile.

"Well....?" Kaitlyn picked up the rolled-up pair of socks and threw them at her.

Tina held her elbow up to deflect. "Hey!"

"I had to knock you out of that funky stuff." Kaitlyn laughed.

"She wants some of the greeting cards I'm making. She's got art all over her house."

"I bet my mom would want some of them too. Save some for me to show her. What else did you talk about? Cuz making gift cards wasn't something to hold back on."

Tina looked at Kaitlyn. She was right, of course. But why *was* she holding back? This was her best friend .

"She asked all about mom. I told her all the stuff she was involved in. And then," Tina placed her stack of shirts in her drawer "I told her that sometimes I get mad at God. And she said God has big shoulders and she couldn't wait to see how His plan for my life was going to turn out. You know, the old He's got a plan for you and all things work together.... blah blah blah."

"Well, she's right. Remember when I got mixed up with Francisco and how I was sure I'd never find Mr. Wonderful. And look how that turned out. " Kaitlyn ruffled Tina's hair. "Seems like you said the same thing to me back then. About God's plans."

Tina pulled the curtain back to let the sunlight in.

"Anyway, I'm glad you were able to open up about stuff. What are you up to now?" Kaitlyn said.

"I was going to stop by the foundation to give the greeting cards to my dad." Tina tensed up. "Did you see them?" Tina took them from her desk and laid them out.

"Those are really nice! Who was the girl?"

"Just a girl in the waiting room, playing." *Just a girl whose life is getting progressively worse.*

"You really captured her. The look of longing in her mom's eyes. You sure have a gift. These are really good! Maybe you can draw something for us for a wedding prese" Kaitlyn said.

Tina took them back. "Maybe my dad will appreciate them. Anyway, gotta run."

"I'll probably be at Luke's tonight. Don't wait up," Kaitlyn said. Tina nodded and turned her head so Kaitlyn couldn't see her frown.

A half hour later Tina showed up at the foundation office and parked. She glanced at Nate's Lamborghini. *I wonder if I could get him to take me for a ride in that. I bet it would be amazing. Max would have loved it.*

She pushed the front door of the building open with her shoulder, adjusting her bag. Spencer was typing out a text.

"Hey Spencer! Wanna see the cards I made?"

Spencer looked up and set his phone down. "Yeah. Sure."

Tina pulled them out of her bag. He looked at each one, engrossed. "Wow. These are really good!"

Tina beamed. "My dad wanted some to give to donors, or perhaps sell."

"Great idea." He smiled. "Say, did he tell you about the fundraising event coming up?"

"No." *Was this going to be something else her dad guilted her into?*

"Yeah, it's the end of August. It'll be at the Waterfront. There's going to be lots of music, entertainers, jugglers, and good food. Free for families."

The thought of it turned her stomach to butterflies. She shifted to her other foot. "Sounds like a bunch of work!"

"It is, but it's really worth it. You could help us, you know." Spencer turned on a pleading look. It reminded her of Bentley wanting to go for a walk.

"Yeah, I'll think about it." She took the cards from his hands and straightened them. She walked down the hall to her dad's office and sat down. He was on the phone and didn't seem to notice her. *No surprise.* She bit on a hangnail. How long did she have to wait? Obviously, her being there wasn't important to him. She placed the cards on his desk and started to walk off. He finished the call.

"Hey, where are you going? Sorry, I had to take that call. Let's look at those cards." He picked them up and thumbed through them. "These are perfect. You're quite the gal, you know? Did you put your name on the backs? You should do that. People need to know who this talented artist is."

He smiled. And even looked her in the eyes. Could she trust this? Somehow, he would twist this to him being great. Him being the father of a talented artist and deserving of praise.

"Thank you." Nonetheless, his praise had been a long time in coming. She'd take the scrap from his table.

"Spencer says you've got a fundraiser coming up?" *Amazing how a compliment could make you want to be more helpful.* Tina leaned against the door jam and crossed her arms.

"Yeah, we do. I'm sure he filled you in on the details. We could really use your help. I want to get everyone in the office involved. Not just because we need everyone to pull together, but because I want our donors to see the faces behind this organization.

Tina took a timid step towards him. "If you want, I could design some fliers."

"That would be wonderful." He clasped his hands together and smiled.

Tina shrugged. Small steps were better than no steps, right?

She walked to the break room for coffee. Nate was sitting at the table engrossed in a magazine, eating a muffin, a cup of black coffee steaming in front of him. She filled her cup and sat down.

"What are you reading?" she asked.

Nate looked up. "Oh, uh, it's a research magazine."

"You really like that stuff, don't you?"

"Yeah. I do." He glanced up at her.

"What is it that draws you in? You seem pretty passionate about it."

Nate looked at the ceiling. "I suppose it's in the details and experimenting. If you come to a dead end, you can think creatively about how to proceed in a different direction. It's a challenge. I guess I like challenges. How do you have time to volunteer here? Aren't you working?"

Tina studied his square jaw. You could see his dimpled chin under his short cut beard.

"Yeah, I'm a nurse at Mercy. I work three twelve hour days so I have a few days off each week. Where'd you get that muffin?"

"Sorry, it's the last one. Here." He broke off half of it and handed it to her.

The touch of his fingers sent an unexpected shiver through her.

Spencer and Mark walked in. "Hey, glad you're both here. Can we talk about the benefit? Nate, it would be really nice if you could give a little talk about how the research is going," Spencer said.

Nate took a sip of coffee. "I guess I could do that. How many people will there be?"

"Based on last year, I'm guessing several hundred," he said.

"Tina!" Her dad looked like a lightbulb just went on in his head.

"Yeah?" She wasn't sure she liked his enthusiasm. What was he going to drag her into now?

"You need to talk about your experience with Max. It would be the perfect thing for people to hear what it's really like. I'll put you on the agenda."

Tina could hear him chortling to himself as he walked out. Spencer followed him.

"Ugh! That man! I am not going to do that." Tina pounded her fist on the table and stood up.

"I need to get away from here." Tina gave Nate a long look. "Take me for a ride in your car."

"Now?"

"Yes! Does it go fast?"

"Uh, yeah." The look on his face was like a deer in the headlights.

She grabbed his arm and pulled him down the hall. "Let's go."

Minutes later, Nate pushed the button on his fob. It beeped and the doors unlocked. Tina slid into the passenger side. The leather seats were surprisingly comfortable and adjusted to her body.

"Where do you want to go?" Nate said.

"Anywhere. Somewhere that you can show me how this thing moves."

He backed out and followed some side roads to a quiet, long strip surrounded by strawberry fields. "Tell me what's going on with you and your dad?"

Nate gunned the car and they sped past farmhouses and orchards.

"I spent my whole life trying to be helpful. When Max was getting sicker and not able to do as many things, I did everything I could to try to help with him. My dad never paid any attention to me. He never came to any of my school programs or came to see me get my art award. It was like I never existed. And now. *Now* he wants me to come into *his* world. First, he asks me to help here, so I do. He actually complimented me today. First time ever. I don't mind helping. But I am *not* going to talk to a mob about what it was like with Max. That is just going too far." Tina pushed the button to roll down the window and let the wind flow through her hair.

Nate slowed to a reasonable speed. He side eyed her and then pulled the car to the shoulder and shifted to park. He turned his attention to her.

"You."

Tina turned to look at him.

"Are beautiful."

Tears slid down her cheeks. She leaned into him and he wrapped his arm around her. He ran his fingers through her copper hair. She pulled away, searching for something to wipe her nose. Nate handed her a small tissue package.

"I'm sorry. I didn't mean to spew on you."

"I asked." He shrugged. "Better now?"

She nodded.

"Should we head back?"

She nodded again. What had she just done? Not only had she commandeered him for a ride in his car, but did she just share her heart with him? She didn't even know him. And woah now, did he actually hug her and run his fingers through her hair? Tina let out the deep breath she had been holding.

Chapter Twelve

Nate dropped Tina off at the foundation. It was too late to return to work. Besides, what if he ran into Mark? What would he say about his impulsive behavior with his boss's daughter? Nate shook his head. What in the world had he just done? That was not at all like him. Yet, when Tina had grabbed his arm and propelled him to his car, what should he have done? Told her she was crazy? Said he had work to do? The thought of taking her for a ride and showing off his pride and joy made him smile. It was worth whatever the consequences.

And when he dropped her off and she held his gaze, it was all he could do to not plant his lips on hers. And if he had? Would it have been so bad?

He pulled into the middle of the lane to avoid a couple on a tandem bicycle.

Heck, he hadn't dated since he was in high school. Wasn't it about time? It wasn't just that she was gorgeous. It was, well, what was it exactly? Her vulnerability? Her confidence? Her sense of something bigger. He couldn't exactly put his finger on it, but she was starting to play on his heart.

Turning down his road, he passed mansions with manicured lawns, pristinely trimmed hedges and slate walkways leading to huge, decorative doors. Nate's house was nice, by all standards, but not quite to the level of his neighbors. He vowed his would be a real house in a nice neighborhood. No more trailer park for him. So far, his vision of what life would be like beyond his youth had come to pass.

The screen on his car alerted him to an incoming call from his mom.

"Hey mom, what's up?"

"Nathan, I hate to bother you, but I went out to my car to take Mitzy to the store to get some dog food, and I had a flat tire. Could you be a dear, and come change it for me?" Nate could hear his mom exhale her cigarette smoke. Was she never going to give up that nasty habit?

"Sure. I was just heading home, but I'll be over in a few." He was glad he lived within striking distance and he could be there for her. Especially since his dad was no longer in the picture. Thank the Big Guy for that.

He rounded the corner and changed directions. This was just going to be one of those days that he rescued damsels in distress. He buffed his shoulders, pride on his face.

And what about Tina? She only had her dad. Mark was capable and strong. Not needy like his mom. They should have a good relationship. What was holding them back? There always seemed to be friction between them. Like the other day when Tina and Mark were having a conversation when she was drawing in the waiting room. With her dad, Tina never displayed her strong sense of confidence like, say, when she was talking to Spencer or some family in the counseling room.

He pulled in behind his mom's '60's Buick. The blue paint was mottled with age and the white roof no longer held the sheen. He had loved riding in the massive back seat when he was a kid— so much room to lay down or stretch out. He wondered if his old gum was still stashed in the silver ashtray on the door.

He got out of his car and walked to the front of hers. Yep, flat all right. He was glad he had chosen a pair of jeans and t-shirt today. He wouldn't have wanted to crawl around on the ground and dirty up his dress clothes.

He opened the screen door and peeked in. "Mom? I'm here."

Mitzy ran up and started barking.

"Mitzy! Stop! It's just Nathan." Loretta picked her up and stroked her head. Mitzy looked up at her and licked her face. "I'm so glad you're here. Is there anything you need?"

"Nope. I'll get right to it." Nate put his ear buds in and turned on a podcast. He rummaged around in the trunk for the jack and spare tire. Hoisting the heavy tire out of the trunk he rolled it to the passenger side of the car. He set up the jack and levered it up until the tire was just above the ground. Using the tire iron, he unscrewed the lug bolts and slid the flat off. Out of the corner of his eye, he saw a man go to the front door. *Probably a neighbor.* He noticed his dirty, worn shoes. He set the new tire in place and tightened the bolts.

Nate heard shouting from the house. He pulled out his earbuds and yanked the front door open. Mitzy was barking her silly little head off.

"Get out of here. I don't have no money, and even if I did, I wouldn't be giving it to you," Loretta said. She stood, arms crossed, in the middle of the room watching the man tear the cushions off the couch and throw open the drawers on the end table.

"I know you've got money stashed. You always had some tucked away somewhere."

Nate recognized that voice. The man started rummaging through the kitchen, looking in drawers, lifting the lid off the cookie jar. Finding nothing but crumbs, he threw it to the floor where it shattered. Mitzy started yipping. Pots and pans hit the floor.

"Get out of here, Alvin! You have no right to be here," Loretta yelled. Mitzy bared her teeth and bit at the man's leg. He kicked her off him. Mitzy yelped and ran to Loretta.

Rage filled Alvin's face as he turned on Loretta and shoved her. She fell against the corner of the table, screaming as she slid down to the floor. Loretta held her hand to her head as blood trickled down her face. Cowering, she gave Nate a pleading look.

"Dad! Stop!" Nate strode into the kitchen and shoved his wretched excuse for a father to the wall. Nate looked at Alvin's face—pocked and needing a shave. His greasy, uncut hair hung limp around his face. Alvin struggled to free himself, exerting strength Nate couldn't imagine an emaciated man could have.

"You need to leave. Now!" Nate's muscles tensed, adrenaline filling his frame.

"You think you can order me around? You're just a little mama's boy. I ain't leaving until I have money," Alvin snarled.

Better think again about calling me names. Nate straightened his shoulders and forced a calming breath.

"Come out to my car and I'll get you money," Nate said. He needed to lure his father out and away from his mom.

Alvin followed him out and suspiciously watched as Nate opened his car door and reached for his phone. Alvin looked around and spotted the tire iron.

"That punk thinks he can pull one over on me?" Alvin mumbled.

Before Nate could react, Alvin picked up the tire iron and smashed in the rear window. Just as Nate lunged for him, he heard sirens. Alvin struggled out of Nate's grip and turned and ran as two officers hastened out of their car. The larger one chased after Alvin.

"I didn't do anything! Let go of me!" Alvin protested.

The other cop walked up to Nate and moved his sunglasses to rest on the back of his head.

"I'm officer Ron. You okay? The neighbor heard screaming and called 911."

"Yeah, but my mom needs to see a doctor. He gave her a good shove into a table."

Nate led Ron into the house. Loretta reached her hand out and Nate pulled her to her feet.

"Let me get something to wipe that blood." Nate pulled a dishrag out of the drawer and held it under warm water. He dabbed it gently on her cut, noting the huge goose egg forming. "Let's sit you down here on the couch. Do you want something for pain?"

"Yes. Look in the bathroom for me," she said. Nate returned with a glass of water and some tablets.

"Mom, I am so sorry. I didn't know it was him. I would have come in sooner."

Loretta put her hand on Nate's stubbly cheek and locked eyes.

Ron hiked his pants up to rest upon his lean hips. "Do you know that man?" Ron looked from Loretta to Nate.

"Unfortunately, yes. He's my dad."

The officer shook his head. They turned and watched the officer lead Alvin, arms behind his back locked in handcuffs, to the police car.

"Looks like he'll have a place to cool off for a bit. I can call an ambulance," Ron said.

"No, I'll take her. Thank you." Nate held out his hand and shook Ron's.

Ron started for the door and turned.

"You'll need to call your insurance company. You're not going to be able to take her in your car with the window all smashed." He pulled out his phone and dialed for an ambulance.

Nate felt a lump forming in his throat as he examined the shattered glass and dented rear. He choked down tears. He glanced at his mom. Tears trickled down her face.

"Hang in there, mom. We'll get you fixed up."

It wasn't enough to hurt his mom. Again. But to smash his car? When was this ever going to end?

Chapter Thirteen

Tina stood paralyzed in the parking lot of the Batten Foundation and watched Nate drive that slick car away. What in the world had she just done? What was she thinking? She just grabbed this guy she barely knew and commandeered him into taking her for a drive. Then she had the nerve to spew all her pent-up anger towards her dad onto him. What kind of guy allows just any girl to force him to drive her somewhere in a fast car?

Her phone rang. "Hey Kaitlyn."

"Hi Tina," Kaitlyn's voice held a hint of worry. "Where are you? You're late. Did you stop at the store?"

"No, but we've got some talking to do. I'll be home in a few," Tina said and hung up.

She drove home lost in a fog. She fingered her locket. *Mom, was that the stupidest thing I've ever done?* She was reminded of the time in high school when she asked a guy to the prom. She had been so nervous, but he had actually said yes, and it turned out to be a fun night. That is until she found out he only went with her because he didn't know how to say no.

But was this the same thing? Okay, I admit I did force

Nate into taking me in his car. And making him drive fast. That might have been a little stupid. Well, a lot stupid. But mom, he listened to me talk about dad. And you're not here anymore. I know it wasn't your fault you died, but I miss you so much! She pounded the palm of her hand on the steering wheel.

Tina pulled into the driveway.

"Hey, you're home. Finally." She skipped up to Tina. "I've got news! We've got confirmation on our wedding venue. Guess what, guess what?" She jumped up and down.

Tina put down her bag and sat on the bar stool. "What?"

Kaitlyn's face beamed. "Luke's arranged for our honeymoon."

"You're dying to tell me. Out with it!" Tina worked at embracing Kaitlyn's joy. She wanted to be happy for her. She *was* happy for her. She just wanted her cake and be able to eat it too. Still have the secure friendship she had enjoyed for all these years but let Kaitlyn fly. Move on. Without her.

"We're going to Iceland! Isn't that going to be cool? We get to see the Aurora Borealis, go hiking, rent bikes and ride to the waterfalls, see the Viking Museum..."

"That sounds really awesome. Really. You're taking me with you, right?" Tina's lackluster responses paled in the light of Kaitlyn's enthusiasm.

"I actually suggested that to Luke and he just gave me the look—you know, the one where he raises his eyebrow and shakes his head?" Kaitlyn laughed. "He does that a lot, you know."

"I can see him now. He's probably not quite used to your exuberance." Tina smiled. "But he loves you. You're going to have so much fun. Come on." She took Kaitlyn's elbow and guided her to the living room. "We've got other stuff to talk about."

Tina sat her down on the couch and plopped down beside her, shoulders touching.

"What kind of other stuff? What's going on?" Kaitlyn's eyebrows knit and her nose scrunched up.

"Well," Tina dragged out the word like it was a ride on a roller coaster. "I did something really stupid and impulsive."

Kaitlyn smiled. "That would be the Tina I know and love."

"No, this was really dumb. You know how mad my dad makes me sometimes?"

Kaitlyn locked eyes with Tina. "What did he do this time?"

"I don't really mind helping with the foundation. But there's this big event they're planning. I said I'd make fliers for it, but then dad came in out of the blue and said I was supposed to get up in front of hundreds of people and tell them what my experience was with Max. He didn't ask, he just told me. He was just going to put it on the agenda without even seeing if I wanted to or not."

"Rude." Kaitlyn clenched her fist in the air, ready to pop Tina's invisible dad.

"Right? So, this is where the dumb part comes in. Nate was in the break room with me and we were just making small talk when this happened. When dad told me that and then walked out, I was ready to blow a gasket. I had to get out of there. I was so mad!"

"How mad?"

"Sooo mad!" Tina's hands formed tights fists and she tightened her shoulders and clenched her teeth.

"Ha! I made you laugh!" Kaitlyn punched her playfully in the shoulder. "You're not to the stupid part yet, though," Kaitlyn said.

"Yeah, well, so I grabbed Nate's arm and asked him if he could take me in his car, somewhere really fast, so I could feel the wind in my face and shake off my anger."

"And he agreed?"

"Uh, not exactly. It was more like I forced him. Like I didn't really give him a choice. The next thing I know we're driving down the back roads by the strawberry fields at eighty miles an hour and I'm spewing my guts out to him."

"What did he do? What did he say?"

Tina held Kaitlyn's gaze. "He listened. Then he pulled the car over." Silence.

"Spill it."

"Then he said I was beautiful."

"He's right! Then you..."

"I started snotty crying. And he put his arm around me and ran his fingers through my hair."

"Did he kiss you?"

"No."

"Did you wish he did?"

"Kinda. I don't know. Yeah. Maybe."

Kaitlyn leaned over forehead to forehead. "It would be okay to have a guy in your life. But I need to meet him first before you go any further so I can give my approval." She smiled.

"Yeah. Okay. Good." Tina took a breath and shuddered.

"Breathe." Kaitlyn drew her hands down in front of her face and let out a deep breath. "Can't wait to hear how it goes the next time you go to the foundation. That should be rich."

Tina punched her in the arm and scowled. Rich wasn't exactly the word Tina would have used. No matter what her dad said, she was *not* going to get up in front of a million people and bare her soul about life growing up with Max. No way. Not ever.

Chapter Fourteen

The hospital waiting room was packed. A small girl with an ear infection, a teen holding onto his dad as he hopped in, his leg apparently broken. An old woman in a wheelchair with an oxygen tank by her side.

Nate looked at the bright lights in the emergency room where his mom waited. The hard plastic of the formed chairs couldn't have been more uncomfortable. He rubbed his aching muscles, tight from holding them close to his body to avoid touching the slovenly woman next to him, puffy bruises around her eye, a sure indication of abuse. A boy, maybe ten years old, threw up in a trashcan his mom had grabbed just in time.

The odor was more than Nate could take. He needed to get away. Maybe a cup of coffee would help. Judging by the constant swish of the sliding doors and unending activity, it was going to be a long night before his mom would be seen.

"I'm going to get a cup of coffee."

His mother nodded, her face pinched with pain. He hated leaving her like that, but if he didn't get some caffeine, he wouldn't be able to help either of them. He staggered down the hall, cursing his dad under his breath, not paying attention to where he was going.

"Nate?" It was Tina. She stopped in front of him. "What are you doing here? What's going on?"

His stomach froze. This was the first time he had seen her since *that* day where he took her for a ride. She looked adorable in her scrubs covered in little foxes that matched the red of her hair.

"Tina! Oh, hey." He ran his hand through his hair. "It's a long story." Was he ready to share this trauma with her? What if it didn't end well? She might push him away and that would be the end before anything ever really began.

"You look like you got run over by freight train." Tina gave a half grin. "Sit down here. You want coffee? Something to eat?"

"Do I look that bad? I could use a cup of coffee. Maybe a sandwich." He ran his hand through his hair and sat down on the amber vinyl chair. A scripture on the table said *God is our refuge and strength. A very present help in trouble.* Was that true? How about the Big Guy step in and take his dad down?

He watched Tina go to the empty counter. He checked the time— nine thirty. They'd been here for five hours.

Tina returned with a steaming cup of coffee and a ham sandwich. She set packets of mayo and mustard on the table next to him. She left and returned with a mocha for herself and a cup of soup.

"Do you want to talk about it? It's okay if you don't. You look exhausted." She put her spoon into the broccoli cheese and blew on the steaming bite.

Nate locked eyes with her. "My mom called this afternoon and wanted me to fix her flat tire. It should have been a quick fix and then I planned to work out at the gym." Nate sighed. "So much for those plans."

"I had just replaced the tire when I saw a man going into the house out of the corner of my eye. I thought it was a neighbor." He paused to take a bite of his sandwich.

"It wasn't?"

"No. It was my dad." His face was scrunched up in disgust.

"I take it you don't care for your dad?"

"That's an understatement! When he's not high on meth, he's halfway decent. The rest of the time he's a complete monster."

Tina sipped on her mocha. "Go on. I'm listening."

"He was screaming at my mom and tearing the house apart looking for money. Then he shoved her, and she hit her head. She's still waiting in ER." He looked in that direction.

"Woof. I get frustrated with *my* dad, but it's a problem the size of a gnat compared to you. That is terrible. How did you get him to leave?"

"I lured him outside. I told him I had money in the car. He must have seen me pick up my phone cuz the next thing I knew," Nate paused. His muscles tensed and he took a breath. "He smashed in the rear window of my car with a tire iron and ran to the front and damaged the hood and my engine." His voice was barely a whisper. He put his hands on each side of his bent head.

Tina reached out and put her hand on his shoulder. "Oh Nate. Not your car! You love it. You must be devastated."

He moved his hands to the table. "A neighbor called 911 and the cops hauled him off. I had to call an ambulance for my mom. I couldn't even drive her here."

"Is this the first time it's happened? I mean, abuse?"

"Nope." His lips were tight. "This has been my life since I was in grade school. I hate him. I lay in bed at night thinking of how I could shoot him in a dark alley, or poison his food, or hire a hit man. My mom has scars all over her body from his beating her up." He left off the part about how many scars he had. He finished off his sandwich and basketball tossed the wadded wrapper into a nearby garbage can.

"Hey, I thought you worked days," he said.

"I do. But they were really short-handed, so they called me in."

"I better get back to my mom. Hopefully, they've got her checked out and we can go home." He stood to leave. "Thanks for the sandwich and coffee. I needed that." He took a step, then turned. "And the listening ear."

"Turn-about is fair play, right? I'll see you Thursday when I come volunteer. Hang in there. I'll be praying for you."

Nate walked a few more steps, then turned. Tina gave a little wave. He returned a weak smile. Maybe her prayers could help him come to terms with the cards he had been dealt, but he had his doubts.

Nate unlocked his front door, took off his shoes and set them neatly next to the door mat. He rubbed his hand through his hair and rested it on the back of his neck. Then he plopped onto his couch, legs spread out in front of him and crossed his arms as if to protect himself from further pain. He took in a deep breath and blew out his mouth. He stared at the floor, oblivious to the swirls in the carpet.

Five wasted hours to get his mom through the hospital ordeal, a call for an Uber to get her home safely and then tucked into bed. His dad knew how to suck the life out of the people he should have loved.

Chuck let out a squeak and studied Nate through the bars of his cage. He cocked his head as if asking what the matter was.

Nate sighed. It was hard to hold in his anger when a soft, furry pet looked longingly at him. He got up, opened the cage door, and gave Chuck a peanut. Chuck grabbed it eagerly and tore into it.

"What am I going to do, little buddy?" He stroked Chuck's head. "I hate this anger that boils up in me. I don't want to be that person who lives each day holding a grudge." Chuck gave a little chirp.

Nate shut the cage door and latched it. He told Alexa to turn off the lights and set his alarm for six a.m., then headed to bed. He'd worry about getting a rental car tomorrow. Maybe he should take the day off. The cure for the disease would just have to wait another day. Besides, Tina wouldn't be there until Thursday. He didn't want to miss a day with her.

Chapter Fifteen

It was one of those sunny days that greet you first thing in the morning like a fresh cup of roasted coffee. It made you want to spread your arms wide and embrace life. Tina was glad today was a nurse day and not her volunteer day. She wasn't sure she was ready to face her dad.

She scanned her name tag and pushed the button for the elevator to the surgery ward. The doors opened and Peter was standing there, eyes glued to his phone.

"Hey," Tina said.

"Oh, hi! Just looking at a text from my dad. He wants me to come home and mow the fields this weekend. You wanna come ride a tractor with me?"

"Boy, sure sounds like fun, but I think I'll pass. Maybe you can find yourself a hot date on Farmers Only who would love to help." The elevator stopped and they got out, but not before Peter nudged his shoulder into her. Tina laughed as she regained her footing.

"What? It's not a bad idea, you know."

"You should sign up for...." Peter looked at the ceiling.

"For what? You guys already tried that, remember?" Maybe

it was possible she didn't need to sign up for a dating site. Thinking of Nate's arm around her still sent tingles through her.

"Anyway, we both know how that turned out for Kaitlyn," Tina said.

"And you think *I* should sign up?"

They walked up to the white board announcing the surgeries for the day. Transport walked by pushing a man on a stretcher. His filthy sandy hair had worked itself into dreads and hung off the edge. He looked like he'd worn the same set of clothes since Clinton was in office.

"The skunks on my family's farm smell better than he does," Peter whispered and waved his hand back and forth in front of his face.

Tina laughed.

The man grimaced and cried out.

"Hurry, you gotta help me. I can't stand this pain! Give me the good stuff."

Daniel came up behind them and placed his hands on each of his friends' shoulders. "Looks like we're in for some fun this morning." He offered a broad smile.

Peter rubbed his hands together and looked at Tina. "Let's go. It's a beautiful day to save a life. They followed the stretcher into an empty patient room and stood by as transport carefully slid the sheet under the man to the bed.

"Careful! You could have dropped me. Do you even know what you're doing?"

The two men in transport put on their poker faces. Best not to interact with this guy.

"Tell me your name. What have we got going on here?" Tina asked.

"Randall. I got hit by a school bus. Can you believe that? What do you think went through those little kids' heads?"

Expletives flew like a burst water balloon. "Give me some meds now or I'll have your job! And don't you try that Tylenol or oxy crap, I want the good stuff, you know what I mean!"

"Woah now, partner. We're here to help." Daniel reached out to pull the bloodied t-shirt over Randall's head. His arm hung limp, making it difficult to accomplish.

"Where does it hurt?" Tina asked.

"My arm. Obviously. Your eyes not working?" More expletives.

Tina wasn't sure whether to laugh or give him her best scowl.

"Anywhere else? How are your ribs? Your legs?"

Randall felt his ribs with his good arm and then tried to move his legs. He let out a scream.

"I can't feel my legs. Nurse, you better fix me, or I'll call my lawyer. I swear, every time I come in this place you people mess something up. Don't you know how to do your jobs?"

As Daniel put Randall's scruffy backpack into the cabinet, a bottle of Jim Beam rolled onto the floor.

"Hey! Don't touch that! That's my medicine! If I come back and even a drop of it is gone, I'll sue."

It took both Daniel and Peter to gently maneuver his pants off. Both tibias had been shattered and were sticking through the skin.

"I bet you like what you see, nursey." Randall's slimy smile revealed teeth which hadn't been brushed since the ice ages.

"Whoa there, partner, take a step back, no need to be creepy," Daniel replied. His lips tightened.

Tina stifled a snort. She loved working with Daniel and Peter. As irritating as they could be, it was nice to have them in situations like these when patients lost all sense of decorum. Well, in this case, there obviously wasn't decorum to be lost.

She immediately thought back to a time when a totally out

to lunch old grandpa ran down the hall after her buck naked in the middle of the day and Peter stepped in to save her, dressed courageously in the John Deere scrubs Kaitlyn's mom had made. Talk about a way to ruin a good lunch. But that's one thing about nursing. There's never a dull moment.

"Daniel, can you and Peter take over? I'll call the surgeon with a report."

They nodded as she left the room. In the hall, she leaned over, hands on her knees and head hung low. *Maybe surgery isn't the floor for me.* She took several deep breaths and went to the nurse's station where she put in a call to Dr. Roberts.

When she returned, Daniel had Randall prepped for surgery. His scraggly dreads were pulled into a pony and tucked into a bouffant cap and his tattooed arms and legs had been bathed with umber betadine. Transport carefully moved him back onto the stretcher to take him to the surgical ward, but not without screaming and vocabulary your average grandmother would have washed your mouth out with soap for.

"Take five," Peter said. It will be a while before Dr. Roberts is ready for us to join him. Let's see if there's any goodies in the staff room."

"How in the world did he get hit by a bus, anyway?" Tina said, leading the way.

"You couldn't smell the booze on his breath? That guy had been drinking like nobody's business," Daniel said.

"He probably stepped off the curb right into the bus. I feel for the bus driver and kids. They'll probably have nightmares for weeks." Peter grabbed a cup from the rack and poured himself coffee. The steam rose and he breathed in the fragrance.

Kaitlyn stuck her head in. "Hey, somebody loves us! They brought scones!" She put one on a napkin and joined them.

"Remember the time when we were on nurse Rached's

floor and that guy came in higher than a kite on meth?" Tina said. She dunked her scone in her coffee.

"That could have been any one of guys coming in on meth." Peter took a bite.

"I know which one you mean. He was the guy who was hallucinating and tried to get away by climbing through the ceiling panels," Daniel laughed.

"And then fell through the roof and onto the floor!" Tina held her side. "I know we shouldn't be laughing but it was so funny to see the expression on his face—like what he had been doing was perfectly normal and how could this happen to him."

"Well, that's one good thing about this job. You always have stories to tell," Daniel said.

"True that," Kaitlyn said. "Hey, we need to have a game night. We haven't had one for eons."

"Yeah. How about a barbecue. Daniel's got a grill," Peter said.

"If you bring the steaks—didn't your dad just butcher a steer?" Daniel turned to Peter.

"Yeah, he actually did. I'm going there this weekend. I'll bring some back."

Tina pulled out her phone and checked her calendar. "Next Friday work?"

"That'd be great. I'll double check with Miya," Daniel said.

"Ooohh, you could invite Nate," Kaitlyn put her hand on Tina's and fluttered her eyelashes.

Tina could feel the blood rush to her face as everyone turned to look at her. Peter cocked an eyebrow. "Nate, huh? Is someone homing in on my territory?"

"Keeping secrets from us, are you?" Daniel said.

Tina flipped Kaitlyn's hand off hers.

"It's just a guy at the foundation." Tina ran her finger around the rim of her coffee cup.

"Okay. Well. Invite him over. Let's see if we approve," Daniel said.

Three heads nodded.

Anxiety shot through Tina. Was she ready to take this to the next level? Then again, these were her best friends. If they didn't approve, that would be a sure sign to stop before things went any deeper.

An assistant peeked his head in the door. "Surgery's ready."

"Okay, team, let's move 'em out," Peter put his cup in the sink as the rest followed suit.

Chapter Sixteen

Tina jogged in place waiting for the light to change. The morning sun reflected off the cars as they whizzed by, convertibles with the tops down and occupants with their hair blowing in the breeze. It looked fun—so relaxing and free.

The light turned and she jogged on ahead, glancing at a small barking dog behind a front fence. She couldn't believe, of all the random nights to pull relief, she ran into Nate. That confident, I-can-save-the-world face he wore at the foundation was not evident. He looked like he'd been run over by a Mack truck. She guessed in a way, he had. Spencer had said something about him being abused but seeing him like that. It was like he was carrying a ton of cinderblocks on his back. She wanted to fix that. To remove them one by one. She wasn't exactly sure how she was going to do that, but she'd talk to Papa God and see what he thought. He always gave her guidance when she asked.

Fixing things. Her dad had suggested it was time to spread Max and her mom's ashes. She was ready to let go of Max. But her mom? She felt like she'd be losing her if she let her ashes go.

They were all she had left. Her fingers wrapped around her locket.

Tina rounded the corner and saw Martha pulling weeds in her garden. She was humming something. What was that song? She thought she should know the name of it. It was catchy, whatever it was. Tina slowed and walked up her slate walkway, making sure not to startle her new friend.

"Good morning, Martha." Tina rested her hands on her hips. Martha stood up and smiled.

"Tina, good to see you." She removed her garden gloves, dirt on one side, purple floral design on the other.

"It's good to be out in the early morning before it gets so hot. I love summer, but, whew, sometimes it's best to be inside." Tina wiped her brow with the back of her hand.

"Yes, these weeds keep me busy!" She set down her hori hori on the brick border, careful to point the sharp end of her Japanese tool towards the house. "Would you like to come in for a glass of iced tea?"

"I'd love that." Tina followed her up the wooden steps and through the screen door. "What was that song you were humming? It reminded me of my grandma."

Martha took some glasses from the cupboard and a glass pitcher of tea from the fridge.

"Peace Like a River. It's one of my favorites." She poured and handed a glass to Tina.

"Let's go sit on the back porch. It's cooler there."

Two wooden rocking chairs were situated to overlook the manicured lawn and professionally landscaped border. Purple heather, borders of pink and purple petunias, lobelia, and dinner plate dahlias. Tina imagined Martha and Robert sitting out here, enjoying an evening. Her mom would have loved this. It was so peaceful. She fingered her locket and thought again about spreading her ashes. Would that finally put things to rest?

"So, what's new in your life?" Martha asked. She took a sip of her tea.

"I think I told you my roommate's getting married in a few months. I'm going to miss having her around."

"You guys are pretty close?"

"Like sisters. I guess. I never had a sister, but if I did, it would be like her." Tina sipped on her tea.

"I had a sister. She was a year younger than me and we were awfully close. She died a few years ago. It nearly broke my heart. First Robert who was my best friend, and then Mary. It really left a hole."

"I bet you've been lonely." Tina looked reflectively at the porch railing, then down at her hands.

"Yes. At times. But thank goodness for God. He says he'll be your husband and best friend. So, when I get lonely, I just start talking to him." She smiled.

Tina looked at her. The soft wrinkles in Martha's face. The wisps of grey hair, curling down. She was so calm. So, satisfied. Tina wanted to be like her when she grew old. Tina brushed a lock of hair out of her eyes.

"I'm starting to realize that about him, too."

"Well, is your friend moving far away?"

"No, actually, she's just moving a few blocks from here. I'm really excited for her. It's not going to be that bad having her gone. It's just that she won't always be there. She's going to have a new life. Without me."

"Sounds like you're feeling left behind."

"Yeah, I guess." Tina set her cup down. "Can I ask you something?"

"Sure, of course."

"Was Robert cremated? I mean, you don't have to tell me if you don't want."

"Yes, he was. Why do you ask?"

"My dad thinks it's time to spread my brother Max and mom's ashes." Tina held a finger to her lips and started chewing her nail.

"How are you feeling about that?"

"I don't know. I think it would be good for my dad. He needs to move on."

"And you think that won't happen until they're spread?"

"It's like he's stuck. It seems like he's holding onto them. Like it's always there—the elephant in the living room." Tina frowned and ran her fingers through her hair. She watched her ice cubes as she swirled her tea, avoiding Martha's eyes.

"And what about you? Are you feeling a little bit stuck too? It would be natural for you to feel that way."

"I don't know. Maybe." She set her glass onto the side table.

"Grieving is not easy. It's hard work." Martha rocked back and forth. "How is your relationship with your dad?"

Tina's eyes flitted as they followed a robin up to the tree branch. "It's okay. Kind of. Well, not exactly that great. I always felt like I was just a third wheel, ya know? All the attention was always on Max or mom. And I get it. They were way more important than me. I always felt like I was just a shadow."

Martha studied Tina until she locked eyes with her. "I can see how you would feel that way. But I would bet that your dad loves you way more than you would ever know. And maybe, I don't know your dad, but maybe he distances you because he's afraid he'll lose you too."

A tear ran down Tina's cheek. She swallowed over the lump in her throat and ran the back of her hand over her cheek to wipe the moisture. Martha set her glass onto the table.

"Tina, dear, I'll be praying for you. This is really hard. Your daddy God is bigger than this. And He desires healing for you and your dad." She stood up. "Come here and give me a hug."

Standing together, Tina felt the warmth of Martha's arms

envelop her. She wrapped her arms around her waist and wished she could stay there forever.

Martha pulled away. "You are welcome here anytime. Let me know how things work out."

"Thank you. Really." She took a deep breath. "You are just what I needed."

Martha smiled.

Tina walked out to the front porch, her fingers waving timidly at Martha as she shut the door. What would Kaitlyn do when she faced hard things? Tina braved a smile, straightened her shoulders, gave a ptooey, pretending to spit over her shoulder and then broke into a run. The warmth of the sun, like powerful arms enveloped her, reminding her that Papa God was right there watching over her, filling the gaps like waves filling divots in the sand. It was a good reminder that there was Someone who was by her side and would help her get through anything.

Chapter Seventeen

Tina sat in her car a few extra minutes, checking her texts, stalling before she went into the foundation. This was the first day that she had been back since her joy ride with Nate. And, she hadn't talked to her dad since then. Was he going to be mad? Or worse, pull a matchmaker role. She opened her car door, took a deep breath, and stepped out.

Her conversation with Nate at the hospital hadn't gone badly. Things *should* be alright, shouldn't they?

Spencer nodded at Tina and resumed checking in a new family.

"Tell me your names please." He typed in the form—David, Megan, Noah.

The little boy, Noah, held onto the back of his dad's legs, jumping to try and climb on his back. David hoisted him up and sat him on his shoulders. Noah's blue eyes sparkled.

"Look dad, I can touch the ceiling!" He ran his small fingers over the ceiling tiles.

Megan grinned up at him. "Careful." She looked back at Spencer. "Noah loves being up there. David is so tall he feels as if he's on top of the world."

"Cute kid, that's for sure," Spencer said. "Looks like I have everything I need. You can take a seat in the waiting room. The counselor will be right with you."

David set Noah down and he ran to the bookshelf, selected a dinosaur book, and ran back to his parents.

He looks normal to me. They better enjoy it while they have the chance. Tina glanced over her shoulder towards Nate's office. Should she go in there and say hi? Maybe not. She'd just wait and see what happened. She took two steps down the hall and then turned. Why not? We're just friends, right?

"Hey Nate, good morning!" Nate looked up from his computer and knocked some Styrofoam balls onto the floor where they rolled across the floor.

"Oh, hey! Come on in." His eyes brightened.

Were his hands shaking as he bent down to retrieve the balls? Tina smiled. Oh, that she should have that effect on a guy.

His office was almost as large as her dad's with two lounge chairs and a huge picture window overlooking the Willamette River. A person could spend their days daydreaming sitting in his chair.

Tina sat down at the edge of the chair across from him, leaning forward, her hands beside her knees resting on the front of the cushion.

"How's your mom?"

"She's okay. They finally got her stitched up and she's back home. She's been in the ER so many times they know her by name." A wan smile played on his lips.

"Well, glad they were able to fix her up. You doing okay?"

"Yeah. I guess. My dad being there threw me for a loop. I'll get over it." Would he? He obviously wasn't over it now.

"You wanna talk about it?" She sat back and waited for him to look at her.

"Not really. There are cures to be found and more important things on my mind."

Tina was hoping that she was one of those important things.

She pointed to the structure on his desk. "What's that? It looks cool."

"I'm making a model of the molecular mechanism of juvenile batten disease." Nate had taken skewers and attached small colorful Styrofoam balls creating a web. Each ball was labeled with several letters.

It was Greek to Tina.

"It looks very sciency. That's a word, right?" She laughed.

"Ummm. Maybe."

Tina smiled at his lopsided grin. She was glad she could erase the strain on his face if only for a short while.

"What are you up to today?" Nate leaned back in his chair and put his feet on his desk, his hands resting behind his head.

"Gonna start work on the fliers for the fundraising event. Hey, mind if I sit in here to sketch them? I can be quiet as a mouse." She batted her eyelashes.

The corner of his mouth quirked up.

"Yeah, I guess. I'll have my head in my computer, so I won't be particularly good company, though."

"That's okay. I just don't want to sit alone. I'm more creative that way." She set her tote bag on the floor and stood. "I'm going to get a cup of coffee. Want one?"

"Sure. Just black." He handed her his insulated mug with the batten logo on the side.

Why hadn't her dad given her one? Maybe she just wasn't special enough.

She walked down the hall toward the break room, hoping to sneak by without her dad seeing her. He had to know about the great escape. But this was just wrong. Why should she feel anxious when she was around him? She wasn't a little girl. She was helping him out, for pity sake. And anyway, hadn't he suggested she pair up with Nate? Tina straightened her shoulders and peeked into his office.

"Hey dad." He looked up from his desk.

"Oh hi, honey. I'm glad you're here. Do you think you could work on those fliers today?"

"I guess you read my mind. That was my plan."

"Say, have you thought any more about when you want to spread your mom's and brother's ashes?" Mark had his hands clasped and twiddled his thumbs.

Tina looked at the floor. "Not really." The very thought made her uncomfortable.

"It's okay. I was just wondering. Let me know when you decide, and we can make a special day of it."

"Yeah." She held Nate's coffee mug up. "Going to fill this up and get to work." Tina backed out of the office and headed down the hall. He hadn't made any reference to Nate and her taking off. Maybe he didn't even know. Had been oblivious. All that worry for nothing.

She returned and settled into Nate's office. She pushed the armchairs end to end and pulled out a large sketch pad. She slipped off her sandals, sat on one chair and bent her knees, resting her bare feet on the other chair. Her pedicured teal toenails matched her blouse.

"Make yourself at home, why don't you?" Nate's lips curved in a half smile.

Tina wrinkled her nose and smiled.

"I think I will!"

She pulled out her charcoal pencil and began sketching. She looked out of the window, trying to picture what she should draw. Kids and their families. Maybe some balloons. Spencer had said there'd be jugglers and musicians. She was deep into her project when a little person came into the office.

"What's that?" Noah asked. He picked up one of the skewers and started to wave it around.

"It's a model of a gene. Want to help me finish it?" Noah nodded. "Here, take that skewer and poke it into this blue ball." Noah poked it gently and picked up another skewer.

"Can I poke this one into this green ball?" He picked up the smaller one.

"Yes, and then let's join them together."

Tina watched them. Spencer had said Nate was good with kids, but she was still surprised at how gentle and patient he was with Noah.

Tina tore off the page and started a fresh page, quickly sketching Nate and Noah, capturing Noah's curiosity.

"Hey there, Tiger. It's our turn to go." Dave took Noah's hand and turned to Nate. "Hey, thanks for entertaining him."

"No problem. He's a cute kid."

David threw him a smile and they walked out with Noah telling him all about building a model of a gene, just like the one inside of him.

Nate took a sip of his coffee. He pressed his lips together.

"What are you thinking?" Tina asked.

"He is a cute kid. I just can't stand the thought of one more kid having to suffer. I really have to put the pedal to the metal for a cure. I'm not sure where the breakthrough will come, but it has to come soon."

"You're going to come up with something great, I know it."

"Why are you so confident?"

"Cuz I've been praying for you and God answers prayers."

"I just hope you're right. That little boy needs a cure."

Tina nodded. Yes, he does. And that big boy needs to know that God answers prayers too.

Chapter Eighteen

Nate took a final look in the mirror, ran his hands through his hair and decided his beard trim was acceptable. Going to a barbecue with Tina shouldn't make him nervous. She was becoming a fairly good friend. Tina said she'd invited Spencer too. Nate could pal around with him if he needed to. He ran his sweaty palms down his cargo shorts. Was he supposed to bring something? It was a potluck. He checked his cupboard and snagged an unopened bag of Goldfish. He grabbed his wallet and key fob and headed to his car. He stopped, went back into the house, and grabbed his guitar. It was a barbecue, right? He'd have it just in case.

The auto repair shop had done an excellent job. It was hard to tell that his baby had been beat up. He ran his hand over the smooth hood. Why couldn't he repair his relationship with his dad as easily as they fixed his car? He knew why. There wasn't any repairing to be done. There had never been a relationship so how could you fix something that never existed?

He double clicked his fob and slid into the driver's seat. "Take me to Tina's." Funny how you could get used to talking to an inanimate object. He had put Tina's address and number into his phone last week when she had invited him to the barbecue. He smiled. Maybe, if everything went well tonight, he might take her on a date. A movie and dinner? She likes to run. Maybe they could do the 10k coming up. He drove down Tina's street and stopped when his car told him he had reached his destination. He checked himself in the mirror one more time and got out.

Tina met him on the front porch. She looked gorgeous, her curly red hair flowing over her shoulders, covering the thin straps of her top. She carried a pie.

"Ready? Did you bake that?" That smile. He wanted to hold onto it. He opened the passenger door and moved the Goldfish into the back seat.

"Did you bake those Goldfish?" She cocked her eyebrow and slid in.

Nate felt his cheeks burn. "Uh, I didn't really have anything to bring."

Cars lined the street at Daniel's. Maybe they could slip in unnoticed. This was a little out of his comfort zone. Tina guided him through the house and into the back yard where camp chairs were set out and food filled a picnic table.

"Help yourself to something to drink." She pointed to a cooler.

Nate pulled a can of sparkling water out and popped the tab. It was a beautiful evening with the slight breeze taking the temperature down to a comfortable level. He scanned the large yard. The buzz of conversations filled the air.

"Daniel, come meet Nate," Tina said.

Daniel, easy going and confident, walked over and shook his hand and patted him on the shoulder with his other hand.

"Finally, I get to meet the famous Nate."

Nate watched as a red glow worked its way up Tina's cheeks.

"Famous? Hardly." Where was that idea coming from?

"Tina talks about you all the time." Daniel grinned. "Only good things—no worries."

"Sit over here." Daniel nodded to an empty chair. Nate sat and placed his can into the holder. Daniel waved Peter over. "Peter, this is Nate. You know, Tina's friend?"

Peter smiled and gave a nod. "We're just getting ready to start a game of cornhole. Tina, you in?" Peter asked.

She shrugged. "Okay, you're in. You can be on Nate's team. Daniel and Miya will be on the other team. Where's Luke and Kaitlyn?"

"Did I hear my name?" Kaitlyn said. She pulled Luke over.

"You're on the other board. Go get Spencer and Claire. They'll complete your team. I'll be the judge." Peter strutted towards the board putting his thumbs through pretend suspenders.

Nate grinned as he watched Peter. Tina's friends seemed to have a good mixture of personalities.

"How good are you at this game?" Nate said. "I mean, if you're going to be on my team, I need to know that you're not going to bring me down."

Tina put her hands on her hips. "Really? I'm fairly sure you won't let *me* down.".

Did he just start something? Just *be cool Nate. You don't need to be the Damien Lillard of Cornhole.*

The game went into play with each team member tossing their bean bags. Tina threw hers. It landed on the board. She gave a whoop and a fist pump. Nate took his bean bag. Should he show her up? Why not? A little competition was fun. He tossed his bag. Into the hole. She turned and they slapped hands in a high five.

"We're a good team, you and I. Keep this up and we'll win the round," she said.

Nate was starting to feel like winning the round wasn't all he wanted to win. Just watching her made him want to smother her in kisses.

As his opponents tossed their bags, he glanced at the other team. Kaitlyn and Luke were whispering, looking his way. Good things? He sure hoped so. He had to win the hearts of Tina's friends if he was ever going to get anywhere with her.

"Spencer, come over here. You've got to meet Luke. He works at Healthy Kids and organizes their events. You guys have a lot to talk about." Tina put her hand on Spencer's shoulder and led him over.

"Nate, I'm starved. Let's see what our options are," Tina said.

There was enough food on that table to feed an army. This could be the beginning of a good thing—Tina and her friends and food. A good combination. Nate loaded his plate with savory steak, potato salad, and scooped fruit from a watermelon carved into a basket.

"I'm going to have to go back for dessert. I'm not going to be able to pass up that blackberry pie," he said and winked.

"Better just put your plate down and get some now, cuz it won't last," Daniel said. "Our girl Tina is quite a talented baker." He patted her on the back.

That grin of hers. He was never going to get tired of soaking it in. Tina glanced at Nate and quickly back to the pie.

♥ ♥ ♥

Dinner was over and they moved their chairs around the fire pit.

"This whole night would be perfect if only we had some

music," Kaitlyn said. She let out a sigh and gazed at the night sky.

"Hey, I know someone who plays guitar," Spencer said. He looked at Nate. "You didn't happen to bring yours with you, did you?" Nate's cheeks flushed. "You did, didn't you. Well, go get it!"

Tina's mouth fell open. Judging by that look, he guessed Tina didn't know he played.

Conversation was buzzing when Nate returned to the back porch. He pulled out his guitar and left the case on the end table. As he turned around, the circle of friends was now silent, eyes closed and each had thumbs up in the air. Standing behind Tina, he faced Kaitlyn who seemed to be the only one with her eyes open. Obviously, he had walked into some sort of game. Then Kaitlyn let out a squeak and the whole group erupted into laughter.

"So guys, how about some tunes? Any requests?"

♥ ♥ ♥

On the way home Nate turned to Tina. "So," he said, drawing out the word like it was a piece of taffy. "What was that game you were playing when I came back? It looked like you had to be one of the cool kids to play."

Tina bent her leg and slid it under the other one. She leaned against the door to face him. "Were you feeling left out?" she asked.

"A bit."

"I loved your music. You're really good at guitar, you know?"

"Are you skirting the question?" Nate raised one eyebrow.

"Caught me. Okay. It was a vote." Tina looked at him to judge his reaction. "To, um..."

She paused and wrapped her hand around her fingers.

"Yes."

"Alright. They were voting to see if you were okay for me." Words spewed out like a waterfall. Tina held her shoulders in, waiting for him to react.

Nate burst out laughing. Tina started to chuckle. Tears started running down his cheeks and he pulled the car over, afraid he would cause an accident.

"Tina." He shook his head. "You are unbelievable." Nate took her hand.

"You're not mad?"

He planted a kiss on it.

"How could I be? I just got voted into the Tina club. I'd be crazy to not want that."

Chapter Nineteen

"Where do you want me to put this box?" Tina asked. She was in the middle of the bustle of unloading sound equipment, boxes of promotional materials, crates of water and lots of cords.

"Just set them over on the stage." Her dad pointed with his chin to the portable stage just erected overlooking the Willamette River along Naito Parkway.

She watched a couple with a Golden Retriever pulling on his leash, headed towards a flock of geese. She laughed as they started honking and spreading their wings, like they needed to fight off a vicious threat.

Tina grabbed another box from the van, Batten Foundation boldly lettered on the side. She could have designed a better logo if her dad had only asked her. She watched as a tour boat docked nearby. Where were the occupants from? Maybe it was just a day trip of locals.

"Do you want me to take that?" Spencer reached out for the heavy load. "You should just go and unload these. We can handle the boxes."

Tina headed back to the stage. She stood in one spot just

staring at a box. Where was Luke when she needed him? He was the one with all the experience of putting on events. He would know what all this stuff went to. IV's she knew. Catheters she was a master at. Sound equipment? Foreign territory. As if on cue, Luke showed up.

"Tina!"

"Hey— where should I start?" Tina felt the tension in her shoulders release. She didn't mind helping with this event. But she had a nagging feeling that somewhere along the line her heart would be laid out on the table.

"This box. It's all yours. Not a clue."

Luke laughed. "I got this."

"Hey Tina." Nate set a folding table down. "Mind helping me set this up?"

"Finally, something I can be successful at!" She grabbed one end and helped turn it up.

"Are you going to speak this afternoon?" Tina asked. Nate pulled the legs out and latched them.

"Yeah. Just a little bit about the current research. You?"

"Not planning on it. I intend to man the table with water and brochures. No desire to get in front of a microphone." *And bare my soul to the world.*

"I know. It's not my favorite thing to do either." He brought the box of brochures to the table.

"Did you bring your guitar? You seem so comfortable when you're playing and singing."

"Actually, I did. I wrote a little song. I hope it's not dumb."

Tina smiled at the peek into his inner little boy.

"I can't wait to hear it. It'll be great, I'm sure." Nate nodded, eyes focused on the brochures.

♥ ♥ ♥

Tina and Kaitlyn sat on the newly mown grass. They watched pigeons tapping the sidewalk where a family threw cracker crumbs. Squeals of delight came as the toddler tried to pet one.

"I could sit here all day soaking up the sun. It feels so good to relax." Kaitlyn nodded her head in agreement.

"This last shift was pretty crazy, wasn't it? I mean, here we had a code and meanwhile that guy from some jungle comes in with that big boil on his neck."

"I know. It was gross. Then when Dr. Roberts lanced it." Tina shuddered. Instead of puss it had been a massive larvae wriggling underneath. She scrunched up her nose. "It was so huge— the size of a fifty cent piece. I couldn't believe it."

"Then when it started wiggling," Kaitlyn let out a squeak, "I about jumped out of my skin!"

"What was it, a foot long when it unraveled?" Tina held her stomach as she joined in with Kaitlyn's contagious laughter.

A shadow fell over the two of them. Tina looked first at his running shoes and then up to well-built muscles.

"I hope that laughter wasn't aimed at me!" Nate drew in.

"Just nursing war stories. Never fear," Kaitlyn said and let out a final laughing hiccup.

"Everything is all set up. We've got about an hour till we're scheduled to begin. Want to go for a walk?" Nate said.

"Sure, I'd love to," Kaitlyn said and began to stand up. Nate cocked an eyebrow. "What? You had someone else in mind?"

Tina punched her in the arm. "Oh, I wish I could, but I can't. Luke and I have a lunch date." Kaitlyn gave an exaggerated wink.

Nate reached both hands to pull Tina up. She brushed off her shorts.

Tina walked down the sidewalk with her hands by her sides. She glanced at his hand connected to muscled arms. Protective. She felt herself longing to touch them. She quickly turned her eyes away.

"How's Spencer holding up? He's running around like a chicken with its head cut off," Tina said.

"He's in his element. Especially having Luke's help. They're quite a team."

They stopped and leaned on the railing overlooking the water. Large freight ships were moored. A sailboat slid by with massive sails, a woman in sunglasses and broad brimmed hat sitting on the deck.

"Do you ever think of getting away? Traveling somewhere?" Nate said.

"Yeah, sometimes. Kaitlyn has gone to Honduras and is going to Iceland for her honeymoon. I've never really gone anywhere. But yeah, it would be nice to travel somewhere. Where would you want to go?"

"I don't know. Maybe take trains through Europe. I wouldn't want to drive on the wrong side of the road. But I'd consider riding a bike so you could really see everything. Then again, I've imagined myself hiking in the alps. I'd have to get in shape first," he said.

Tina chuckled at the serious look on his face.

"What?"

"You're always so serious! You should have a dreamy look in your eyes when you think of where you might want to go."

"Yeah, I guess so. But, where would you want to go?" He followed her gaze as several seagulls flew overhead.

Tina fell silent and watched the small waves lapping the

shore. She hesitated and glanced up at Nate. Did she want to share that with him?

"Well," she began. "There's a certain beach. The water is clear and turquoise. It's beautiful. At least in the photos."

"Where is it?" The seagulls had landed and were hopping on the sidewalk next to them pecking at spilled popcorn.

Tina took a breath. "It's in the Dominican Republic." She pulled her arms back from the railing and gripped it with her hands.

"That sounds pretty. You haven't been there have you?"

Tina shook her head. "It's where my mom dreamed of going. Max filled all her time. And then she died." Tina fingered her locket and felt her throat choke up. She swallowed. "That's where I want to go to spread their ashes." She looked away.

Nate took his hand and placed it on hers. He stared at the water. It seemed like minutes passed in the silence. But she was okay with that. Somehow in that small gesture, she felt safe and her heart protected.

Chapter Twenty

A crowd was beginning to gather, watching a volunteer walking on stilts juggle balls. He was dressed in a clown outfit complete with a multi-colored wig and striped pants. A small band of folk musicians were tuning up their guitars, fiddle, and hammer dulcimer. Families watched sugar crystals form into strands of blue cotton candy. A girl in a wheelchair reached for it, a grin filling her face.

The band struck up a lively tune of *Dancing with Bears*. A woman with a floor length flowing skirt and ribbons woven into her long grey hair grabbed the hands of several children and began to dance to the one-two-three rhythm.

"Come on, let's dance!" Tina grabbed Nate's elbow and steered him towards them.

He stood and looked at her, not sure what to do with his feet or hands. She placed his right hand on her waist and his left in her hand, smiling as she showed him how to waltz.

"You can't tell me you've never danced!" Tina laughed.

"Yes, I could. I've never been around this kind of music. Where did you learn to do this?"

"Middle school P.E. They made us do it. We said we hated it but I have to admit it was pretty fun."

Nate soon got the hang of it and pulled back to send her into a little twirl.

"Woah, quick learner. Next we'll have to learn to tango."

The song ended and they grabbed some water. Tina looked over at the unmanned brochure table.

"Yikes, I better get over there to my post!"

"Yeah, I better get my speech together," Nate said.

"Welcome everyone," Spencer boomed over the mic. "We're really glad you've joined us today. We hope you're enjoying the entertainment and free food."

Heads nodded.

"I'd like to introduce you to Mark Halverson, the executive director of the Batten Foundation. As many of you know, Mark is no stranger to the trials and hardships this disease brings upon families. He's made it his life's work to create an environment where people can express their fears and experiences and offer hope. Mark, come on up here."

Tina watched her dad stand a little taller with a broad smile on his face. She looked at the crowd. You would have thought he was some kind of hero. *They just don't know him like I do. But then again he's there for them.*

"Thank you, Spencer," he said. "He's done a great job of putting this event on, don't you think?" Applause.

"Those of you with family members working their way through this disease know what an uphill battle it is. I know there are also people in the crowd who have been faithful supporters of the foundation. For that, we are most grateful. We couldn't do this without you."

Family groups pressing forward, not to miss a word, wanting to spot those who have contributed hope to their lives. More applause.

"I hope you can look around and into the eyes of those you are helping. Then tell your friends to open up their wallets!" Laughter.

"Next, I'd like to introduce you to the most important person on our team, Nate Bronson. He is our researcher who will find the cure for you."

Cheers and hollers.

"Nate! Come on up here."

Nate walked onto the stage and glanced at Tina, his eyebrows raised in a what-have-I-gotten-myself-into look.

"Hello everyone. I'm much more comfortable behind a computer or a book than standing behind a mic."

Laughter.

"I feel extremely excited that we've made a small breakthrough in our research. A recent cure was found for Huntington disease, which is close in structure to batten. We hope we're on the right track to a cure. Maybe even this year."

Tina could feel an aura of hope surround them. Nate reached for his guitar and adjusted the strap around his shoulder.

"I've written a song for you. Enjoy." Nate glanced at Tina before he began strumming.

Tina rested her elbows on the table and put her hands on her cheeks. This guy. He writes songs? She was beginning to think her first impression of him was on the wrong track.

I look into the face of my infant
　Eyes the color of the sky
　Tufts of hair like his mama
　Little baby don't you cry.

. . .

You fill our days with wonder
  Our hopes lie in your hands
  We watch you grow into a toddler
  Visions of so many plans

Nate is singing about babies? He's so tender. What kind of dad would he be?

You little one, you are my baby
  We love to see your smile every day
  No matter what life brings we will love you
  We'll be the ones to show you the way

This isn't the way we predicted
  We thought your life would be secure
  But still we will love you every minute
  As long as you're here we'll endure.
  We will love you every minute
  In our arms you'll be secure.

Nate picked the last chord and set his guitar down. You could have heard a pin drop. He stepped down from the stage and walked to the back of the crowd. Mark walked onstage and took the microphone.

"Nate, that was beautiful. Thank you. You really know how to speak for all of us. Rather, sing for all of us."

Gentle laughter.

"And now, I have a lovely young lady who has a few words to say."

Tina looked around. She didn't see anyone who would be speaking next.

"Tina, come on up here and share your story."

He didn't just do that did he? I told him I didn't want to speak! Her arms wrapped around her stomach. *What should I say? She looked around for someone to rescue her.*

"Don't keep the crowd waiting, sweetheart." Mark walked towards her holding out the mic.

Tina's feet felt like she was slogging through thick muck as she made her way up the steps. He held the mic out to her. Her hands were shaking as she took it, a pleading look in her eyes. Mark turned and walked off the stage leaving her alone, front and center.

"I'm not sure how to follow up after Nate. He was good, wasn't he?" A trickle of sweat ran under her arms.

Smiles encouraged her.

"I suppose most of you know that my older brother had batten. He was my best friend. At one point I became his older sister and did things for him. It wasn't always easy. I'm sure you folks know that. But he was a beautiful person. Even though life wasn't the easiest, there was no doubt in my mind that he was meant to be in our lives. I guess if there was one thing I could say to you, it's to find something good in every day. Life could change at any moment and you can't get them back."

Spencer stepped onto the stage and took the mic.

"Thank you, Tina. And thank you everyone for coming."

Applause.

Tina felt like her legs weren't going to carry her to her table. She fell into the chair and let her forehead fall to her chest. Tears trickled down her cheeks. Strong hands began rubbing her shoulders. She took a minute to compose herself and looked up at Nate.

"You did it. You sounded good up there and you shared from your heart. It wasn't easy, was it?"

"Sometimes I hate that man! He knew I didn't want to go up there." Tina slammed her fist on the table. Tears streamed down her face and she sniffed, wiping her cheeks with the palms of her hands.

Nate grabbed a napkin from a nearby vendor and handed it to her.

"Maybe he thought you needed to talk about it."

"Or maybe he just wanted to embarrass me in front of a hundred people," she said tightly.

Nate's thumbs worked their way into her tight muscles.

Tina could feel herself start to relax. "Thank you Nate. I'm sorry. He just brings out the worst in me."

He kissed the top of her head. "He's all the family you've got."

Tina crossed her arms on the table and rested her head on them. Nate was right. Her dad was all the family she had. But did that make it right for him to force her into things before she was ready?

Nope. Not ready. She was just. Not. Ready.

Chapter Twenty-One

Tina sat in the back seat with Miya as Kaitlyn's sister Maggie drove their parent's SUV east on Hwy 26 towards Mt. Hood. It was one of those days when you couldn't help but smile. Gorgeous sunny day, a few puffy white clouds. Tina relaxed her shoulders and sighed. She needed a girl's weekend.

Maggie cued her tunes and all four girls joined in singing *Going to the Chapel* at the top of their lungs. They erupted into laughter.

Maggie turned on the blinkers and made a lane change getting closer to the ponderosa pines lining the road. "We should start a quartet. Miya, your voice is amazing! And Tina, where did you learn to sing harmony?"

Tina reached her hand out and placed it on Kaitlyn's shoulder. "Yeah, we could sing at your wedding, Kaitlyn. What do you think? I'm sure Luke would love it."

"Mm, maybe not." Her freckled nose wrinkled as she shook her head. "How much further, Maggie?"

"We just passed the sign for Marmott and the cabin is only a few miles from there." Maggie nodded her head towards the sign.

"Good— I gotta pee. That iced coffee went right through me," Kaitlyn said. She wiggled in her seat.

"Like dad says— 'gotta pee so bad my eyeballs are swimming'," Maggie laughed.

They rounded the corner and drove down a long dirt road bordered by bracken ferns and huckleberries. The vine maples were beginning to show their fall colors. Maggie parked and the girls piled out of the car. A full wrap around porch bordered the log cabin and a green metal roof protected it from the rain and snow. They climbed the steps and followed the deck to the back where it overlooked a flowing stream.

A fish jumped and Kaitlyn smiled. "Luke would love this place!"

"Yeah, but he's not here, is he. Just us girls!" Maggie bumped her shoulder into Kaitlyn.

"You couldn't have picked a better place for a bridesmaid weekend." Kaitlyn gave her sister a side hug.

Each grabbed their bags and groceries and made their way inside. The stairs heading to the open loft had rails made of stripped logs, accenting the raw log walls to the vaulted ceiling. The windows overlooked the woods and stream. A blue jay squawked, and hummingbirds flew to a feeder hung from the rafter.

Maggie and Miya set the groceries on the granite countertops and started putting milk, eggs and lasagna in the fridge and wine on the counter.

Tina and Kaitlyn made their way upstairs. The master bedroom had a king-sized bed with a log frame and was covered by a quilt decorated with bears and pines. It faced huge picture windows overlooking the stream. Kaitlyn held Tina's gaze.

"You're thinking of your honeymoon, aren't you," Tina said.

The corner of Kaitlyn's mouth turned up. "You are! I knew it."

They laughed.

"This will never do unless we all sleep in the same bed," Kaitlyn said. "We need to be in a room together. What fun is a slumber party if we're all separated?"

They moved down the hall to the next room.

Kaitlyn threw open the door. Sunshine filtered through the trees creating interesting shadows on the beds.

"Two sets of bunkbeds! I get the top." They tossed their bags onto their beds and returned downstairs where Maggie and Miya were sitting on the couch.

"...was going to have a naked guy pop out of a cake," Maggie said and let out a chuckle.

Miya turned to see Kaitlyn at the foot of the stairs, her eyes large. She put her hands on her hips and stomped over to Maggie.

"You wouldn't!"

"Wait!" Maggie said, shielding herself. "I was going to say, but I knew Kaitlyn wouldn't want that." Maggie put her arm around Kaitlyn's waist. "See, I know you."

Kaitlyn rested her head on Maggie's shoulder while Tina watched with envy. *This is what it would have been like if I'd had a sister.*

"Okay," Maggie said, rubbing her hands together. "Let's get this party rolling. I brought everyone a bag of goodies on the coffee table."

They rushed to the table. Tina pulled out a pair of sunglasses that said *Bride Tribe* and put them on. She struck a model pose. "We'll have to wear these to our nail appointment." She held out her hand showing her nails.

"Ooo la la— pink silky robes!" Miya said. She held hers up against her chest.

"I hope there's chocolate in there." Tina reached to the bottom of the bag, then smiled as she held out a cellophane bag of truffles.

Maggie shooed everyone upstairs to change. "Enough of this. Let's go soak in the hot tub, then nails and I've got a stack of romance movies cued up." Thoughts of Nate invaded Tina's mind. Snuggling with him on the couch, her mom's quilt wrapped around them watching Hallmark movies. Maybe a cup of hot cocoa. And cookies...

♥ ♥ ♥

The warm water enveloped Tina, allowing her to release the aches in her neck and shoulders. She laid her head back resting it on the edge of the hot tub and closed her eyes. Getting away was good. A change in scenery. She hadn't realized the amount of angst the batten event had built up in her.

She should have been happy to share about her experience. What held her back? Why couldn't she just separate her experience with her dad asking her to do it? If he loved her, he would see that she wasn't ready to share publicly. Then again, if she loved him, she would honor his request willingly, right? Life was so confusing.

The others slid into the water, laughing.

"Taking a nap?" Kaitlyn nudged her and handed her a glass of wine.

Tina fingered the beaded ring placed on the stem— her name etched into a small leather strip. "Just thinking." She glanced sideways at Kaitlyn. Now wasn't the time to fill her in on the sordid details and Kaitlyn had been so busy with Luke she hadn't had the opportunity to share her heart. "This is really nice. Getting away."

"I know, right? Not have to wipe any butts or give any shots."

"Or take any blood," Miya said.

"Woof, your jobs are gross! I'll just keep to my boring job as a secretary." Maggie set her glass down and stretched her arms out on either side of her.

"Okay Kaitlyn, I mean, Mrs. McCarthy, what are you most looking forward to?" Maggie asked.

Kaitlyn looked up towards the sky. "I'd have to say being with Luke 24/7. I want to fix breakfast for him. Or have him bring me coffee. I want to share every moment." She sighed.

All the things Tina would miss about Kaitlyn as a roommate.

"A little more snuggle time?" Tina gave an exaggerated wink and watched red creep up Kaitlyn's cheeks.

"Who wants to make a bet at how long it will be before she's pregnant?" Maggie's eyebrows raised.

"Let's see, wedding at Thanksgiving." Miya started counting months on her fingers. "I'd say a baby by August." They laughed.

"What about you guys— it looks like I'll take the lead. And proud of it! Who else wants kids?" Kaitlyn said

Eyes darted from one to another.

"First things first," Miya said. "But yeah, eventually I'd like to have some kids. I'm not sure about Daniel."

"Not me." Tina looked down and kicked her feet, gently moving the water. "I don't want to take the chance on having a kid with batten." She looked up, her eyes on Kaitlyn.

"Understandable. Okay then. So, Kaitlyn," Maggie said changing the subject, "What is Luke's worst habit that's gonna drive you nuts in ten years?"

"That's an easy one. Whenever he has a pen in his hand, he clicks it. He doesn't even have to be using it—he can just sit in front of the computer, or tv and he picks up a pen and click click click. It drives me batty!"

"That's an easy fix. Get rid of all the clickable pens!" Tina said.

"We could give him a big box of all kinds of non-click pens for a wedding gift," Miya said.

Kaitlyn laughed. "He probably wouldn't even know why he was getting them!"

Tina wondered what crazy bad habits Nate had. She'd have to keep an eye out for them.

"I'm starting to turn into a prune." Maggie looked at her wrinkled fingers and poked Tina. "Let's head to town and get a bite to eat, then get our tootsies done."

Tina ran a brush through her hair. She enjoyed the extra attention her red hair garnered. Max's hair had tinges of red, but hers was full on like her mom's. She changed into her silky pink robe wishing it had been teal to accent her hair and climbed onto the bottom bunk. Today had been the kind of fun she had needed. They had laughed as they wore their sunglasses to the nail salon, aware of the secret glances of those around them. Going out to lunch. When was the last time she'd done that?

The bed creaked as Kaitlyn climbed up the ladder and snuggled in. Maggie turned off the light as she came in. The full moon shone through the windows and cast amber light across the floor.

"I'm scared," Kaitlyn moaned.

"Kaitlyn, it's not even dark in here," Tina said.

"No. I'm scared of getting married. What if he finds out that I floss and sometimes forget to throw the string away? Or that I don't always make the bed? Or I don't replace the empty toilet paper roll?"

"Calm down. Really?" Maggie said putting on her big sister voice.

"He's just gonna have to get used to it. Those aren't the real worries of life, my dear," Miya said.

"Have you guys even had a fight?" Tina asked. She would know if they did, wouldn't she? Thoughts of heart to heart conversations scrolled through her mind, none leading to anything of magnitude.

"Not really. Well, kind of. There was that time when I thought he stood me up for coffee but really it was cuz his mom was in the accident and my phone died and he couldn't get ahold of me."

"But you kissed and made up and everything was happily ever after, right?" Maggie said.

"Yeah. I guess I'm just nervous. I want Luke to be my forever guy. I don't want anything to go wrong."

"You just have to take things day by day and be intentional about your relationship," Miya said. "That's what keeps Daniel and I together."

"Tina, are you seeing anyone?" Maggie asked.

"Yeah, Tina, how about Nate?" Kaitlyn said, her voice lilting.

Tina felt blood rush up her cheeks.

Miya chimed in. "Yeah, he's pretty cute. When he pulled out his guitar at the potluck it was like he turned into another person." She adjusted her pillow.

"How do you know him?" Maggie asked.

"He's a guy who works at my dad's Batten foundation. He's

a researcher trying to find a cure. I met him when I was volunteering." Tina raised her head and rested it on her hand.

"Have you gone on a date?" Maggie asked.

"Not yet," Kaitlyn said. "But she will. I can see it in the stars." She leaned over the edge of the bunk and wiggled her eyebrows at Tina.

"We've had several meaningful encounters. I wouldn't mind going out with him. He can be pretty serious. But I suppose I could try and break through that," Tina said. She felt warmth spread through her chest.

"Meaningful encounters? Do tell," Miya said. She sat up in her bed and rested her back against her pillows. "I hope this is juicy."

"Well, I kind of made him take me for a fast ride in his Lamborghini."

"Yeah, she wanted to escape her dad and grabbed Nate. Forced him to take her away. Poor guy didn't know what hit him!" Kaitlyn laughed.

"Okay, so it was a little impulsive. Then another time we had some good talks when he drove his mom to the hospital."

"So are you guys just friends? Or is this heading to something more?" Maggie asked.

"Something more," Kaitlyn jumped in.

"I'm starting to think it might be something more. We'll have to wait and see." The shadows hid Tina's slight grin.

Later that night, listening to Kaitlyn's soft snores, she propped herself up and stared at the moonlight.

God, is this who you have for me? Mom used to pray for my future husband. Could this be him?

She lay back down. *One step at a time. No reason to rush things. She knew she could trust Him on this journey. If Nate wasn't in His plans? She'd just have to leave that up to Him.*

Chapter Twenty-Two

Nate cradled a steaming cup of coffee in his hands. Rain was coming down in sheets and splattering against the kitchen window. He shivered. Maybe he should turn on the heat. Fall weather had definitely set in. Good thing the weather for the batten event had been nice. A day like this would have meant postponing it. That would have meant missing the opportunity to spend time with Tina. And seeing the twinkle in her unfathomably deep green eyes.

Did she really ask him to dance with that silly song? What was it? Something about bears. He couldn't quite remember because he had been so focused on not stepping on her toes. What he could remember was the scent and softness of her hair. The touch of her hands.

She didn't seem to mind when he had rubbed the knot out of her shoulders. He had hesitated at first, not sure if that was getting too personal. Small steps. He should just keep things slow and easy.

Chuck started squeaking, wanting attention. His black eyes gazed at Nate and his paws were held out in anticipation.

"Hey little buddy, you hungry?"

Chuck's black eyes stared at him.

"Here you go, here's a little nugget." Chuck grabbed it greedily and began munching.

Nate's phone buzzed. He grinned as he read the text from Tina.

<Hey Nate>

<Hi. What's up?>

<Kaitlyn and Luke wanted to know if you and I wanted to go to the pumpkin patch this week >

Nate looked out the window.

<What's the weather supposed to be like?>

<It should clear up tomorrow>

<Sounds like fun. Should I pick you up?>

<Does that mean I get another ride in your fancy car?>

Nate grinned. Would this be considered a date? He could see her cocked eyebrow luring him into the promise of fun and adventure. He could hear the lilt of her laughter and he was determined to do whatever it took to make this more than just a friendship.

* * *

Tina had been right. The rain had stopped and the clouds had drifted away. A rainbow shone in the distance. It was a sign of hope, right?

Tina was watching out the window as he pulled up. She stepped outside and pulled up the zipper to her sweatshirt. Her hair was tied in a pony, the breeze blowing the few tendrils hanging loose into her face. Nate got out of the car and opened the passenger door. The fragrance of her lotion made his breath catch.

"Hey, did you wear some slop shoes?" Tina said. "It's probably muddy from the rain."

"I hadn't thought of that." His eyes traveled to his shoes. "These aren't that great. Should be fine."

Tina slid inside. As he started the car she told Siri to take them to the Gunderson Pumpkin Patch, the one Peter's family owned.

"Where are Kaitlyn and Luke? I thought they were coming with us." Nate watched the screen as he backed the car into the street.

"They had to do some errands first. They'll meet us there."

Fields of pasture and apple orchards dotted the landscape. It was refreshing to leave the city for a day. Maples and ash were turning brilliant reds and oranges. They soon came to the Pumpkin Patch sign held by a scarecrow.

Tina rubbed her hands together. "This is gonna be fun!"

They got out and Nate locked the car. "Were we meeting Kaitlyn and Luke here?" he asked.

"Yeah, they were supposed to meet us at the entrance." She scanned the crowd. "Maybe they're running late. Let's just go on ahead. They'll find us."

Nate reached out his hand and Tina took it. She glanced up with a smile that he couldn't help but return.

Assorted sizes, colors and shapes of pumpkins and gourds were displayed on wooden shelves. Corn stalks were tied to poles and a scare crow was perched on the shelf. A high schooler dressed in denim coveralls, auburn hair in pigtails, greeted them and pointed her thumb in the direction of the activities.

Nate looked behind. "No sign of them?"

Tina checked her phone.

"They can't come. Luke's grandpa William needed them." Tina looked up. "I guess you're stuck with just me." She grinned and nudged him with her shoulder.

Nate was sure that was going to be just fine. He returned the gesture, basking in her nearness. They walked to where pumpkins were stacked next to several tall-beamed structures with sling shots fashioned out of rubber tubing and nylon pouches. Sheets were stretched between fence posts as targets.

"Are they actually shooting pumpkins at a target?" Nate's blue eyes widened. "This is going to be awesome."

Tina pulled out her phone and began to record as a crowd gathered to watch. Nate selected a pumpkin the size of a cantaloup and placed it in the pouch. It rolled out and the crowd booed.

"This is not going to be good," Nate said and a crooked smile formed. He placed the pumpkin back into the sling. Tina laughed, a sound that encouraged him to continue.

"You have to get way back."

Nate pulled the sling shot as far as it would stretch. "Crouch down!"

As he did, he lost his balance and landed in the mud. The pumpkin slipped out and rolled away. Tina slapped her forehead with the back of her hand and laughed.

"You didn't record that did you?" He stood up, frowned, and tried to wipe his pants off.

"Sure did! Try again." Her laughter was contagious.

Nate stood tall, puffed out his chest and put it into the sling again. "Third time's a charm!"

He pulled back as far as it would go, crouched down, and let go. This time it flew right into the target. Nate's smile stretched from ear to ear, and he gave a fist pump.

Tina ran up to him and gave him a peck on his scruffy cheek. Nate pulled her to him. He couldn't remember when he'd felt this happy.

"Mister Nate?" Noah tugged on his pant leg.

It took Nate a moment to place him. He recalled letting this kid play with the cell model in his office.

"You were really good! You were so funny when you fell!" He giggled.

"Well, hi there, Noah. You making fun of me?" Nate smiled and looked up at his parents. "Out for a fun day?"

"Yeah, we want to give this little guy as many opportunities as possible before..."

Nate nodded. Yeah, before he went downhill. Nate *had* to find a cure. He bent down to eye level, touched the brim of Noah's baseball cap, and tugged it down.

"Be sure to get a big pumpkin!" He was determined to not let this little guy get any worse.

Nate followed Tina to the hay bale maze. Kids were shouting and running amuck. Nate took Tina's hand as they went down the path, finding themselves making twists and turns leading to a dead end. Nate slid one arm gingerly around her waist and pulled Tina into the hay wall. His hands moved up to her shoulders.

She looked up at him with those clear green eyes, a grin blooming over her lips. His eyes went to her parted lips. He hoped she wanted this as much as he did. He softly let his lips touch hers and pulled back. She leaned into him stretching up on her toes to capture his lips in her own.

"What if we can't find our way out?" Tina whispered.

"I guess we might have to stay here forever." Nate grinned and gave her one more quick kiss before he took her hand and led her back through to the end. *That didn't turn out too badly.*

"Let's get some cider. And a cookie." Tina grabbed his hand and led the way to sit on a hay bale. "You ever been to a pumpkin patch before?"

"Not with activities." Nate looked away. "Going to the pumpkin patch was the one happy event I can remember with my dad. I was in kindergarten and he went with us on a field trip. He took time off work, and we spent the day together. I have a photo of us sitting on a hay bale holding my pumpkin. It was so heavy I could hardly lift it." The memory brought a smile to his lips.

"What happened with your dad?"

"I don't know. I think he got laid off and couldn't find another job. I suppose that's when he started using." He shook his head.

"Is that when your happy memories ended?"

"I guess. I just remember he started hitting on my mom and I'd be so scared I'd hide under my bed." He pulled his shoulders in. He hadn't ever really talked about this. Could he trust her?

"That must have been awful. Didn't you have anyone you could tell?"

The hurt always just under the surface.

"I was always afraid to tell. Sometimes," he paused and licked his lips. "Sometimes I had bruises from him grabbing me. I always wore long sleeves to cover them up. I didn't want my teachers or anyone to know. I had friends who had gotten put in foster care and I didn't want that to happen to me. I needed to be home for my mom."

"That's a pretty big burden for a little boy to carry." Tina put her hand on his arm. "Did you ever reach out to God?"

Nate looked at her. "I went to Sunday School with a neighbor. They had all these great stories about Jesus and said what a good friend he was. But when I'd go home, I wasn't ever seeing him stop the mess in front of me." He leaned his elbows on his knees.

She trailed her hand down to cover his hand. "I know. I pray a lot about how to fix the relationship with my dad. I mean, it's nothing like you and your dad. But sometimes I feel like I'm invisible to him and he only sees me when he needs something."

"Sounds like we both have problems feeling loved." Nate put his arm around her and pulled her close where she rested her head on his shoulder. He may not feel loved by his dad, but he was starting to feel loved by this beautiful girl. Maybe that was enough. For now.

Chapter Twenty-Three

Tina parked and turned off the wipers on her car. The rain was coming down in buckets, gathering fall leaves and swirling them down the street. She pulled up the hood to her raincoat and zipped it hoping she could get into the building without looking like a drowned rat. Her pulse raced as she looked forward to volunteering today. Maybe she should ask her dad if it would be okay to come twice a week. Any excuse to see Nate.

She pushed the glass door open and stood in the entryway shaking off the drops. She hung her coat on the hook and wiped the water out of her eyes and a stray wet lock off her forehead.

"Well good morning sunshine!" Spencer said. "You have the same cat-caught-the-canary grin as our friend Nate. Something going on between you two?" Eyebrows raised.

Tina felt the warmth of her blush. "Wouldn't you like to know." She sat down. "How do you think the event went?"

"It was sure great to have Luke help out. He's a wizard at those things." Spencer glanced at his computer.

"I knew you'd hit it off."

"I thought it went well. People were smiling. That's always a good sign. I think they really liked Nate's song." Tina smiled. She hadn't noticed how people were reacting she had been so caught up in listening to every word and strum. "Did it bring in much money?"

She leaned against the wall.

"Actually, yes. It was our biggest fundraiser of the year." He leaned back in his chair. "Tina, I know you didn't want to speak, but what you said was heart felt and made a connection with people. Thank you for doing that."

Tina looked down. She nodded. "Uh, thanks." She moved past his desk. "Guess I'll see what needs to be done today." She didn't want to go there—talking about her past. This was supposed to be a good day.

She headed down the hall and peeked in at Nate's door. He was deep in thought, reading a periodical. She smiled remembering him searching for something to sit on before he placed his muddy rear end on the driver's seat of his precious car.

"Hey you."

He looked up. His smile was bright. A good sign. She wanted to give him a peck on the cheek but wasn't sure about going public yet.

"Tina! Hey." She sat down. "I really enjoyed yesterday."

"It was fun, for sure. I told Kaitlyn all about it." She gave a mischievous grin.

"All— as in *all* about it?" Nate's eyebrows raised. She'd let him think she had, anyways.

"What are you working on?" Deflect.

"More research. Did you know that you could combine gene therapy with bone marrow transplant for batten disease therapy?" Those serious eyes.

"I have no idea what that means. Glad you do. Call me tonight." Tina pursed her lips and blew him a kiss. She forced herself not to skip down the hall. If Spencer could tell she was twitterpated, it wouldn't be long before her dad figured it out and she wasn't quite ready for that to happen.

She went to the storage and collected cleaning supplies. The windows were dirty— not a good reflection on this place. People shouldn't be distracted by anything. They had enough dirt in their lives to worry about.

She finished up the front offices and headed down the hall, glancing into her dad's office as she passed.

"Tina, that you?" He set his newspaper down.

"Yeah dad." She held up the window cleaner. "Just tidying up a bit."

"Come on in. Sit down, honey." She set the spray bottle down and sat on the seat edge of the teal armchair, not wanting to get too settled in.

"What's up?" She dug her fingers into the cushion.

"I've been giving some thought to spreading Kristina's and Max's ashes." He glanced out the window at the rain. "Where do you think we should do it?"

Tina's eyes travelled to the corner of the ceiling. Was he ready to do this? "She loved the beach." She couldn't bring herself to say mom. Somehow it seemed an invasion of Tina's connection to her, to share that word with her dad. The ache was always there.

"I was thinking the same thing. There are lots of beaches. Did you have a specific one in mind?"

Was he really asking for her opinion? She swallowed. "You know that really beautiful photo in the travel magazine? The page she cut out and put on the fridge? It had such clear turquoise water and white sandy beaches." She leaned into the chair back.

"Yeah. Where was that, anyway? There are a bunch of places with that kind of ocean." He leaned back in his executive chair and put his hands behind his head. Was he actually keeping eye contact with her and not being distracted?

"Punta Cana. You don't remember that was her dream vacation?" How could he not remember?

He looked absently out the window. "I guess I had other more important things on my mind."

Tina twirled her hair around her finger. "Well, could we go? I know it's a long way, but I really think that's where we should spread her ashes."

"Yeah. I guess so. Let me think about the best timing."

"It just has to be after Kaitlyn's wedding in a few weeks." Tina stood up and took a few steps, then turned. "Thanks dad."

A broad grin filled his face. "You are welcome."

Chapter Twenty-Four

Tina sat in her red armchair, feet propped on the footrest watching the autumn leaves swirl and dance on the lawn. She loved the colors cascading in piles, maple seed helicopters twirling down. Remembered visions of her, Max and Kaitlyn jumping in piles of leaves and laughing till their guts hurt invaded her mind. She could still hear giggling and see their smiles. The sound of crinkling leaves.

Kaitlyn walked in with a cup of hot cocoa, whip cream swirled on top. She went to the window and smiled. "Remember when we used to jump in the leaves?"

"You read my mind. Yeah, that was so much fun!" Tina followed Kaitlyn's gaze. "Dad would tell us to rake them, and we'd pile them high. At least it seemed high when we were young."

"I love fall, all bundled up in coats and scarves. The air so crisp." Kaitlyn turned and sat down on the couch, grabbing the quilt, and snuged herself in. "Thanks for a wonderful weekend."

"It wasn't me— Maggie did all the planning."

"Yeah, but I'm sure you helped with some of it. It was really fun to have girl time." Kaitlyn set her mug down.

"It was. It seems like we've been two ships passing in the night."

"True. How are things going at the foundation? You and your dad getting along?"

"Yeah, I guess. He brought up spreading mom's and Max's ashes." Tina fingered her locket.

Kaitlyn straightened her position. "How are you feeling about that? Where would you spread them?"

"It needs to be done. We need some closure. Remember that magazine photo mom kept on the fridge? The one with the beach? It's in Punta Cana. I want her to have the chance to go there." Tina rubbed her moist hands on the upholstered arms of the chair.

Kaitlyn nodded. "That's a long trip. Are you ready to spend that much time with your dad? He'll probably control every aspect."

"I'm sure. I don't know. I just want to get it over with." Tina glanced at Kaitlyn. She was probably right. Her dad always wanted to make the decisions without regard to her thoughts. But then again, he had asked her where she thought they should spread them. Was he softening? Her head tilted, and lips formed a straight line.

"Understandable. Moving on. Did I see a glint in your eye talking about Nate?"

Tina flushed. Why would she do that with her best friend, the one who knew her deepest thoughts?

"May-be." She sat up straighter and turned. "And what the heck? You were supposed to be at the pumpkin patch. Wait. You set us up, didn't you? You lied to me!"

Kaitlyn laughed. "It wasn't really a lie. We did go and visit Luke's grandpa. We just thought it would be a good way to get you guys together. It worked, didn't it?" Kaitlyn's shoulders shook as she let out a giggle. She pulled her knees up and adjusted the quilt.

Tina threw a pillow at her. "Yeah, I guess I have to concede that."

"Well, what happened? What did you do? What did he say?" Kaitlyn leaned in.

Tina looked at the ceiling. "It was fun. You should have seen him trying to launch the pumpkin in the sling shot. It was hilarious!" She reached for her phone. "Here— watch this." She handed her phone to Kaitlyn who started with a chuckle and ended with a guinea pig squeak when he landed on the ground. She wiped the tears from her eyes.

"Quite a guy, that Nate."

He *was* quite a guy. Tina couldn't help the grin spreading across her lips. "And then we went through the maze. With a brief stop along the way." Tina sipped her coffee.

"And?"

"And... he kissed me." Tina shrugged like it was an everyday occurrence. No big deal.

A ghost of a smile on her lips.

"Did he now?" Kaitlyn put her finger to the corner of her pursed lips. "And?"

"And," Tina paused. "It was amazing. I keep imagining what it would be like to be with him every day. To look into his sky-blue eyes each moment. For always." Tina sighed.

Kaitlyn let out a chuckle. "Twitterpated. That's what you are!"

"Not like you aren't? Three more weeks till your wedding." It was Kaitlyn's turn to blush.

"Hey," said Tina, "I was going to visit Martha this morning. Want to go with me? We could take some of those Halloween cookies you decorated. She's really sweet. You'd like her."

♥ ♥ ♥

Martha greeted them with a broad smile. "Well now, what brings you girls out on this crisp fall day?" The porch rail had been decorated with a garland of leaves and the door with a hand painted wreath.

"We thought we'd stop by. Kaitlyn made cookies. Oh," Tina glanced at her friend, "This is Kaitlyn, my roommate." At least for a few more weeks.

Kaitlyn stretched out her hand. "Tina's always talking about you!"

"Well come in. I just made a fresh pot of coffee." Martha had set a vase of fall leaves on the coffee table. Her knitting project sat on the couch.

"You knit? My mom used to knit." Tina picked up the piece and examined it. "Looks like you're making a sweater. I love the colors. The cable design is so intricate. You should give me a lesson or two. " Her mom had taught her the rudiments of knitting. Tina looked down and felt her shoulders shrink in. She hadn't picked her needles up since her mom had died. Maybe she should try again. She could make a scarf for Nate.

"I'd love to! Let's see, I'd have to fit you into my busy schedule..." Martha smirked. She handed them their coffees and set a plate of cookies on the table. "What have you girls been up to, besides nursing?"

"Kaitlyn's getting married in three weeks."

"How exciting! Tell me about your man." Martha had a way of seeing you, like she could reach right down into your soul.

"His name is Luke. He works for Healthy Kids. I met him

while caring for his grandpa William who has diabetes. He lives alone." Kaitlyn looked at Tina like a lightbulb just went off.

"Would you like to come to my wedding? We have extra spots." Her mouth turned in a mischievous grin.

"Oh, I wouldn't want to impose." Martha put her hand on Kaitlyn's.

"It would be okay. Really." Her eyes twinkled like the small strand of lights inside the vase.

"Well, it *would* be nice to get out."

"It's settled then. I'll drop by an invitation for you."

Tina held Kaitlyn's gaze over the rim of her coffee cup, a knowing smile in her eyes.

Chapter Twenty-Five

"Where do you want me to start?" Tina looked around at the moving boxes piled in Kaitlyn's room. How could she have accumulated so much stuff in just a few years?

"You can start taking down the photos and I'll start on the closet."

Tina placed a box on the bed. Photos had been collaged and strung up on all four walls. She let her eyes roam over them. Twenty-five years of Kaitlyn. A whole lifetime of Tina, intermingled like two streams flowing into the same river.

She unclipped the photo of her getting on the kindergarten bus. Tina had been clinging to her mom, tears streaming down her cheeks. Kaitlyn, sitting in the front seat of the bus, had watched her through the window. Tina's face had been in stark contrast to that adorable handmade dress her mom had made for her. Kaitlyn couldn't stand to let someone be distraught. She jumped from her seat and down the steps.

"It's going to be okay. Come on, I'll be your friend," Kaitlyn had said. She put her hand on Tina's shoulder.

Tina's mom's face had transformed from concern to gratefulness.

"See?" she'd said. "You already have a friend. Hop on the bus. I bet this nice little girl will let you sit with her."

That had been the first day of years of hugs, laughter, plans, sorrow, and joy.

Photos of Kaitlyn and Maggie giggling, playing with their dog, family photos with her parents and seven siblings including two brothers who were constantly teasing her. Kaitlyn's family had been such a contrast to her own. There was always something going on–making crafts, canning fruits, going to the park for bike rides. It was Kaitlyn who invited her to youth group where she cemented long lasting relationships and learned to love a different Father.

Tina's mom was busy, but always with causes—parent club, committees, and then with Max. She smoothed out the bent corner of the photo. When Tina needed a restore-her-joy-day she would spend it with Kaitlyn. She blinked away the moisture in her eyes.

"Okay, I've got all my clothes in boxes. I'm just going to leave the stuff in my drawers and move the dresser like that." Kaitlyn's shoulders raised as she gave a sigh and sat down on the bed next to Tina. "You okay? You lost in memory world?"

Tina blinked back the remaining tears and looked up "Yeah. Look at this one." Tina held a photo of the two of them. They might have been seven.

"I totally forgot about that!" A laugh escaped Kaitlyn's lips. "We got into my mom's dress up box."

The photo held the image of Tina putting a wedding veil on Kaitlyn, dressed in a way too big satin dress and high heeled shoes.

"You should use this somewhere at your wedding! I'll keep it aside," Tina said.

This moving out business. It didn't have to be the end. It was just another chapter. She set the photo aside. Look at how many things they had done together. Those experiences were the glue that held them together. There would be new adventures and shenanigans ahead. It would just be different. And that would be okay. Tina relaxed her shoulders and felt all the stale thoughts inside her whoosh out in a big gusty sigh. Kaitlyn put her hand on Tina's and made her own whooshing sound. Tina burst out laughing and they hugged until they cried.

That was okay, too.

The morning had begun with mimosas and a spread of pastries, omelettes, and fresh fruits. Then proceeded through setting up the reception area, hair styling and makeup, followed finally by helping Kaitlyn into the dress that transformed her from every day to princess. This would be the Cinderella moment that would have a magic wand spreading glitter and lights. Smiles and laughter had filled each moment. Tina couldn't contain the joy she felt watching her bestie's dreams being fulfilled. What better guy than Luke to take Kaitlyn into the next chapter of her life?

The music began and Tina took slow steps down the aisle. She spied Nate sitting midway on the bride's side. He was probably feeling out of place— he didn't really know anyone here other than those he met at Daniel's potluck. It was brave of him to come and sit alone. Sure, he'd met everyone, but they were up front on the platform with the bride.

Tina smiled as she envisioned Nate becoming one of the gang. She took her place with the others and watched everyone rise as Kaitlyn, arms linked through her dad's, his eyes beaming. Was there a little moisture in the corners of his eyes? Kaitlyn focused on the man of her dreams as she made her way down the aisle. Luke's face could hardly contain his grin.

Nate couldn't have been more handsome. She'd never seen him in a suit before and she thought he cleaned up pretty nice. She caught his eye and held it. A crooked smile formed on his lips. Was this relationship leading to them walking down the aisle? It was too soon to let her thoughts travel down that road. They'd only just begun seeing each other. But oh my. It wouldn't hurt her feelings if things continued this way. She swallowed to keep from letting drool slide down her chin.

The pastor turned. "And now, Luke, did you have some words for Kaitlyn?"

Luke held Kaitlyn's hands, his eyes locked to hers.

"Kaitlyn, I've been drawn to your curly brown hair and energetic smile since our first bike ride. I never thought I'd be lucky enough to get to know you and spend time with you. You have brought laughter, new perspectives, and a deeper faith into my life. I can't wait to spend the next seventy years with you through ups and downs, joys, and sorrows. Whatever life may bring. You are my everything. I will never stop loving you."

Tina handed Kaitlyn a tissue to wipe her tears. It wouldn't do to have mascara running down her beautiful face. Tina eyed Nate. He was leaning over, his forearms resting on his legs, intent. His face was so serious. She didn't know what thoughts were swirling around in his head, but she did know what was going on in hers. A longing she couldn't put aside.

⋆ ♥ ⋆

The dinner was amazing. Kaitlyn's mom Kate, Maggie and her aunts and a few uncles had all joined in to cater the food. Prime rib, homemade rolls, a very small amount of greens for those who felt a need to include what Kaitlyn described as disgusting plants fit only for cows and sheep. It turned out Luke's co-worker, Gracie was a wiz at baking and decorating. She'd made one small cake which sat upon a tower of varieties of individual smaller cakes, each decorated with enticing swirls of chocolate, whip cream and mousse.

Tina scanned the room as Nate headed to the dessert table to bring her a delicacy. Happy chatter, clanks of silverware and the clink of glasses filled the room. Her eyes landed on Martha whose animated hands were describing something to Luke's grandpa William. His eyes twinkled as he gave rapt attention to his new friend. Leave it to Kaitlyn, the matchmaker.

"I hope this is what you wanted," Nate said. He handed her the gorgeous multi-layered delicacy. Tina closed her eyes, licked her lips, and swallowed.

"This might be the highlight of the wedding." She grinned and slid her fork into the delightfully rich concoction and savored the bite.

"Good?" Nate smiled. He opened his mouth and pointed. "Put it here."

Tina slid a bite into his mouth.

"Not bad."

She gave him a playful slap with the back of her hand as he reached for her fork.

"Go get your own!" she said and thought better of it. "Do you want me to get one for you?"

He shook his head. "No, I'm fine." He put his hand on hers and smiled.

The Bent Shingles took their places and began to play. Tina recognized some of the staff from her unit at Mercy strumming guitars and a mandolin. Luke took Kaitlyn's hand and swirled her around the dance floor. He pulled her to a stop and leaned in, his lips close to hers. She lifted her chin, ready to receive his kiss when her dad tapped her shoulder.

"May I step in?" her dad said.

Luke bowed and stepped back—lips turned up in a smile. The song began slowly but soon turned into an energizing swing beat where her dad started swirling, flipping, and spinning her around. They flowed together like they had done this a million times. Tina crossed her arms over her chest as she watched them. Why couldn't she have that kind of relationship with her dad? She shook off a memory of her and her dad silly dancing in the living room when she was, perhaps four? She wasn't sure. She wondered if it was still in him, the idea of having fun together.

Nate reached over, pulled her close and kissed the top of her head. "Dance with me?" he said, pulling her from her reverie.

She nodded. This was the distraction she needed to pull her thoughts away and refocus on the joy of the moment.

"I promise I won't step on your feet!" He took her hand and guided her to the floor where laughter rang out and all her cares were washed away.

Chapter Twenty-Six

Nate downed the last swallow of coffee, rinsed his cup, and placed it in the dishwasher. The sun was just beginning to peek rays between the few clouds and bare tree branches. He wanted to get a run in before work. Nate wiggled his feet into his running shoes and headed outside. Cold air hit him, and he was glad he had opted for his sweatshirt and a pair of gloves.

As he ran, he replayed Kaitlyn's wedding. He was no stranger to going places alone, so when Kaitlyn invited him, he immediately said yes. Besides, sitting alone gave him opportunity to stare at Tina. Gaze at Tina? Fix his eyes on her? All the above. He just wanted to soak in her beauty. Did she even realize how beautiful she was? Her hair was pulled back with some kind of girly thing-a-ma-bob allowing a few tendrils to fall down. She was absolutely stunning in her teal dress. It accented just the right curves and he had had a hard time switching his focus from Tina to Kaitlyn and Luke.

Nate paused at the intersection, jogging in place until the few cars passed. Was that what true love looked like? He sure hadn't seen that in his parents. Come to think of it, he hadn't ever observed that with anyone in his life. Would it even be possible that he could have head-over-heels-in-love experience with Tina? He wasn't sure. He was having a hard time focusing on his research because thoughts of her invaded his every moment. Maybe that's what love was. Putting everything aside and focusing on someone other than yourself.

The band had been good and they seemed to have a lot of fun together. Dancing. It wasn't something he'd had much experience with. But music and the energy it brought loosened him up. Made him laugh.

Tina always teased him about being too serious. He supposed he was. All scientists were serious weren't they? Well, dancing with Tina put him in his happy place. Being near her. Taking in the fragrance of her hair. The touch of her hands. Her jade eyes locked with his. Her full, delicious lips...

Nate rounded the corner, slowed, and cooled down in his front yard.

He'd have to call the yard person to clean up all the maple leaves before the rain made it impossible.

Nate stretched and rolled his shoulders. He had been leaning over his desk for what seemed like hours poring over statistics, reviews of clinical trials in animals and then volunteers. He and others had determined a list of potential benefits verses side effects. They had narrowed treatment down to enzyme therapy. So far so good. Were they close enough he could suggest little Noah proceed with a trial? Research hadn't shown any horrible side effects. Maybe some nausea or headaches. But this was a treatment, not a cure.

Nate shook his head. No, he had to keep working on this. A

picture of Noah laughing with him at the pumpkin patch came to mind. His sparkly blue eyes, straight brown hair. Noah and others like him needed a cure. It needed to be sooner than later.

He walked down the hall to the break room to get a cup of coffee. Habit made him glance at the chair Tina sat in when she was there. He felt a little lost without her bubbly smile and cheerful ways. He filled his cup and stopped by Mark's office.

"Nate." Mark looked up from his computer. "Have a seat. What news do you have for me?" Nate always wanted to leave Mark with hope. Research was such an excruciatingly long process and too often hope seemed elusive.

"I've begun neonatal trials on rats to determine which gene triggers the disease and then we could try to replace it. This gene triggers interference with a cell's capability of recycling necessary molecules. So, if we can replace it in the fetus, we can prevent the disease." Nate leaned back and placed his hands behind his head.

"That is exciting news. A little over my head but it sounds like you're onto something. That doesn't, however, help those with the disease already."

Nate kept his eyes trained on Mark, but in his head Tina was shouting, *See? This is what he does. Always has some kind of Debbie Downer to end the conversation with.*

"Yeah. Well, I'm working as fast as I can." Nate stood and turned to leave. He had to keep himself positive and not read anything into that last remark. Mark was, after all, the one who gave him a paycheck.

Mark pushed back from his desk. "Say, it appears you and my Tina are becoming an item."

Nate paused and slowly turned. Where was this going to lead? Nate had thought often about whether it was okay to date the boss's daughter. His shoulders relaxed as he noted the hint of a smile forming on Mark's lips.

"Yes sir." Nate felt like a deer in the headlights. His mouth went dry. This was, after all, his first real relationship. How was he supposed to know the protocols? It wasn't like anyone in his life had instructed him on relationships.

"Well, I can't think of a better guy than you for her to date." Mark let out a small chuckle. He straightened the papers on his desk. "Thanks for stopping by."

Nate walked back to his office and plopped in his chair. He whooshed out a long breath. His phone buzzed.

<Hey, how's your day going?>

<Tina! Wouldn't you like to know!>

<You made a breakthrough?>

<Not yet- getting close>

<Don't hold me in suspense. What?>

<Nothing special. Just your dad asked if you and I were an item> Smile emoji

<He what??? What'd you tell him?>

<I loved you and couldn't stop thinking about how cute you were in your bridesmaid's dress and how I just wanted to be with you all the time. You know, stuff like that>

Wait. Had he just put in writing he loved her? He'd already pushed send. No reply. He waited, watching. Seconds ticked by.

<Sorry, Kaitlyn just interrupted me. You didn't really say all that to him, did you?>

Nate's sigh of relief was audible.

<No. When he asked, I said, yes sir. That's all.>

<Did you just call my dad sir? Really?>

<I panicked, okay??>Cockeyed eye emoji.

<What did he say?>

<He smiled and said he couldn't think of anyone better for you than me>

<Well, for once he's right. See you tonight?>

<Indeed> Smiley kiss.

He gave a fist pump. He'd passed the second test—the first being acceptance from Tina's friends. Things could only get better from here.

Chapter Twenty-Seven

Tina closed the car door with her behind and carefully balanced a plate of fudge and tote bag. The fudge would probably have traveled better in a plastic container, but she wanted to present it on the traditional decorative plate. If she had brought the container and the plate, she'd have to remember to take the container home. And the plate later. Too many details.

She was glad for the covered hospital parking garage as the rain was coming down in buckets. Kaitlyn was going to be so proud of her, not only remembering to bring Christmas decorations for the unit but making fudge all by herself. The house had been so lonely since Kaitlyn had moved out. Too quiet. The kitchen too clean. The dish cupboards too empty. Tina's attempt at fudge was a conscious step to move on.

"Do you need help?" Daniel had sidled up to her, his hand out ready to take the plate.

"Yeah, could you take my bag?" Tina wrestled the tote off her arm and held the plate away from him.

Daniel took the bag. "You're not going to trust me with the fudge, are you?" His shoulders, usually so strong drooped and he put on his best puppy dog eyes. "I thought you were my friend."

"Don't try to pull those sad brown eyes on me. I just think it should at least make it to the break room before half of its gone. I know you—a chocolate addict through and through."

"Hey now, what about Kaitlyn? She's never passed up chocolate. Ever."

"She's not the one trying to help me right now either." Tina laughed. "What's on the schedule for today?"

"Did I just hear my name? In conjunction with chocolate?" Kaitlyn sidled up to them. Her eyes shone. Marital bliss suited her.

"Two surgeries," Daniel said. "A twelve-year-old with a shattered arm and an appendectomy."

They walked into the break room where Tina uncovered the plate and set it on the table. She pulled a snowman and some holly from her tote and thoughtfully arranged them. Then put her tote in her locker.

Out of the corner of her eye, Tina watched Kaitlyn lock eyes with Daniel and pointed to the fudge with her chin. Tina stifled a laugh. They each silently snuck a piece and stood back just as Tina turned. Daniel had popped his in his mouth. Kaitlyn had curved her hand around hers and hid it behind her back. She looked up at the ceiling and began whistling.

"Okay you two. You both look like the cat that ate the canary." Tina tried to put on her mean mom look.

Kaitlyn started to giggle. Daniel swallowed his chocolate, his Adam's apple bobbing.

"Did you just bring this in to tempt us?" Kaitlyn said. "Cuz if you did, that would just be mean. I know you're not that kinda person." She batted her eyes.

"Well, how is it? Did it turn out okay?" Tina asked.

Kaitlyn popped hers in her mouth. "Yeah, I guess it'll do."

"We gotta get to work before we eat it all. Save some for Peter and the others."

Tina adjusted the blood pressure cuff on Krystal's arm. She could have wrapped it around twice since her arm was the size of a toothpick.

"Sit tight while I take your blood pressure. There are a few things we need to do before your surgery." Krystal's whole body was rigid. Her left arm looked as if it had been put through a meat grinder. Bits of torn muscle and bloodied broken flesh. What had happened to her? This wasn't just a fall down the stairs.

Kaitlyn straightened the pillows and laid a warm blanket over Krystal's body.

"How's that? Are you more comfortable?"

Krystal gave an imperceptible nod. Her dark eyes darted back and forth.

Tina removed the cuff and took the young girl's temperature. Her BP was high. Maybe she was just anxious about the surgery.

Daniel popped into the room. "Well, who do we have here?" He looked at the chart. "Miss Krystal." He smiled. "How old are you? Ten?"

"Twelve." It came out in a bare whisper. Daniel sat down on the chair next to her.

"I'm a bad guesser." He glanced at Tina, then Kaitlyn. "Can you tell us what happened to your arm?"

Krystal pulled herself in tighter and stared straight ahead. Her lips were a tight line.

"Where's your mom and dad?" He looked at Tina. "Did someone tell them they could be in here with her?"

"They're not at the hospital," Tina said.

Daniel's eyebrows knit together.

"Okay sweetheart. Walk us through what happened to your arm." Tina said. She moved a chair close to the bed and sat down.

"I fell." Krystal breathed out the words.

"Where were you? At your house? At school?" Tina's words were gentle.

"At my house."

"Who was with you?"

"My dad." Krystal gave a slight shudder and looked away.

Tina looked at Kaitlyn and Daniel, glanced at the door and gave a slight nod towards it. She might get farther with Krystal if they were alone.

"Krystal, sometimes kids come into the hospital with injuries and bruises, and they say they fell. They're scared to tell what really happened. They don't want anyone to get in trouble."

A tear slid down Krystal's gaunt cheek. No way was this just a fall. She had to coax the story out of her. Had Child Services been notified?

"You're in a safe place here. It's important for you to tell me what happened so we can take the best possible care of you."

Krystal looked out the window, her teeth pulling in her lower lip.

"Alright, I'm going to ask you some yes or no questions. You can just nod." Tina folded her hands in her lap.

"Okay." Krystal winced as she repositioned her mangled arm.

"You said you were at home when this happened, right?"

A yes nod.

"Was your mom there?"

No.

"Was your dad?"

Nodded.

"Was anyone else there?"

No.

"Does you house have any stairs?"

No.

"Do you think you can tell me what happened?" Tina asked.

Krystal looked towards the door and then hesitantly began her story. "I was home alone. My mom was at work—she doesn't get home until two in the morning—and my dad came home."

Her eyes traveled to the window.

"He got really mad because I was supposed to do the dishes. I was going to. But I had an assignment I needed to finish first. It was due the next day." Krystal's fingers clenched the blanket.

"Okay, go on." Tina crossed her legs. She wanted to look relaxed to put Krystal at ease. But her mind was racing. Did her dad grab her? No, even if he had broken her arm, it wouldn't be all mangled. Did she have siblings who would have been around?

"He started yelling. He does that all the time." She looked absently at the corner of the ceiling. "I hurried to the kitchen to start washing dishes, but then he grabbed me because I wasn't fast enough." Tears welled up in her eyes. "Then he..."

Tina put her hand on Krystal's.

"He..." She started sobbing.

Tina handed her some tissues and stroked her dark hair. Krystal wiped her eyes and blew her nose. "He drug me to the back yard and pushed me into the fenced kennel with his Rottweiler." Her eyes grew large. "I screamed and screamed but he just walked away and left me there. He didn't even look back and then I heard his old pickup start."

She trembled as she touched her arm. "He did this to me. I started kicking the dog and finally climbed the chain link fence and got away. I hate him! How could he do this to me?" The mix of fear and loathing in her eyes was nothing Tina had seen in anyone before.

Tina swallowed. Climbed the fence? She had to have been desperate and full of adrenaline to have gotten over it with a damaged arm. Tina had to stay calm—hard to do when her heart was racing. She hated to admit it, but at this moment, she hated Krystal's dad as well.

Tina dug her fingernails into the palm of her clenched fist. "Did your dad bring you to the hospital?"

"No, it was my neighbor. No one lives near our house. My arm was killing me, but I ran down our long road to their house."

"The sun goes down early now. Was it dark then?"

"Yeah, but there was a bit of the moon peeking through the clouds. I was so scared. I kept looking behind me because I was worried my dad would catch me heading over there." She shuddered.

"Donna, my neighbor came out on the porch and saw me coming. When I showed her my arm and told her what happened she drove as fast as she could to the hospital."

Daniel came in. "Dr. Roberts is ready for you, young lady. We're going to wheel you into the surgery room and get you all fixed up good as new."

Yeah, we can fix her arm, but it's going to take much more to heal her heart. There's only One being I know who can do that.

Chapter Twenty-Eight

"Do you have everything you need? Passport? Swimsuit? Charger?" Kaitlyn said.

Tina was relieved that Kaitlyn had come over to help her prepare for her trip with her dad. Kaitlyn could look through the windows of her heart and she knew this was no time for Tina to be alone.

Kaitlyn had loved Tina's mom almost as much as Tina did. In fact, she had always called her Kristina-mom. This act, this going to spread her ashes would bring closure to her as well.

"I think so." Tina hesitated and then pulled open a drawer. She wrapped her fingers around the object she had hidden. "Just one more thing." She glanced at Kaitlyn and sat down on the bed. She took in a deep breath and opened her fingers to reveal the little red race car.

"Was that Max's?" Kaitlyn took it from Tina. "I remember he used to play with this all the time. Never left the house without it."

Tina nodded. "I hid it." She traced the curves on her bedspread. "My dad had put it on their shrine in his house. I wanted to have something of Max's to remember him by."

Kaitlyn sat next to her and wrapped an arm around her shoulders.

"Was that wrong?"

"Wrong to take it? Of course not. I don't get it. Why is this bothering you?" Kaitlyn stroked a loose hair from Tina's face.

"I just took it. I didn't ask. I was afraid my dad would think it was stupid or something."

"Your dad is the one who put together the shrine. He, of all people, knows how much items help you remember the person you loved."

Tina slowly nodded. Maybe Kaitlyn was right. It just had seemed like she had violated something. Maybe her dad's trust? She wasn't sure but keeping the secret had made her feel like she had some control. That she could hold onto Max in some small way. A way that was hers only.

Tina stood. "Well, anyways, I'm going to put it back and see if he notices." She stood and looked around the room once more. "I guess I'll take off. He was going to make me breakfast before we go."

Kaitlyn drug Tina's suitcase down the stairs to the front door and gave her a long hug.

"I'll be praying for you. I know this is going to be tough. More so the time spent with your dad than the spreading of ashes, but it's gonna be fine. Remember to breathe." Kaitlyn pressed a piece of chocolate into Tina's hand.

"Say goodbye to them for me."

Together they wiped the errant tears from each other's eyes.

♥ ♥ ♥

Tina pulled into the driveway. She could see her dad through the window and knew he'd be fixing breakfast for her. Why did she feel so nervous? It was just her dad. She popped Kaitlyn's chocolate into her mouth.

"Dad?" Tina rolled her suitcase and set it by the entryway.

"In the kitchen!" The sweet smell of fried onions wafted through the air. What was it about enticing food that brought comfort? Tina shook her head. As much as she wanted to feel wrapped in love, a nice breakfast wasn't going to be what brought that to fruition.

"Whatcha making?" Tina leaned against the counter watching her dad stir the potatoes in the cast iron pan. The tiny kitchen contrasted with the one in their old house. Her mom had loved that kitchen with the granite counters and the huge island. There had been plenty of space to spread out all the ingredients and supplies. And room for Tina to work side by side making muffins to go with potato soup, or chocolate chip cookies.

The sun, just coming up, filtered through the leaves and left a yellow cast through the window of her dad's kitchen.

"Eggs and potatoes. Muffins are in the oven." Mark wore a half apron over his brown corduroy pants. "Say, could you run upstairs and look in the closet. Pull down a suitcase for me and set it on the bed."

"You haven't packed yet?" Tina was incredulous. They had to be at the airport in a matter of hours.

"There's plenty of time."

She headed down the hall to his bedroom. Surprisingly, the bed was made. She paused to let her eyes sweep the room. A photo of her mom and dad sat on the dresser. It must have been taken at the beach before she and Max had been born. Her mom looked adoringly at her dad. *Mom, I want to see what you saw in dad. I want to be able to look at him that way.* She moved to the walk-in closet. A row of dress shirts hung, button sides all facing the same direction and organized by color. A few pairs of slacks and a whole lot of cords were folded and hung over hangers. Tina imagined this is what Nate's closet looked like. Minus the cords. But totally organized.

On the opposite wall, the one that had been her mom's, there was only one garment hanging. Tina took a quick breath. It was her mom's red wool coat. She gingerly took it off the hanger and slid it on. She hugged the fronts together and breathed in her mom's fragrance still lingering in the threads. Tina leaned back against the wall and closed her eyes. *I miss you mom. You don't even know.* She opened her eyes and slid her hands in the pockets. Her fingers wrapped around a small envelope. Her hands began to shake as she read her name in flowing script. Had her mom meant to give this to her before she died?

Tina muffin,

I remember the day you were born. Your dad and I were so excited to meet you— you had that full head of red hair and hazel eyes. They hadn't turned green until you were nearly one. You were such a delight. Even when you were a toddler, you liked to help mommy pick up toys and do the laundry. I remember you climbed into the dishwasher to reach a cup and I snatched you up before you fell. You started crying because you were just trying to get a cup for daddy's coffee.

And you were such a big help with Max. I sometimes think that your childhood was stolen from you because we had to focus so much on him. I'm so sorry. I wish I could have changed all that. I feel like I neglected you. And now, muffin, I'm going to leave you.

Life is not always what we believe it should be. I would never have imagined that things would end this way, and with me being short of forty. I always thought I would see your wedding and laugh with my grandkids. I guess God had other plans.

What I want to leave with you is this. Appreciate every

moment of every day. Enjoy life. Take care of your relationship with your dad. He's all the family you've got. Remember that despite what you see, God's got his best in mind for you.

I love you, sweetheart. Always remember that.

Mom

Tina fingered her locket. Why hadn't she gotten this letter years ago? It had been in the one piece of clothing that had randomly been saved? God must have known she needed this today.

"Tina, breakfast is ready." Tina found the suitcase, slid it down and placed it on the bed. She removed the coat and hung it up, placing the letter in her hip pocket. She headed to the kitchen.

"Dad, I found mom's coat in the closet. You still have it?" He looked up at her as he placed her breakfast on the placemat in front of her.

"Yeah. She loved that coat, and I just couldn't get rid of it."

"I found a letter in the pocket. To me. Did you know it was there?" *Had he known and never given it to me? Tina clenched her fists.*

"A letter? No. I never thought to look in her pockets. It must have been meant for you to find it now, just before we spread her ashes. How serendipitous." He poured them each some coffee, sat down and reached for her hand. "Pray with me?"

Tina gave an imperceptible shake of her head. She let out a breath and relaxed her shoulders. When was the last time they had prayed together? Quite possibly never.

"Lord, thank you for the opportunity to take this trip. May it be safe and fruitful. And bless this food."

He squeezed her hand and grabbed for a muffin.

"Looks good, dad."

Breakfast was over. They hurriedly cleaned up and put

everything in the dishwasher. "I need to hurry and pack. It won't take long. Could you gather Max and Kristina and anything else you think appropriate to bring from the other room?"

Tina walked into the living room and stood frozen as she looked at the table. She fingered Max's car, still in her pocket. She took it out and set it on the table.

"Here Max. I brought your race car back. I hope you haven't missed it. We're going on a trip— you and mom and dad and I. We get to fly on an airplane and go to the beach. I think you'll like it there." Her lips curved up.

What should she do now? Were they just going to put Max's box and her mom's sea green urn in their suitcases? Or carry on? Would they get stopped through security? They weren't supposed to buy extra tickets for them, were they? Hopefully, her dad had these things figured out. She certainly didn't.

♥ ♥ ♥

After arguing about which parking space to take, standing in line for eternity for security, clearing their passports, and safely getting Max and Kristina through, Tina and her dad were finally on the plane and soaring above the clouds. Tina couldn't imagine what it would have been like trying to take Max through in his wheelchair. He was so much easier to transport now. She felt a little twinge of guilt. Was it okay to think that? Max would have thought it was funny.

She leaned her head against the window, trying to imagine where they were. Was heaven really up here? And how did it work exactly? As soon as they died, did their spirits just whisk up into the sky? What did their spirits even look like? And then did they get new bodies as soon as they arrived? That's what her mom said about Max. That when he died, he would get a new body and be able to run and jump and play like never before. She hoped he had found friends and loved that special room Jesus had made for him. At any rate, to be wrapped in His arms was more than she could imagine.

"What are you thinking about, muffin?" Did her dad just call her by her nickname? She couldn't remember the last time that had happened.

"I was just wondering about heaven and trying to picture them up there."

"It's hard to wrap your mind around, isn't it?"

"Yes indeed." She set her tray down as the steward handed her a drink and peanuts.

"This is nice, spending time with you. I get so focused with the foundation I forget to let you know how much I appreciate you. When I watch you interact with the families it does something to me." He put his closed hand on his chest.

Tina glanced at him. Was he going to get all warm and fuzzy? She wasn't quite ready to open her heart to that possibility. What if she did and he pulled away? She felt fragile, like a finely formed glass vase that could be dropped and shattered at any time.

"Tina, when I think about Max and how you were always there for him... Not just him, but such a help to your mom and me. You'd entertain him and make him smile. And that smile would take the edge off the pain for us."

Tina stared at her tray. She couldn't move. Couldn't look at him. This was the only time in her life that she could remember him talking to her. She just wanted to listen. To soak in it.

"And then when Kristina got sick, well, it about did me in. I was so angry at God for taking everyone away. I started to get depressed and felt like I could hardly hold anything together. I knew she needed me. The foundation needed me. And you needed me. But I forgot about how much you needed me because I felt pulled in so many directions and I didn't feel I had what it took to just be your dad. You got left by the wayside."

He took a sip of his drink, his voice sunk to a whisper. "It's taken this trip to stop and think about things. I wake up every day worrying that something will happen to you as well. I guess I just pull back because I can't stand the thought of losing you."

Tina took her napkin and wiped the tears running down her cheeks. She stared down at her tray.

"It just always seems like you only talk to me when you need me to fix something or do something for you." She took a hiccuping breath. "And when you basically forced me to get up on stage in front of all those people and bare my soul." Her voice dropped to a hoarse whisper. "You had already lost me. What were you thinking? You certainly weren't thinking of me and whether I was ready for that or not. I was mortified!" Her fingernails dug into the palms of her hands.

Silence. He didn't know what to say, did he? She saw herself putting on a pair of boxing gloves and pummeling him. Pounding him into the ground.

"Tina." Just one word. He breathed out. "I haven't been that great of a dad. I am sorry. Really sorry."

Tina reached her hand towards his and stopped. Mark slid his on top of hers and gave a tentative smile.

Like Nate said, she and her dad were the only family they had. Through God's grace, this final trip for her mom and brother would bring beauty from ashes.

Chapter Twenty-Nine

Tina read directions from maps on her phone. The rental car didn't have navigation. His usual git-er-done serious driving had somehow turned into a leisurely scenic drive in this country of spectacular lush surroundings. They traveled down a dirt road, tall coconut palms casting long shadows. Turning into the drive of their airbnb, they saw the roof covered with palm fronds. The stucco siding was painted orange and deck chairs surrounded a crystal-clear pool.

Mark held the door open for her. Tina got out and placed her hand on her heart. "Mom would have loved this!"

"Yes, she would have!" Mark said. He smiled. A man, his brown bare feet covered in sand, welcomed them, and held out a bucket with a squid floating in some water.

"Hola amigos! Quisieres estes? You want?" He adjusted his floppy hat. His dark eyes looked intently into theirs.

Tina peeked into the bucket and stepped back. The squirming tentacles and soft pinkish flesh were a little too close for comfort. She wrinkled her forehead and shook her head. Mark smiled.

"Thank you, but no." The man bowed a nod and left.

"Holy moly! I wouldn't even know what to do with it!" Tina said.

"I'm sure our friend Google would have great recipes," Mark said and stepped inside.

Tina grabbed her bag, wheeled it inside and changed into shorts and a tank top.

"Let's get settled and then we can go buy some groceries. There's a full kitchen," Mark said. "Hopefully, they sell something other than squid!"

♥ ♥ ♥

The bright sun sparkled on the crushed seashells interspersed in the dirt road. Mark held out his pinky to Tina. She glanced up at him and caught his smile, then held her pinky out to hook with his. This was nice. This was the dad she had longed for. Slowly the hard shell around her heart was beginning to dissolve.

"Remember that time we went to the beach? Maybe you were too little, but it was you, your mom and Max. Before we realized he had batten. You were walking, so you must have been around two, maybe three." They headed down a path towards the beach. "You guys made an intricate sandcastle with little seashell doors and a moat around it. It even had a little bridge and Max had put one of his matchbox cars on it." Mark smiled.

"I think I remember that. Mom was wearing a red ball cap with her pony pulled through it."

Mark nodded.

"Was that the time when I ran into the waves and got

knocked down? All I can remember is being surprised and water rolling over me. I tried to stand up and got knocked down again." Tina looked up at her dad and out at the surf. "You pulled me out of there, didn't you. You saved me."

He had been there for her when she needed it. When she was small. At what point had they lost connection?

"I was so worried I'd lose you, muffin."

"I wish we could go back to those days. You used to read stories to me and taught me how to ride a bike. And one time at the beach, mom had bought these awesome kites..."

"That was when we realized something was wrong with Max when he stumbled into the tide pool."

Tina picked up a shell. "It had to have been hard for you and mom, looking after the both of us. It was probably a good thing that Max died before mom got cancer. I can't imagine what that would have been like. I watch families come into the hospital with chronic illnesses all the time. It's hard to keep their hopes up."

"It was. But honestly, Kristina and I starting the foundation kept us focused with a common purpose."

It was good to finally have a conversation with her dad and understand where he had been coming from.

"Come on." Tina grabbed his hand.

They laughed as they ran to the waves and jumped into the clear aqua water. The waters swirled around her ankles and the salt spray tickled her skin. Tina scooped up some water and splashed it at her dad. Mark reciprocated. He slogged through the water and picked Tina up and threw her into the oncoming wave. She squealed, went under, and came up laughing.

"We better get back and change so we can get groceries. Remember, that's where we were headed?" Mark said.

Tina wrung out her dripping hair, twisted it and tied it in a knot on top of her head. She thought about her mom and Max, enclosed in urns. She was glad it was just her and her dad. Should she feel guilty?

***

Tina pulled a sleeveless shift from her suitcase and held it up. Yes, this would do. A little more formal than shorts and tank top. Her mom would approve.

Her dad sat on the patio in a wicker chair drinking a cup of coffee. "Ah, Tina. You look nice. Come join me. There are some pastries on the counter and I made a fresh pot of coffee."

Tina walked over to him and gave him a peck on his head.

"Thanks dad." She wore a satisfied smile. This was the day. The day to spread ashes and finally put her family to rest. She hoped it would be the beginning of a new life. For her. For her dad.

It wasn't like she would ever forget about either of them. It's just that it had been hanging over their heads for so long, like a black cloud. Always present no matter how hard she tried to push it away. No, this *was* going to be a new start. She would be intentional about her relationships— with her dad and with Nate. And now when thoughts of her mom or Max snuck into her mind, she would see smiles, or laughter, or encouragement. She let out a cleansing breath.

***

A slight warm breeze rustled Tina's hair as they walked down the beach. Her mom's urn was cool and light as she hugged it to her. Her dad held Max close to his heart.

"Let's head to that little cove," Mark said and nodded towards it.

The white sand was warm between her bare toes. This was it. This was the perfect place for her mom to rest. Yes, she knew her mom was already in heaven. But the thought of her spending eternity on the beach warmed her heart.

"Remember how mom could always find something to be cheerful about? Even when she was going through chemo? When we shaved her head, she started laughing so hard tears ran down her cheeks." A smile lit her eyes.

"Her light always shone. Her glass was always half full. Even when Max started to decline, she championed him. She always saw what he could do, not what he couldn't." Mark paused to look at Tina." And you were so good with him. At one point it was as if you had become his big sister."

They reached the cove and settled on the sand. The warmth of the afternoon sun wrapped around Tina's bare legs. She nestled the urn into the sand and watched the waves curl and crash.

"The ocean is kind of like our lives, isn't it. It's calm and then works itself into a rhythm of crashing waves, then spreads itself thin," Tina said.

Mark nodded. "And then it recedes and rejoins the strength of the mass."

Seagulls squawked overhead and sandpipers ran across the wet sand looking for insects to eat.

"Look at the sky. It's really pretty—oranges and pinks." Tina stood up. Mark joined her and put his arm around her waist.

"It's really gorgeous. The perfect time..."

"It's time, isn't it," Tina asked and brushed the sand off her legs. She reached her hands out to Mark's.

"I think we should say the Lord's Prayer before we spread them."

As we forgive those who trespass against us.

Thoughts flooded her mind. I forgive you dad for what you did or didn't do. Or what I thought you did or didn't do. I hope you forgive me too.

For thine is the kingdom, the power, and the glory forever.

Tina hadn't been sure what she'd find when she carefully removed the lid to the urn.

She reached in and took out a handful.

"I thought they would be grey. Look, they're white. And they feel like coarse sand, not soft like wood ash." She gave a little tilt of her head.

Mark opened Max's urn. "Okay little buddy. Time for you to join mom."

They each took a handful, counted to three and tossed them into the air. The breeze carried them away.

"Goodbye mom. Goodbye Max. I love you." Tina wiped her eye with the back of her hand. Mark turned towards her. Tina felt warmth in the embrace of her dad, something that hadn't been shared since before her mom got cancer. This hug was different from any of the others. Neither one was tense, only soft and open to each other. This. This is what she had longed for. Finally righted in their relationship.

Chapter Thirty

The December air was chilly. Nate glanced at the temperature— thirty-two degrees. More than chilly. His down jacket and the scarf Tina had knit him were definitely the right choice. He was grateful for the warmth and security of his Lamborghini as he headed north on I-5. Plows had cleared the roads of the fresh snow that had fallen the night before. It was romantic. And beautiful. Almost as much as that girl riding beside him. He glanced at Tina snuggled under a fuzzy throw.

How did he get so lucky as to find a girl like her? She was cute, funny, intelligent, and seemed to fill the gaps where he lacked. Like the other day when he was telling her about his research. He was sure she didn't have a clue what he was talking about, but she was a good listener and asked intelligent questions. Research he understood. It was where he excelled. Relationships? That was another thing. He found himself observing the variables as he did in research. If Tina reacted a certain way to something he said or did, he would note what triggered her smile. Or her frown. And then adjust at the next encounter.

Nate smiled. His *Tina* research was producing exceptional results.

"Do you mind if we stop at the next town? I could use a mocha and something to eat," Tina said.

"Yes. Of course. I could use a break as well. We'll stop in Ellensburg . It's a couple more hours from there."

"I am so pumped!" A broad grin filled her face." "I've always wanted to go to Leavenworth. My parents were always going to take us, but, well, you know how things went down."

Nate nodded. "You haven't told me yet how your trip went. Was it okay?"

Tina crossed her legs and turned towards him. "It was more than okay. I was so anxious about spending that much time with my dad and, I don't know, just the thought of spreading their ashes and the finality of it all."

"But it turned out okay?" He stole a glance at her.

"Yeah, it did. The island is beautiful! The jungle and all the different kinds of plants. All kinds of birds. And lizards. And the ocean is gorgeous! The water is crystal clear aqua. We got to scuba dive and saw so many beautiful fish and even some dolphins. We should do that together sometime! You'd love it!"

Do that together? He'd do anything together with her. Especially if it led to a future.

"That sounds amazing!" He turned his blinkers on and passed a semi-truck.

"It was." Tina snugged her wrap tighter around her. "We stayed in this airbnb that was right on the beach. It was surrounded by coconut palms and had a pool and outdoor barbecue. The weather is so nice—I wore shorts and a tank every day."

Nate could just picture that. Her shapely figure in a tank top. Maybe they should go scuba diving. He'd love to see her in a bathing suit. He cocked his eyebrow.

"What are you thinking about?" He gave her a crooked smile.

Tina raised one eyebrow and glanced out the side window.

"What about spreading the ashes?"

"I carried mom's urn and dad carried Max's. It was surprising how light they were. Anyway, we took them down the beach where no one was and then sat down on the sand. We just talked about all kinds of things we remembered about each of them and when we ran out of memories, we said the Lord's Prayer. Then we opened the urn, took out handfuls and let the breeze carry them away." She looked vacantly out the window.

"How did that feel? Was it weird? Or just a relief to let them go?"

"Kinda everything. It was a little weird. But I just imagined how much my mom loved to be on the beach and that made it all okay. Their souls weren't in the ashes so really, they didn't care. They were already in heaven in their new home. But your imagination takes you away to what you think they would have wanted."

A new home in heaven. What did it take to get there? He was sure he wasn't good enough and hoped that end game didn't depend on that.

Nate took the turn off to Ellensburg, and pulled in at a coffee shop. They got out and stretched. Nate gave Tina a quick kiss and wove his arm through her elbow, steadying her as they walked through the snowy sidewalk.

From their table, Nate watched Tina admire all the Christmas décor. There was even a beautiful hand carved creche on the counter. Nate took note— Tina loving Christmas was something to add to his observations.

"Kaitlyn would love this place. She'd be taking photos of everything to duplicate for her new home."

"You miss her, don't you?"

"I do. I know she's just a few blocks away, but it's just not the same." Tina wrapped her hands around her hot mocha.

"You told me about spreading ashes. You didn't tell me about how things went with your dad."

"It was actually amazing. When we were on the plane, he and I had a 'talk'. Well, maybe I did more listening at first. But he just opened up to me on the plane and said he was sorry that I had gotten lost in the crowd with everything going on." She pushed a strand of hair under her beanie. "He told me he was afraid that he would lose me too and that's why he pulled back."

"Wow. That must have been kind of a hard talk. I'm not sure I could do that with my dad." He ran his hand through his short scrubby beard.

"But Nate," she put her hand on his knee. "You should. I wish we hadn't waited this long. There's a part of the Lord's Prayer that says, 'forgive us our trespasses as we forgive those who trespass against us.' It really hit me, and I was able to forgive him. I realized that my lack of forgiveness was holding *me* hostage. It was really freeing." Tina had folded her napkin into an accordion.

"Maybe this was just the right timing. Anyway, it opened all kinds of conversation. We even talked about you!" She gave a nervous giggle.

"Like, what a great researcher I am?" She wouldn't have talked about them, would she?

"That, and what a great guy you are to have in my life." He wanted to memorize the sparkle of her eyes.

"What did he say?" He took a sip of his peppermint latte. Tina had coaxed him into something more than his usual boring black coffee. Did he really want to know?

"He was excited that I had found someone and that it was

you. I think he wishes you were his son." She gave an exaggerated wink.

Nate was beginning to wish he were Mark's son as well. Son-in-law.

♥ ♥ ♥

Leavenworth was all it was made out to be. Every store was Christmas. Literally thousands of lights twinkled in the trees, shops, and eateries. Nate slipped his hand in Tina's as they walked to the gazebo to hear a violinist and choir sing Christmas songs. He snugged her close, enjoying her fragrance.

"Let's look in the shops. I want to find a good ornament to give my dad to remember this year." Tina smiled.

He lightly kissed her forehead before they moved towards the German Christmas markets. Hundreds of people surrounded them, their chatter and laughter adding to the magic of the moment. Tina settled on a Santa ornament dressed in swim trunks with a scuba mask. He was holding a clear ball with some sand. The perfect pick. Which ornament would he pick out for his dad if things were different? He quickly blew that thought away and chose a pekinese for his mom.

"Come on! We better head to the sleigh ride—don't want to miss that!" Tina tugged on his elbow.

Nate smiled. She was as giddy as a little kid. Being here with her almost made him want to run and skip, something he couldn't ever remember doing. In fact, he couldn't remember a time when he'd been excited about Christmas. It had never been something to look forward to. His mom would pull out the old silver tinsel tree she got at a Goodwill and he'd hang a loose stocking from his drawer. With any luck it would hold something other than a single piece of candy. Any Christmas celebration lasted less than fifteen minutes with them each opening their one present.

They stopped to watch the reindeer in a fenced in area. He hadn't realized that they were so small. No wonder it took eight of them to pull the sleigh.

The sleigh, beautifully carved and delicately painted pulled up in front of them. The driver, wearing a double-breasted green coat and an elf hat leant a hand to Tina. Once seated, Nate wrapped his arm around her shoulders. That move had become such a comfortable one. The feel of her fingers melded into the feel of his own.

The draft horse decked out in a collar of jingle bells began to move which brought the music of jingling ringing out with each clop of its hooves. The sky darkened and tiny flakes of snow began to drift down landing on their hats and coats. Never in all his days had Nate thought he could experience this love for anyone. He couldn't stop himself from smiling.

Chapter Thirty-One

Tina looked around her living room. Nate had helped her bring home a Christmas tree, chosen from Luke's Healthy Kids Tree Stand and set it up. They not only strung the lights on the tree but bordered the ceiling with festive colors.

Christmas had been her mom's favorite holiday. She said you could judge a ceiling of a house by how tall a Christmas tree you could put in there. Her dad had always made her and her mom wait until the day after Thanksgiving to go out into the woods to find the perfect noble fir. It was a whole family affair —toastily wrapped warm in scarves and mittens, hot cocoa, carols. Until Max got sick and then Christmas, like everything else in their lives, seemed to fall to the wayside. Tina shook herself.

Her friends would be over soon to decorate the tree. She had placed a tub of lights and the few decorations she had in the middle of the room. Nate had set up a folding table with the makings for decorations. Scissors, paper, string, glue sticks. Don't forget the glitter. Pinterest had become her new best friend.

She nodded and made her way to the kitchen where she lifted the lid to the crockpot and breathed in the aroma of her homemade clam chowder, her mom's recipe. The timer went off and she put on her Christmas hot pads to take out the cinnamon rolls. Nate had set everything in place for the makings of hot buttered rum.

The doorbell rang and Kaitlyn and Luke entered before she had a chance to answer to door. Just as it should be. She missed Kaitlyn's dog Bentley barking his greeting. She really missed having Kaitlyn here as a roommate, hanging her stocking, putting out candles, twirling through the living room when it was all decorated.

"Hey! Hang your coats up and come on in." Kaitlyn gave Tina a hug. Nate patted Luke on the back.

"Wow! You really outdid yourself! You must like Christmas as much as Kaitlyn. Every nook and cranny at our house is filled with Christmas stuff." Luke smiled and hung his coat on the rack. "Did you know she even put a gift under the tree wrapped in a blanket! What's that all about?"

Tina grinned. "It's a family tradition. Your wife and I always wrap the special present that way." She glanced at Kaitlyn. Tina was glad that Kaitlyn was extending a part of their relationship into her new life.

There was a knock on the door and Peter, Daniel and Miya let themselves in.

"What do you want us to do?" Daniel asked. He followed his nose to the kitchen and lifted the lid to the chowder.

"Mm hm."

"Set out some bowls and there's Christmas napkins in the drawer."

Tina reached for her phone and cued up Christmas tunes as the others showed up and made themselves at home.

It's Beginning to Look a Lot Like Christmas came on. Kristina's favorite. Kaitlyn gave Tina knowing glance.

"Okay everybody, dish up!" Tina said.

"Wait," Peter held up his hand like a policeman at a busy intersection. He puffed up his shoulders. "I'll lead grace. Be sure to join in!"

He fisted his hands and raised one arm and to the tune of the Superman Theme Song began,

"Thank you Lord, for giving us food."

He held his other arm up.

"Thank you Lord, for giving us food."

He began to move like he was flying.

"For the food we eat and the friends we meet. Thank you Lord, for giving us food."

The room filled with laughter.

Nate had his arms crossed over his chest. Tina nudged him.

"You didn't join in." She wore a teasing grin.

"Uh," he tilted his head and raised his eyebrows giving her a quizzical look.

"Come on, you should be getting used to these guys."

"Uh, yeah. Think I'll dish me up some soup."

Tina gave him a peck on the cheek and a hug.

* * *

"That was delish," Kaitlyn said and pulled Tina aside. "How was Leavenworth?" She glanced at Nate.

"It was amazing! I don't think he ever had a real Christmas. It was so magical."

"What was so magical?" Nate sidled up to Tina and put his arm around her.

"You are." Tina looked up at him. "Come on, let's get those decorations going. We've got stuff to make paper chains, snowflakes, ornaments—whatever your little heart's desire. See that poor undecorated tree? It's waiting for your masterpieces."

"Okay, let's try this."

Tina showed Nate how to fold a strip of paper in half and make cuts that were half inch apart.

"Now open it."

He held it up and it separated out and extended. "Look, if I twist the bottom, it looks like a DNA model!"

"That's the spirit! Let's try a snowflake."

Nate watched Tina as she folded a piece of paper and began to snip.

"Well, come on." She handed him the scissors.

"I'm not sure I know what to do."

"Surely you made these when you were in school!"

"Maybe. I could probably make a good one if you showed me how."

Did he not know how to do this? Tina shook her head and scrunched up her nose.

"Take a square of paper." She took a square and folded it several times to demonstrate.

"Like this?"

"Yeah, just start cutting any way you want to make your design."

He started snipping. "Now unfold it and see what it looks like," Tina said.

He unfolded it and it fell into four separate pieces. Nate held his hands out.

"See, I have no clue how to do this."

Tina couldn't help but laugh.

"Okay okay. Go get your guitar. You know how to do that!" She smiled as she cleaned up the scraps.

Daniel and Miya were joining strips of paper into chains.

"I've got to find somewhere else to live. My landlord just raised the rent and it's way more than I can afford," Miya said.

"Maybe you two should just get married," Peter said and gave an exaggerated wink.

"It's probably in the plans, but not quite yet..." Miya said. She glanced at Daniel and taped another strip to the chain. Daniel raised an eyebrow and busied himself with his strip.

"Well now, lucky for you I just might have the perfect solution," Tina said.

"Really? What?" Miya looked up at her.

"You can move into Kaitlyn's old room. And I'm sure it'll be less money than you're paying now."

Daniel put his arm around Tina's shoulders. "Now that's what friends are for."

"Oh, wait a minute. That would mean Daniel would probably be over here all the time. Let me rethink that." Tina nudged him.

"He's a good cook," Miya said.

That might not be so bad. And Daniel would be a good influence on Nate as well. She looked at the ceiling seeing the possibilities.

Tina sat on the couch next to Nate who was picking chords to *Away in a Manger*.

"That is really pretty."

Now this is what Christmas is supposed to be like.

"Hey, want me to teach you a few chords?" He set the guitar in her lap and placed her hands in the right position. "You have to hold your fingers like this and press hard. That's right. Now strum with your right hand."

Tina tried it and smiled. "Not perfect, but I might be able to learn. That is, if you're willing to teach me. It might take an awfully long time." She gave him a mischievous grin.

"Babe, I'm willing to do anything as long as it's with you!" He planted a kiss on her lips. "That's good, cuz I have a song I want to teach everyone and I need you to play it." She handed the guitar back to him.

"Okay everyone, gather round. I've got a new version of Twelve Days of Christmas." Tina handed out sheets with the lyrics and they all chimed in.

"On the first day of Christmas, Mercy gave to me, one crazy floor to work on.

On the second day of Christmas, Mercy gave to me, two poops a flying on that one crazy floor we work on." They laughed as they continued with Kaitlyn dramatically singing out five lactulose enemas, four bed alarms screeching, three requests for pain meds, two poops a flying on that one crazy floor we work on."

These guys. Maybe this is what family was supposed to be like. A bunch of weirdos—there for you in a pinch, and there for you for good times. There was no doubt about it. She was feeling blessed.

Chapter Thirty-Two

Tina had just hauled out the tub to put the Christmas decorations in when her doorbell chimed.

"Martha! Come in!" She held a plate of cookies.

"I thought it was my turn," she said. Her eyes twinkled.

"How thoughtful. Here, let me take your coat." Tina set the cookies on the coffee table and hung her coat on the rack. "I have some chai. Would you like me to make you a cup?"

"That would be lovely." Tina chose two red cups and heated the chai, poured in some cream, and handed one to Martha. They sat on the couch.

"What type of cookies did you make?"

She took the saran off the cookies.

"Molasses. Yum. I remember my mom and I made some of those for a school event once."

She took a bite.

"You use real ginger, don't you?" Martha nodded.

"How was your Christmas?" Tina asked.

Martha's face lit up. "Well now, you sneaky girls had it all figured out when you invited me to Kaitlyn's wedding." She put on an impish grin.

"Yeah?"

"William took me to the nicest restaurant. It overlooked the river. We even did a little dancing." Her eyes twinkled.

"Oh, that sounds sweet. I had never met him before the wedding, but Kaitlyn was always talking about him and how great he is. I'm sure he helped Luke become the guy that he is."

"Luke is something, isn't he? He's so thoughtful and full of integrity. What's going on with your friend Nate?"

Now it was Tina's turn to twinkle. "We went to Leavenworth— it was so gorgeous. The lights, the snow, the sleigh ride. All of it." She wasn't sure she wanted to tell her about the snuggling and kisses. "He gave me these diamond earrings." She pointed to her earlobe.

"Those are beautiful. They show off the sparkle of your eyes, dear." She set her cup down. "Can I help you take down your decorations?"

"That would be nice. Usually Kaitlyn would help me, but, you know, with her being married..." Tina shrugged. She scooted the tub closer to the tree and smiled as she took down the paper ornament Nate had made and placed it in the tub. She wondered if someday her adopted kids would want to hear the story of it. That is, if things led the way she hoped.

"Do you have any kids? Grandkids?" Tina asked.

"No. We tried but no luck. I'm sure Christmas would be way more fun with them. But, the Lord knows what's best."

"How did you know you wanted to marry Robert?"

Martha unhooked an ornament and placed it in the tub.

"Well, now that's a good question. We had been dating for nearly a year, which in my day, was a long time. My friends were getting married after only a few months, or at most, six."

"Did something hold you back?"

"Actually, yes. I loved everything about Robert. He was handsome, strong, had a good job. He was well liked by everyone. My parents thought he was the best thing since sliced bread."

She paused and looked at the tree top star.

"But he didn't grow up going to church. He didn't know how important a relationship with God was. He used to tease me about praying about everything before I made any decision."

"Nate's the same way. When I tell him I'm praying for him, he just kinda shrugs. It makes me sad." Tina unplugged the lights and began to unwind them. "But you married him anyway."

"Yes. I decided it was better to have a good man that didn't believe than to have one I wished I hadn't married."

"Did he ever believe?"

Martha smiled. "Yes. He eventually started going to church with me. He realized where my joy was coming from. Tina, just keep being you. Of course, keep praying about it. God will make it plain to you if Nate is the right guy."

* * *

"Pass me the garlic." Tina separated several cloves and handed them to her dad. She watched him set the knife blade on its side and crush the outer layer before peeling it off, releasing the pungent, savory smell. Today was Mark's birthday and she couldn't describe the peace she had being with him.

He had set up his tablet on the counter so they could watch a cooking show and make dinner together. They had decided on beef stew. Good smells were already emanating from the cast iron dutch oven as he sautéed the garlic, onion and now the dredged meat.

"Do you want me to sprinkle in the thyme and basil?" Tina asked.

"Yes, and I'll get the carrots chopped."

Tina looked up and smiled. Little bits of grey were beginning in his dark hair. She suspected if he didn't shave, there would be a lot more grey there as well.

"Dad, I'm glad we got things smoothed over. You've become the dad I always wanted."

Mark set down the knife and held Tina's eyes.

"Aw honey."

He blinked back the bit of moisture forming.

"I've always loved you so much, I just was afraid to show it."

Tina put her arm around his waist and rested her head on his shoulder.

After they had finished putting the ingredients into the pot, Tina led him into the living room.

"Come on, I've got your present. You can open it now while the stew is cooking."

She handed him a package and he peeled off the tape.

"A photo book!" He looked up and a slow smile spread through his face.

"I scanned in some of the old photos and had a book made." He opened the cover and read the inscription.

To you dad, so we'll never forget.

"Our wedding picture? Where'd you find that?"

"It was in a box of photos. Look how young you were!"

"Your mom was nineteen and I was twenty. I guess that was pretty young."

"Her dress is so beautiful." She wished it were still around so she could try it on. It didn't necessarily mean she had a reason to wear it. But who knew?

"Where did you meet mom?"

"I never told you that story? She was my friend Rick's sister. I needed a date for Homecoming and Rick suggested Kristina. I never even thought of taking her on a date. She was just Rick's little sis." He smiled. "Turns out she was much more than that."

"I never would have put that together. Uncle Rick. Hmm."

"How about you, sweet pea? How are things going with Nate?" His eyebrows raised.

"Good. Great. We went to Leavenworth. It was so beautiful. I think that was one of the best Christmases I've had in a long time."

"You're falling for him, aren't you?"

"I'd say more like fallen." She looked out the window. The moon was peeking through the bare branches of the oak tree.

"He's so smart. And thoughtful. He really loves his mom."

"And his dad?" He put his arm around her shoulders and gave a squeeze.

"Not so much. He's a meth user and is abusive."

"Really? Does that worry you?"

"If I'm honest, a little. I don't think Nate would ever be like that. But his dad put his mom in the hospital several months ago. What if he did that when we were together?" She shivered.

"That's a concern. But nothing the two of you can't manage together if you love him." He pulled back and gave her a questioning look.

Tina couldn't help but smile. She hadn't let herself think that word. But his saying it was like opening a door to sunshine after days of rain.

"I'm not going to tell you what to do, but if I were you, I'd keep doing what you're doing. And," he put his arm around her , "I wouldn't mind having him for a son-in-law." He winked.

"I think the stew's probably done. We better eat while it's just right."

Let's just leave that subject alone for awhile.

Chapter Thirty-Three

Nate gazed out the window of the plane at the patterned landscape below. How many children below would benefit from the cure he had found. He knew Noah would, and if he were the only one, it would be enough. So many hours had been invested. So much research and clinical trials. A slow smile spread over his lips. He had to admit his perseverance and intelligent mind had been a strength. The fact he could use them for good? Well, that was what he was cut out for. He sat up a little straighter.

Tina checked the screen in front of her to see how much further to Boston. She snugged her arm through Nate's and rested her head on his shoulder.

"Thank you for inviting me to come with you."

"I can't think of anyone I'd rather have by my side." Nate kissed the top of her head.

"Your mom will be so proud of you. I'll be sure to take lots of pictures." Tina sat up. "I bet your dad would be secretly proud of you too." She glanced at Nate. He tensed up.

"As far as I'm concerned, *he* doesn't ever need to know anything about me and what I do." His lips curled in disgust.

"Did I tell you about the girl we had in surgery a few weeks ago? Her arm was all mangled—looked like it had been put through a meat grinder. I'd never seen anything like it."

Nate turned and rested his back in the corner so he could face her.

"What happened? That sounds awful."

"It was. She didn't want to tell us, but I finally was able to coax it out of her. Apparently, she hadn't done her chores and her dad got mad and locked her in a chain link enclosure with his dog. It sounds like it was trained to be vicious."

Nate's eyebrows knit together. "The dog chewed up her arm?" He pulled back. "What a jerk!"

"I know, right? When she got through telling me the gory details, I seriously felt hate for that man. I've never felt that before. For anyone."

"Yep." He looked away.

"That's what you feel towards your dad, isn't it." Her voice was soft. Maybe she was beginning to see what his life was like. Still, Nate felt like he wanted to scoot as far away from this conversation as he could. He couldn't help it. Every time he even thought of that man he had to shake it off. Try to reconcile? That wasn't ever going to happen. He was evil. Right now Nate only wanted to concentrate on the good things in his life— like this girl by his side. And receiving a well-deserved award.

Nate couldn't believe all the vendors and hubbub in the convention center. Tina had insisted they stay in separate rooms. Not his idea of what this trip was going to look like, but he respected her wish and was surprised at how it increased his longing for her.

Now, after a breakfast of croissants and eggs, and a snowy walk through Boston Commons, here they were. A twinge of anxiety zinged through him when he thought about the presentation he was to give. When they had notified him that he would be receiving an award and expected a presentation, he never dreamed it would be in front of so many people. Highly respected ones, at that. No, he was just a geeky science guy. His comfort zone was in the lab or reading research.

They meandered past displays of new medical devices, pharmaceuticals and employment opportunities.

"Is any of this interesting to you?" Nate asked.

"Actually, yes. It's like this huge other world has opened. So many things I never knew existed. We could use some of this stuff at Mercy."

"Okay, cuz I didn't want you to be bored."

"Not gonna happen. I'd go anywhere with you Nate Bronson!" She bumped shoulders with him and grinned. Nate wrapped his arm around her and pulled her close.

He checked the time. "We've got to be at the next presentation in ten. I want to see how Dr. Langston presents and see if I need to tweak anything before I give mine this afternoon.

♥ ♥ ♥

Nate adjusted his tie and walked to the podium where he checked the mic.

"Good afternoon ladies and gentlemen. There was a time not so long ago when there wouldn't have been researchers who were women in the audience. A change we deeply appreciate."

Emboldened by their smiles, he continued. "I'm here today because someone believed in me enough to guide me into a focus where I could truly be of use to society. Today I would like to present my findings with you for a cure to batten disease. We can now take the missing enzyme and replace it directly into the brain."

Nate's eyes were animated, and his hands waved through the air as he explained the finite details of his research as evidenced in the trials. The nods of approval and voracious applaud filled him with joy from his head to his toes.

He thanked everyone and stepped down. His eyes scanned the room to find Tina who was heading his way. A woman, dressed in a black fitted dress and stiletto heels stepped up to him and held out her hand.

"Nate, this is such exciting news! I am so glad to be here and have the opportunity to meet you."

"Thank you," Nate glanced at her name tag, "Roberta. Have you been researching this as well?"

"I'm a neurologist at Langone Hospital in New York. And yes, our hospital has been conducting years of research in this area. You seem to be just the person we've been looking for to join our team. Would that interest you?"

Nate couldn't believe this incredible opportunity. This hospital was the gold standard. Not only would there be a pay increase, not that what he was receiving now was bad, but beyond that, he could work with world renown researchers. This was a dream come true.

"Would I? Absolutely!" Nate said.

"Could I meet you for dinner? Six o'clock?"

Tina walked up and slid her arm through Nate's. Roberta glanced at her.

"You're welcome to join us, of course." Tina looked up at Nate who gave an enormous grin.

Nate looked over his breakfast menu. "What looks good to you, Tina?"

"I'm going all out with the crepes and strawberries. And yes, I want the whip cream!"

The waitress brought their coffee and took their orders.

"You were amazing up there, giving your presentation like it was something you did every day. When you received your award—I was so proud of you! I could just burst."

Nate grinned.

"I hope I didn't seem arrogant," he said.

"Nope. Just confident." She put her hand on top of his. "The job sounds interesting," Tina said. She took a sip of her latte.

He looked up and an enormous grin filled his face. "It would be amazing. I'd be working with the best. I'd learn so much."

"New York is pretty big. Are you ready for that?"

Nate glanced out the window. "I'm sure I could figure out how to navigate that. Just get an apartment close to the hospital and take public transportation. That's pretty much what people do."

"What about your car? And when are you going to tell my dad?"

"I don't know. I'm sure there are a few details to iron out. Your dad should be fine. I've finished the job he hired me to do."

The waitress brought his plate and set it down. He dug into the home fried potatoes and eggs.

Tina took a small bite and looked out the window.

"Are you okay? Your eyes too big for your stomach?" He grinned.

She looked down. "Yeah, I guess." Her finger twirled a strand of her hair . "Just not as hungry as I thought."

"Guess I'll have to finish mine and dig into yours." He licked his lips.

"Excuse me. I need to go to the ladies' room." Tina slid out and left. Nate dug into her crepe, tingling with the possibilities awaiting him.

Chapter Thirty-Four

"Peter, tie the back of my gown for me." Tina held the strings up.

"Sure thing." He tied and Tina tucked her wild hair under her surgical cap.

"Mine too?" Kaitlyn said and backed up to Tina.

"Wait for me," Daniel said and backed up to Kaitlyn.

"Who's supposed to tie mine?" Peter said and put out a pouty lip.

Dr. Roberts just shook his head. "Let me know when you goons are finally ready!"

Kaitlyn let out a giggle.

A woman lay on the surgical table, covered with a blue sterile drape. The anesthetist sat near her head.

"Count backwards starting at ten." He placed the breathing apparatus over her nose and mouth.

"Ten, nine, eight, seeeeveeen."

"And she's out ladies and gents. Let the show begin."

"Just a routine appendectomy today, folks. You know what to do."

Tina handed Dr. Roberts the trocar which he used to create

a small puncture in the woman's abdomen. Kaitlyn handed him the laparoscope. They watched as he inserted it into the trocar.

"Showtime," Peter said.

The images appeared on the monitor.

"Woah, pretty swollen."

"Need two more ports." Daniel handed them to doc and watched as he inserted an instrument to remove the appendix.

"How was your trip with Nate?" Daniel asked.

"It was good. They gave him this huge plaque as an award," Tina said.

"Did he get money too?" Peter asked. His eyes lit up.

"Actually, yes. I was surprised by how much."

"That's good, now you guys can treat us to a vacay!" Tina scrunched up her nose.

"Not gonna happen."

"Focus!" Dr. Roberts pulled out the appendix and placed it in the sterile bag Tina held.

"Okay, close this pretty little thing up, gang. Just look at those tiny little holes. She'll never even know I was in here."

♥ ♥ ♥

"How *was* your trip?" Kaitlyn asked. They walked through the door at Coffee Corner and found a seat.

"It was amazing. Boston is a beautiful old city. Full of history. We don't have anything like that in the west." Tina pulled out her phone and started showing pics. "Here, look at these. I'll go get our drinks."

She returned with Kaitlyn's borgia and an almond mocha.

"I got a lemon bar and brownie." She set the brownie in front of Kaitlyn.

"Yes! It seems like I can't get enough chocolate lately. I mean, two months of throwing up every day and now I just want to eat 24/7!" She patted her belly. You wouldn't even know she was four months pregnant other than her glow.

"It looks like you had a blast. What about the convention?"

"The center was fun. There were all sorts of machines and medical equipment we could use on our floor. Not so sure we could convince management to buy them for us."

She took a sip of her drink.

"Nate's presentation went really well. There were a ton of people there. I thought he'd be nervous, but I think when he starts talking about what he's passionate about, he gets all wound up and energized."

"I can see him now. What was the audience reaction?" Kaitlyn took a bite of her brownie. Her eyes rolled heavenward, and she let out a deep sigh.

"They loved him. Maybe a little too much." Tina glanced away.

"Tina? What? Did something happen? Did Nate do something wrong?"

Tina swallowed. Her throat was tight. "This lady came up to him afterwards and offered him a job."

"That's good, isn't it?"

"That would be good. If it were in Portland. But it's in New York." Tina wrapped her hands around her cup.

"New York? He's not going to take it is he?"

Tina's eyes started to fill. She glanced away.

"He's thinking about it isn't he." Tina nodded slowly and sniffed.

"But it would be an adventure, right? You could get another job at a hospital in New York. I'm sure you could get one at his same hospital. Then you two could work together every day and have so much to talk about." She set her hand on Tina's.

"I wonder if they have as many crazies in their hospital as we do..." She put her finger at the side of her lips and looked up.

"I don't know. I mean, I really love him. And I want to be with him. He's so excited about this possibility. I don't want to be the one to get in the way of his career. He's completed what he was hired to do at dad's foundation. He *should* move on to another job."

"So, what's the problem?"

Tina thought about their camaraderie earlier that day in surgery.

"I can't leave you guys. I mean, we're the Invincibles. There can't just be a three-some. Now that I've started a good relationship with my dad, how can I go away? Not to mention becoming "auntie" to your little nugget. Now that Miya's moved into my house. What happens there?" Her lips tightened and she shook her head.

Kaitlyn pushed a strand of hair out of Tina's face.

"Yeah. A lot to think about. But I'm here for you whatever you decide."

⋅ ♥ ♥ ♥ ⋅

Tina parked her car in her drive and just sat there, staring at the steering wheel. What should she do? If Nate was seriously thinking of moving to New York, was he intending to have her go with him? Didn't she get a say in any of this? Or did he think more of his career than he did of her?

Their ride home from breakfast had been quiet. It seemed he was just full of thoughts of his future. A future that might not include her. When he dropped her off he had only given her a cursory peck on the cheek.

She shrugged out a sigh and got out.

Miya was standing in the kitchen where she had just hung up her phone. "Hey. I was just talking to Daniel. He's going to come by later."

Tina hung up her bag and plopped down on a chair. She set her crossed arms on the table and laid her head on them.

Miya stopped. "You okay? What's going on?" She sat down across from her.

Did she want to open up to Miya? She didn't really know her that well yet.

"Bad day at work? Something with Nate?"

Tina sat up and ran her hands through her hair, pulling it back. "You know we went to that conference back east for Nate to receive his award." Miya nodded.

"Well, he got offered a job."

"That's good. Isn't it?"

Funny. That's what Kaitlyn had said.

"That he got offered a job, yes. But it's in New York."

"So, he's going to move? Are you going with him?" Miya stood up to get a glass of water.

"I don't know. That's just it." She filled her in on the details.

"Has Nate brought up the M word yet?" *Marriage?*

"No, but I was pretty sure we were headed that way."

"Is it what you want?" She sat back down and handed Tina a glass.

"Yes. I mean no. I mean," she stared at the ceiling, "I want to be with him. But I don't know if I could leave everything here."

"What did he say when you told him how you feel?"

Tina gave her a blank stare.

"You haven't told him?" Miya asked.

"I guess I haven't really had the chance."

"Listen, Daniel and I had a fight not too long ago. You know I've worked nights forever. But I decided to switch to days, so I could work and spend more time with him. It took a while to change my sleep rhythm. Anyway, it wasn't working out like I thought it would. Yeah, I'd see him at work, but he was always busy. Then on the evenings and my days off, he was always hanging out with Peter, riding motorcycles and stuff."

"Ouch. So, you talked to him?"

"Yeah. Basically, he's like every other male on the planet—tunnel vision in what they want to do. He didn't have a clue that's why I changed my schedule."

"So that's why he's coming over tonight?"

"Yeah. It sounds like Nate is chasing after long time goals—recognition, challenge, opportunity. He probably doesn't see any reason you wouldn't want to tag along."

Tina nodded.

"Talk to Nate. Tell him exactly how you feel about this. If he doesn't listen, he's not the right guy for you anyway. Better to find out now."

When she imagined what it would be like to live without him, her chest tightened. Was she ready to let him go? Maybe it *would* be okay to move to New York. Then she thought about what she'd leave behind and shook her head.

Chapter Thirty-Five

Nate stood at the doorway of his office and looked around. He would need to finish up a few loose ends, like telling Mark, and then start packing up. He was consumed with thoughts of this new job. It wasn't that he hadn't enjoyed working at the foundation, but New York had so many more possibilities. His learning curve would be exponential, surrounded by those who were cutting edge. His cohorts here were good, but nothing like at Langone. Last week when he'd had his online interview, he was energized by the depth of the questions they had asked and the scope of their research. Yes, this was going to be amazing.

"Nate, I've got someone here to see you," Spencer said.

Nate looked up and a broad grin filled his face.

"Mr. Nate!" Noah ran up and hugged his knees.

Nate bent down to look him in the eye.

"Hey. What's up? Glad to see you!" He ruffled Noah's hair.

"I wanted to show you my dinosaur." He held out a stuffed triceratops. "I got it at OMSI yesterday."

"You got to go to the science museum? I love that place," Nate said. This little guy tugged on his heart.

"So does he," David said. He reached his hand out to shake Nate's. "We can't thank you enough for all you've done for our son. Because of you, he has a future. We have a future as a family." He pinched the bridge of his nose with his fingers.

Nate swallowed. "It's my job. I'm glad I was able to finally come to a solution."

It was more than a job. It was a way to change lives. This. This is what he was meant to do. To make a difference.

"Noah, would you like to take this gene model? I'm taking a job in New York and can't take it with me."

"Really?" His blue eyes sparkled as he looked up at his dad. "Yes! Do you think I could be a 'scientis' too when I grow up?"

"Absolutely!"

A boy that was now capable of dreaming dreams and having a future.

♥ ♥ ♥

Nate reached his long arms above his head and clasped his hands for a much needed stretch. His eyes swept over the room and he walked down the hall to Mark's office.

"Hey, ready to go?"

Mark looked up from his computer. "Yes, just let me finish and close my computer. I thought we could go to that Mexican restaurant on 7th."

♥ ♥ ♥

Mark handed his menu back to the server and steadied his gaze on Nate.

"I want to take a moment to acknowledge all your hard work and effort. Your diligence really paid off."

Nate fingered his napkin. He wasn't used to being praised.

"Your drive and focus are unparalleled. And receiving that award! That topped it all. It was well deserved."

Nate nodded; the corner of his mouth turned up.

"Thank you. I wasn't sure I could get to the bottom of it. I have to say it was exhilarating when everything pulled together. Research is what I love."

Winning points with this man was a good thing. He could possibly have him for a father-in-law. That is, if things continue with Tina in the same direction.

"Speaking of love.... You and my daughter seem to be a perfect match." Mark grinned.

"She's an incredibly special girl. You did a good job of raising her."

"I'm not sure about that. But I do see the sparkle in her eyes when she's around you. That's not something I've ever seen in her before."

The server set a plate of chimichangas and carne asada before them.

"What's next for you?" Mark took a bite.

Nate took a breath. "So, it seems my job here is through. I've been offered a job at Langone in New York."

Mark set his fork down. "New York. That's a long way from here. Are you ready for big city life?"

Nate nodded. "It is big. But I'm sure I could get used to it. It's the research that's important, not where you do it."

"What about my daughter? She going with you?" He raised a brow.

"Yes of course. I think so. Probably." He sounded like an idiot. She *was* going with him, wasn't she?

"Sounds like you two need to have a discussion about this." Mark took a bite. "At any rate, I'm so proud to be able to claim that you were on our team. You were a game changer for loads of families. You'll be missed."

♥ ♥ ♥

Nate finished loading boxes into his car. There hadn't been that many as most of his work had been in the lab. The computer belonged to the organization and all his files were saved on the cloud.

He carefully boxed up the flier Tina had made and a sketch she had left of him on his desk. His girl had talent.

He closed the trunk, pulled out and glanced over his shoulder one last time. He was going to miss Spencer. And Mark had been such a great mentor. He wished his dad had been like that. Tina didn't know how lucky she was.

Nate stopped at the store and picked up a salad kit and frozen lasagna. Tina was coming over for dinner and he wanted something other than Uber eats. She should know that he at least knew how to turn on the oven. He smiled. Maybe he should get a bottle of wine too. Flowers? Oh, and a candle. Girls liked that sort of thing, didn't they?

He hoped she would like his house. She hadn't seen it yet—they'd always been at her house or out somewhere. He couldn't wait to introduce her to Chuck. Did she like to play cards? Or maybe they could watch a movie. A slip in a few kisses.

♥ ♥ ♥

Just as Nate lit the candles, the doorbell rang. His heart skipped as he opened it. His eyes skimmed over Tina's, cable knit turtleneck and down her brown leggings. Her hair was pulled back with pins letting her diamond earrings sparkle.

"Hey!" He leaned back. "You look amazing!" He drew in for a quick kiss.

"Thanks! Something smells good. I bet you've been slaving over a hot stove all day." Her crooked smile drew him in.

He leaned against the wall, one arm above his head, and watched as Tina took in his surroundings. The color splashed painting, his stark white furniture, the multiple skylights.

"This is not what I expected." Her lips parted and her eyebrows raised.

"Do you like it? I wanted to live in complete contrast to what I grew up with. As far away from a rundown trailer as I could get. When I'm at home, I forget about my past."

A nervous smile flickered across his features. It shouldn't matter if she liked his house or not. But it surprised him at how much it did.

"It's different. The skylights are nice. Especially when it's gloomy outside." She looked around. "Not sure about the white leather couch. I'm more of a comfy home kinda gal." She smiled. Nate thought of her home. Yeah, he could adjust to that.

"Come meet Chuck."

She followed him to a large cage.

"Oh, he's adorable! Look at those big ears and that furry tail. Is he soft?"

"Here, I'll take him out. He's not much of a cuddle bug but you can pet him."

She reached out and felt his soft fur.

"Hey Chuck! Does Nate tell you all his secrets? Does he tell you all about me and how much he loves me?" Tina pressed her lips against a grin as Chuck let out a tch tch tch.

"Hey, no colluding with my confidant." A chuckle escaped his lips. He gently lifted Chuck from her and returned him to his cage.

"What'd you make for dinner? It smells delicious."

She headed to the dining room.

"Flowers? And candles?" She put her arms around his neck and let her lips softly touch his. A ripple of heat flashed through him.

"That's okay, right?" Had he gone too far? He hoped not. He wanted Tina to know how much he cared about her.

"It's definitely alright. Nobody's ever given me flowers before."

She gave him another kiss and slid her fingers along his arms as she pulled back.

"What do you want me to help with?" She looked around.

"Yeah. Umm." He put his fingers over his lips. "I'll pull out the lasagna and we can dish up at the counter." He thought about taking the lasagna from the pan into a serving dish but he was sure that would end up a disaster. He didn't want her to think he was a complete numb nuts.

Tina buttered her French bread. "When do they want you to start your new job?"

They both turned their heads at the sound of the doorbell. Nate checked his phone—an image of a man with his back turned. He wore a knit hat and jeans jacket.

"Who is it?" Tina asked.

"Not sure. Doesn't look like anyone I know." Nate set down his fork and walked to the door. He wasn't expecting anyone. No one ever came to visit unless invited. He pulled open the door.

"Hello son."

Chapter Thirty-Six

Tina followed Nate as he moved to slam the door.
What is he doing here? He's never come to my house before. How did he even find out where I live?

His dad blocked the door with his foot. "Nathan, I need to talk to you."

"I have nothing to say to you." Nate's jaw tightened. He shoved on the door, all the strength of his shoulder pushing against it.

"It's your mom. Let me in. Please."

Nate glanced at Tina at the end of the hall and opened the door a crack.

"What did you do to her this time?" The memory of blood trickling down his mom's cheek flooded his mind.

Alvin's fingers twitched at his sides and his foot tapped against the floor.

"I didn't touch her. I swear. I went to her house and she didn't answer the door, so I went inside and she was lying on the floor."

Nate's first instinct was to think he was lying. But that was always motivated by money or a drug payoff.

"Why didn't you call an ambulance?" Nate's impatience and frustration boiled up inside. What lame excuse could he have this time?

"I couldn't." He looked at his feet.

"You could. Pick up the frickin' phone and call 911! It's that simple."

"If I call, they'll find out I broke parole." His shoulders slumped and he scuffed the cement with his toe.

Nate shook his head and sighed impatiently. It was always about him. Tina placed a hand on Nate's shoulder, pulling him out of the moment. What must she think? This was something he never wanted her to see.

"Tina, I have to go rescue my mom again. I'm really sorry. Call 911 for me?" He told her the address.

"I'm coming with you!"

Nate looked at her, pain in his eyes.

"I'm a nurse. I should be there." She grabbed her bag and followed behind, dialing.

Tina climbed into the back seat of his car, letting Nate's dad sit in front.

"Nice car, son. I see you've done alright for yourself."

His nonchalant attitude was irritating. He desperately wanted his dad to acknowledge him, not for his success, but because he was his son.

Nate's eyes flicked out the side window and he gripped the steering wheel harder, his knuckles turning white. He was not going to enter a conversation with this man.

The red and blue lights of the ambulance flashed their reflection on the trailer window. They jumped out of the car and ran into the house. Loretta lay unconscious on the floor,

Mitzy whining beside her sweat drenched face. Two paramedics knelt beside her.

A woman put a strand of blonde hair behind her ear as she checked Loretta's pupils with a pen light. The other, tall, and muscular, sternal rubbed, digging his knuckle into her chest.

"What are her vitals?" Tina asked. She squatted down beside them. "I'm a nurse."

"Her BP is 40/palp and she's unresponsive." He looked up.

"We need to get her to the hospital right away. Get the stretcher!" the blonde said.

As he ran to the ambulance, the blonde attached oxygen tubes. Tina put her two fingers on Loretta's neck and checked for a pulse.

"How long has she been lying here?" the taller paramedic asked.

Nate twisted his eyebrows as he looked at Alvin.

"Dunno. She was like that when I came by. Maybe an hour ago?"

Nate heard the apology and regret in his tone, noting his black rotting teeth. It had been that long? Nate crossed his arms over his chest. What was wrong with him? Alvin could feel sorry, but that wouldn't stop what he might have prevented. She could die. Nate paced the floor, his jaw set, raking his hair with his hands. She should already be at the hospital if it weren't for this deadbeat.

Loretta let out a groan and her eyes flicked open. She tried to reach for Mitzy, but her arm wouldn't respond.

"She's waking up!" Nate rushed to her. "Mom?" He placed his hand on her shoulder.

Loretta gave an incoherent groan.

"Okay, let's move her," the paramedic said.

They placed Loretta on a stretcher and wheeled her to the ambulance.

"I'll go with her," Tina said. She turned to Nate. "Meet you at Mercy."

The siren screamed as the ambulance sped away.

Nate's eyes narrowed, ready to explode. He had been dealing with his dad's addiction for years. Was this never going to end? He had promised his mom he would always take care of her. It hadn't turned out to be an easy promise to keep.

Nate glared at his dad in the dim rays of the porch light. His greying hair was wiry and thin, bits of it stuck to the sweat on his forehead over his sunken eyes. His sallow skin was covered by scabs and sores.

"You are despicable!" Nate set his hands on his hips, shooting daggers at him.

Alvin was scratching himself again and his eyes darted around the yard like he was planning an escape route. Nate lunged towards him. Alvin tried to back away, looking at Nate, his eyes wide. Nate took a swing, hitting him in the jaw. Alvin fell back against the hedge and swung back, hitting Nate in the gut. Nate grabbed his arm and shoved him to the ground, placing his knee on his chest.

"Get out of here, before I pulverize you." Nate stood, his muscles tense and fists clenched. He moved towards his car. "Don't you *ever* come around here again."

Nate ran to his car, out of breath, sweating and hyped on adrenaline, leaving Alvin coughing and sputtering by the lawn. Somewhere within the house, Mitzy howled.

Nate sped towards the hospital. His eyebrows knit and lips held in a tight line. Rage coursed through him. He hated that man. They should lock him up and throw away the key. People like him shouldn't be allowed to live on the planet.

He turned on his blinkers and sped into the emergency room parking lot. Nate jumped out and ran through the front doors. He was directed to radiology where his mom was getting a CT scan.

Tina stood as Nate entered. "How is she?" he said.

"It looks like she's had a TIA, a mini stroke."

Tina took hold of his hand. "What happened to you?"

"It's nothing." Nate looked down and pulled his hand away.

"There's blood on your hand." Her brows wrinkled as she looked up at him.

"I must have hit it against something," he said and looked away. *Something hard. Like a jawbone.*

Tina wet a paper towel and dabbed at it. Her hands were gentle and soft. A light in the darkness.

Nate glanced at the time and then at his mom. "It's late., Tina. Looks like they have everything under control. Let me take you back so you can get home and get some rest. You've got work tomorrow, right?"

Tina nodded. "They'll call you when they know more. She's in good hands."

♥ ♥ ♥

"I see what you mean about your dad."

Nate glanced at Tina and pulled onto the freeway.

"He reminds me of the patients I had last year on the crazy floor." A small grin grew on her lips. "We had a few choice stories to tell."

"And each of those patients had some family member that had to deal with them and try to pick up the pieces." He rubbed the back of his neck.

"Has your dad ever gone to rehab?" Tina turned towards him and rested her back on the door.

He laughed bitterly and shook his head. "Don't know. The only time I ever interact with him since I've left home is if he's been harassing my mom."

"Maybe you should see about getting him admitted. I've seen people clean up pretty good."

"Did you look at him? You think it's even possible? He's too far gone." Nate snorted derisively and wiped a sweaty palm on his pants.

"No one is ever too far gone, Nate. There's always a chance for redemption."

"I can't see it ever happening." Nate turned down his street.

"Nate," Tina said softly and put her hand on his knee. "I agree that your dad is a jerk. But think about it. If he hadn't gone over to your mom's and found her, she would be dead by now."

The lump in Nate's throat crept higher and he tried to clear it. He knew Tina expected a response, but right now, it wasn't in his power to give one.

He pulled into the driveway. "Can I just let you out here?"

Tina nodded, leaned over, and gave him a peck on the cheek. "I love you Nate. Get some rest. Things will look better in the morning."

But would they? Look at what he had just done. He was no better than his dad, letting rage take over. No, he had to get out of here. Had to take that job. He wasn't going to stay here any longer. He wasn't the man for Tina. She needed someone stable. Not someone who could possibly harm her or, heaven forbid, his future children. He'd start packing tomorrow.

Chapter Thirty-Seven

"We need to talk," Tina said. She shivered. Why did the hospital always have to be so cold? The bright lights of the staff room shone down on her and her pals causing her to squint.

"Now?" Peter said.

"No. Too much to talk about. How about Coffee Corner after work? We can grab a bite."

"Alright. You okay?" Kaitlyn put her hands on Tina's shoulders and looked her in the eyes.

"Yeah. No. I just need you guys, okay?" Kaitlyn gave her a squeeze. A call through the intercom for a rapid response broke the moment.

♥ ♥ ♥

The bell tinkled on the door and Tina led her friends to a corner table in the back. Peter turned his stool around backward and sat on it, his chest pressed into the back. Everyone soon settled in with their orders.

"What's going on?" Daniel said. All eyes focused on Tina.

"What's going on is that last night I went to Nate's for what I thought was going to be a romantic dinner and evening."

"And? That sounds pretty okay," Daniel said. "What's his house like?"

"Big. Contemporary. Lots of white-—couch, walls, counters. Big windows. Not what I expected." Tina stirred the ice in her Italian soda.

"Did he actually fix dinner?" Peter asked. His face registered surprise.

"Kinda. He bought a lasagna and some French bread. He probably put the salad together. Anyway, that part was okay. He even had candles and flowers." She gave a crooked smile.

"Did he propose?" Kaitlyn looked at Tina's hand. No ring.

Tina frowned and shook her head. She took a deep breath.

"He's not leaving you, is he?" Kaitlyn said.

Tina exhaled. "Nate's dad showed up. He told me a little about his dad and that he was abusive. I was not ready for what I saw."

"Was he just coming for a visit, or what?" Peter said.

"Remember all those patients we used to have on Delores' floor?"

"IV drug users? Heroin smuggled in the Christmas ornaments?" Daniel chuckled.

"Leaving AMA for a smoke or hook up with a 'friend'? Peter said.

"Yeah, well Alvin, his dad, would fit right in. Stringy hair. Rotten teeth. Sores."

"Nate's dad? I never would have pictured that." Daniel bit into his scone. "Neither would I. Anyway, Nate didn't want to let him in, and then Alvin told him he found his mom on the floor at her house. I thought Nate was gonna have a coronary." Tina's lips found her straw and she took a sip.

"Why was his dad there? I mean, couldn't he have just called him?" Kaitlyn said.

"I guess he doesn't have a phone. And then it turns out he didn't call an ambulance because he's broken parole and didn't want to get turned in." Tina's eyes widened and she shook her head.

"So, Nate's mom is out cold on the floor of her house. I suppose you called the ambulance." Daniel sipped his soup.

"Yeah, and then we all went in Nate's car to her house. I couldn't believe where she lived. In that trailer court on the south side. You could lean on it and it would fall over. And garbage everywhere."

"You'd think Nate would hire her a housekeeper." Kaitlyn lifted the bread off her sandwich and removed the lettuce and tomato.

"I know, right? Anyway, the ambulance was already there. She was out, low BP and her little dog was whining and licking her face. We got her loaded into the ambulance and I went with her— just wanted to make sure they were doing everything that needed to be done for her."

"What did the doctor say?" Peter said.

"They did a CT scan—TIA's. Gonna keep an eye on her for a few days."

"Pretty exciting night." Kaitlyn put her hand on Tina's. "There's more though, isn't there?"

Leave it to Kaitlyn to sense a bigger picture.

Tina bit her lip. "Yeah. Nate was so angry." Her voice was a hoarse whisper. "I mean really angry. I thought maybe he was going to hit his dad. There were a couple of times when I was actually scared."

"Not good. Not good at all," Peter said. He shook his head

back and forth.

"Has his dad been to rehab?" Daniel asked.

"Apparently not. I suggested it to Nate, but he doesn't think anything would work. And really, I don't think he wants anything to work." She stirred the ice in her drink. "I almost think he hates him."

There was a silent pause. The sound of Peter crunching a chip jolted them out. All eyes turned to him.

"What?" Peter raised his hands in question.

"What are you going to do?" Daniel asked. "He accepted the job back east, didn't he?"

"Yeah. That's the other thing. I really love him and want to be with him, but..."

"But?" Kaitlyn said.

"I don't know. New York is so big and so far away. And I've just started to have a good relationship with my dad. And..."

Tina rearranged the chips on her plate. A lump was forming in her throat.

"And I don't want to leave you guys," she whispered.

"That would be bad. If you left. We'd have to find a replacement for the Invincibles," Peter said.

Tina punched him in the shoulder and let out a choked laugh.

* * *

After a long Kaitlyn hug, Tina got into her Fiat and drove towards home. Maybe it was time to straighten her shoulders and start a new chapter in her life. New York might be fun. There was a lot going on. She and Nate could watch Broadway shows. There were tons of places to eat. And it would probably be easy to get another job. She could always Facetime her pals. It wouldn't be the same, but she could keep up with their lives. Maybe she could even convince them to move to New York and get jobs at her new hospital.

The main thing was, she wanted to be with Nate. Yeah, there were things to be worked out. But she could help him work through things with his dad. Not that her problems with her dad had been anything like his. But still. It felt so good to have a relationship with dad. Surely Nate wanted that. It might take some time ...

Tina parked in her driveway and checked her phone. Nate hadn't called or texted all day. She frowned. Not like him. She'd get settled and give him a call. Hopefully, he would have calmed down.

Miya was in the kitchen standing over a steaming pot of spaghetti.

"Oh, hey. Smells good." Tina leaned against the counter, pulled out her phone and dialed Nate. She frowned.

"Hey Nate, just checking in. How's your mom? Give me a call. Love you."

"No answer?" Miya said.

"No."

"Maybe his phone died."

"Not Nate. He's too organized for that."

Tina sent him a text.

<Hey-— tried to call but it went to your answering machine. Everything okay?>

Miya dished up the spaghetti and offered her a plate.

"Oh, thanks, but no. I just came from Coffee Corner."

"How was your day?" Miya asked.

"Full. Crazy. Nate's mom had to go to the hospital."

"Is she okay? What happened?" Miya set a piece of French bread on her plate.

"She had a TIA. I think she'll be okay." Tina wasn't ready to spill her guts to Miya. And she was surprised at how exhausted she felt.

"I'm gonna head to bed. I feel a headache coming on."

Chapter Thirty-Eight

Tina smiled at the daffodils just sprouting out of the winter ground. She was so ready for spring and to get on with her life. She didn't like transitions and her thoughts were anxious. She waited for a family to exit the foundation door and eased inside.

"Hey Spencer. How's it going?" She shifted her bag and leaned against the window.

"Pretty good. You?"

Tina nodded.

"Have you heard from Nate? I've been trying to get ahold of him, and he hasn't answered. That's not like him."

Spencer shook his head.

"No."

He checked his phone and shook his head again. "I don't see any missed calls or messages. I gotta tell you, it's not the same here without him. When were you guys going to move?"

"Now that's a good question. I'm not even sure I want to move that far away. We were supposed to talk about it the other night when I went over for dinner. But then his dad stopped by and his mom ended up in the hospital. It was pretty much a mess."

"Oh, that's too bad. Well, anyways, good to see you here today."

Tina walked down the hall to Nate's office. She leaned against the doorway, memories of him gushed through her mind. Her sitting on the chair, feet stretched onto Nate's desk while she drew. Him shutting the door to hide the passionate kiss he planted on her lips. Enough of that. She turned and walked to her dad's office. He was seated at his desk, as usual, poring over something or other on his computer.

"Hi dad. Got a minute?" She sat down and set her bag on the floor.

"For you dear? Of course! What's on your mind?" A wide smile filled his face.

Tina's shoulders sagged. "Have you heard from Nate? He hasn't answered my texts or calls."

"You guys didn't have a fight, did you?"

"No. He invited me for dinner and in the middle of it, his dad showed up." She filled him in on the details.

"Woah, now, slow down there, muffin. That sounds like a lot of excitement. How about we go for a walk and you tell me what's going on." He stood and took her hand, pulling her up.

The sky was an unusual blue and a flock of swallows flew in from above them, gliding and dipping.

"Okay, first things first. Why was Nate mad?"

"He doesn't like his dad. I mean he *really* doesn't like his dad. I guess he abused Nate growing up. And he blamed his dad for not calling an ambulance and getting his mom to the hospital sooner."

. . .

Tina avoided a bulge in the sidewalk where a tree root had worked its way under it.

"Why didn't he call? That would seem like a realistic expectation."

"I guess he's avoiding parole and didn't want to get picked up. It's kind of a mess."

"But his mom is going to be okay?" Mark reached down and picked up a chestnut.

"Yeah, I called the hospital and they're sending her home soon. But that's the thing. Why hasn't Nate contacted me to let me know? Why did I have to call the hospital to find out? It's not like it's some big secret."

They rounded the block and were back at the foundation.

"Maybe something happened to him. Have you gone over to his house?" Mark stopped and looked at her.

"No. I guess I hadn't thought of that. Is it okay if I don't do any volunteer work today?"

Tina put her hand on her hip.

"That's what I'm going to do. I'll go over there. Thanks dad. You're the best!"

Tina gave him a peck on his cheek and jumped in her car.

That must be it. Something must have happened and he's at home, or all wrapped up with his mom and caring for her. Or maybe he had to deal with his dad about something. She was sure everything was alright. But still, it wouldn't hurt to go over there and see.

Tina double checked Maps, trying to remember which exit to take. She really needed to talk to Miya about her house. She was sure it would be alright with her landlord for Miya to take over when she and Nate moved. What should she take with her? They'd probably just get an apartment. How expensive would they be? Maybe they could each get one in the same building. She'd have to make sure he understood that she wasn't going to be moving in with him. And when should she give notice at the hospital?

She was glad she didn't have any pets. But what about Chuck? Could Nate take him with? He seems pretty attached to him. Would she have to get a moving van? She couldn't stop her mind from swirling around.

Tina took the exit. Nate's road wasn't far from the turnoff. She smiled at the buds beginning to form on the trees. Slowing, she came to a stop in front of his house. In the front yard was a for sale sign. So that's what's kept him busy. He's just been listing the house. Still, he could have called and asked her to help.

She got out, admiring the newly mown lawn and pushed the doorbell. No answer. She didn't see his car, but she assumed it was always parked in the garage. She tried again. Nothing. She walked to the window and peered in. Her jaw dropped. There was not one thing in the living room. Not a picture. No furniture. No area rug. Did he move already? Without her? He wouldn't do that, right? He always told her everything.

She wandered around to the back of the house and peered in. Nothing. No pots and pans hanging from the rack. Counters were bare. Empty deck where chairs had been. She sat down slowly on the steps and put her head in her hands. God, what is going on? There isn't anything you don't know. Did you want to let me in on this? Obviously, Nate's left me. Did I do something wrong?

Tina glanced at a rhododendron bush, hoping it would

appear on fire, like for Moses. She could use an audible voice telling her what to do. She let out a sob and headed to her car.

♥ ♥ ♥

Tina didn't want their time together to end. Not their time in Portland. Not their time in a relationship. The thought made her head spin. Here they came again, the sobs, racking her body, making her nose run. She hadn't thought it was possible to cry as much as she had in the last two days.

What was she supposed to do now? Get on with her life, she guessed. Which meant, doing whatever she was doing before she got mixed up with that creep. She thought back to when she had first met him and he bumped into her, leaving her pile of papers strewn all over the floor. He was a jerk then. He's a jerk now.

Unstoppable tears ran down her cheeks. If only she didn't love him. There was so much more she wanted to say to him, but now it was too late. She wanted to help him with his mom. She wanted to help heal his past. Dang. She slammed her fist into her pillow. She just wanted to be with him.

Chapter Thirty-Nine

Nate deliberately chose a seat in the back of the plane, hoping the row would remain empty. He wasn't in the mood for some crazy lady asking where he was going and did he have family. If that were going to be the case, he'd have his air pods ready.

He put his carry on in the bin and climbed to the window seat. The stormy, pouring rain matched his mood. He hoped it wouldn't delay the flight. His chest tightened at the thought of his impending departure and he just wanted to get out of there.

Nate checked his phone before takeoff. Twenty-four messages from Tina, six phone calls. He couldn't bring himself to look or listen to them. Yet he couldn't bring himself to delete them, either. Why oh why did he ever let himself get drawn into a relationship with that girl? She was way too good for him.

He knew she'd be worried sick that he wasn't answering. But he just couldn't. This was best. Just leave and save her from the monster he was. If he had told her he was leaving, she would have tried to convince him to wait for her. Convince him that he was okay. Well, he wasn't. She didn't understand the depth of his hurt. And her suggestion to try to fix his dad? That was never going to happen.

Nate put his phone on airplane mode as the plane rolled away from the hangar.

* * *

February temperatures were much colder in New York than Portland. Men wore long wool overcoats and scarves, something he didn't own. He'd just have to tough it out. Spring was around the corner and it should be much warmer then.

Nate stopped in front of an apartment building on east thirty-third street. He toured the available furnished studio. That's all he would be needing since he was alone. He was happy to see a workout room. He had a whole lot of pent-up energy he needed to use up.

Apartment prices were outrageous— twice what his monthly house payment had been. He shrugged. His new salary was more than enough to cover it. Maybe he was paying for the seventeenth-floor view of the city and nearness to Langone. Well, that's just the way it was. He had put his Lambo in storage. There was no need for a car in New York.

He checked the time, arranged for an Uber, and went to the hospital. He was greeted by Dr. Matthias with a firm handshake. She was tall and her straight black hair was held back by a fancy barrette.

"Welcome. We are so excited to have you join our team of researchers. I'm sure you'll find this a more than stimulating environment. We have the best researchers from all over the world."

Her dark eyes smiled as she took him on a tour of the facility and introduced him to his new team.

"I'll let you get acquainted. Could I interest you in dinner tonight?"

Nate's heart jumped a beat. Did he really want to go to dinner with this woman? But then again, if he didn't, it might affect his job.

"I'm sure I could fit it into my busy schedule," he said. He'd just have to set some boundaries. He wasn't about to get himself mixed up in a new relationship.

Nate was enjoying his job. He was able to delve in with passionate coworkers, sometimes working twelve-hour days and repeating it the next day. Always chasing something he knew was right around the corner. Pursuing a cure was all encompassing. Maybe in its own way, it was his addiction.

Having dinner with Dr. Miranda Matthias once a week had become a regular spot on his calendar. She had encouraged him to pick up a few speaking engagements, which he found he really enjoyed. He secretly enjoyed the praises and being able to answer difficult questions with authority.

And thankfully, she hadn't encouraged anything more than a friendship. They talked about a lot of things, but he never shared anything about his past. Or Tina.

It had been three months and he had pushed all thoughts of her aside. He refused to allow his thoughts down the rabbit hole of wondering how she was doing.

"I was wondering Nate, if you might be interested in

helping out with a project a few of us are working on," Miranda said.

She set her menu down.

Nate figured it was probably some other type of research. "Tell me about it."

"A group of us have been remodeling a homeless shelter. We could really use some extra hands. It's fun and feels good to do something for someone else. You might like it."

Nate raised an eyebrow. "Yeah, I guess. I've never done anything like that before and I'm not sure if I know how to effectively use a hammer." He grinned. Had he ever volunteered? Guess it had never crossed his mind.

"Alright, it's settled then. I'll text you the address. Saturday at nine."

Saturday rolled around. Nate pulled out a drawer, looking for something other than his work clothes. Did he even have clothes he could get dirty in? He settled on a pair of older jeans and a t-shirt. He paused when he saw the Batten Foundation logo on the front. He wadded it up and tossed it into the garbage. That was a part of his life that was in the past. He didn't need to be reminded of it. Or of her.

Nate wasn't sure what he had expected to see, but the site was a wreck. Garbage was strewn along the street. Men needing shaves and haircuts and pushing overflowing shopping carts filled the cracked sidewalks. He was tempted to tell the Uber driver to keep going.

Miranda waved at him, and he reluctantly got out.

"Hey, come meet Ricardo and Denzel. They're the ones heading up the project."

"Hey brother," Denzel patted Nate's shoulder. "Glad to have you here. We can really use your help. Tools are over there. Or you can start cleaning up what we've demolished."

Nate nodded. Maybe cleaning up was the better choice. Then on the other hand, as he watched Ricardo with the wrecking bar and sledgehammer, maybe he should get his workout in.

After a morning of demolition, they sat on a makeshift bench atop sawhorses. Ricardo brought burritos from the food cart nearby. Nate twisted open a water bottle and took a swig. It was amazing how much energy this work took.

"How did you two get into this project?"

Ricardo and Denzel shared a glance.

"Miranda talk you into this?" Nate said.

"No," Denzel's deep laugh rolled out. "She's quite a gal, that one." He ran his fingers through his short hair, bits of grey flecked through the black.

"Denzel and I met on the streets." He nodded his chin towards the men on the sidewalk. "Those used to be our people." He drenched his burrito in spicy hot sauce before he took a bite.

"Yeah, I was Ricardo's drug dealer. Heroin. Meth. Whatever he needed."

Nate's hand paused before he took the next bite and stared at them. This is not what he had expected them to say.

"We was gettin' pretty bad. Almost OD'ed once," Ricardo said.

"What happened?" Nate figured once a loser, always a loser. But these guys didn't exemplify that.

"I guess you could say we had a come-to-Jesus moment." Ricardo looked at Denzel.

"Yes indeed, the Lawd just took and lifted us up out of the mire." Denzel slapped his large hand on his knee. "Miranda was working at the soup kitchen, and she got to know us. Then one day she asked if we might want to get cleaned up."

"Langone gave a large grant to a local drug rehab and asked me if I could find people that wanted to participate," Miranda cut in.

"We was not sure we wanted to give up the pookie, tha's right Ricardo?"

"That's right. I needed that rush and it drove me to chase it as long as there was breath in my lungs. Only problem was, my body was wasting away and if it hadn't been for Miranda, we'd both be dead by now. It wasn't easy. It took a lot of work."

Ricardo finished off his water bottle and tossed it into the garbage.

"Yeah, it took me three rounds in rehab before it stuck." Denzel snorted.

Nate studied both men. Except for a few scars on their faces, you'd never know they'd had that past. They looked healthy and fit. Alvin crept into his mind's eye. Could it be possible his dad could get turned around?

Chapter Forty

Tina stood outside the door and raised her hand to knock. She stopped, hand raised. Was this alright? Would she be intruding? No, she had felt a nudge from the Lord and she was going to follow it regardless if it made sense or not.

She could hear shuffling footsteps and the door unlatch. The worn door squeaked open.

"Loretta, hi. I'm sure you don't remember me, but I'm Tina. I was here with Nate the night you went to the hospital."

Loretta held her little dog. "Come in, dear. I was just watching a little television."

Tina looked around the room. It was just as they had left it that night. Dirty drinking glasses on the coffee table. A floor that hadn't been vacuumed for who knows how long. Sagging drapes covered the grimy windows.

"How are you feeling?"

"Alright, I guess. I get dizzy sometimes. Come sit down." Loretta moved some worn magazines from the couch and tossed them on the floor.

"I'd get you something to drink, but I'm pretty worn out. You could fix a cup of tea if you'd like." She nodded towards the kitchen.

"Of course. Would you like a cup?"

"That would be lovely. There's a little sugar in the bin. Tea bags in the drawer."

Tina filled the kettle and set it on the stove. The kitchen was in disarray. What must she be eating? An empty cereal box sat on the counter along with an empty bag of microwave popcorn. Had the hospital sent a home health nurse to her?

Tina washed out two cups. They may have been clean, as they were in the cupboard. But she wasn't taking any chances.

"Here you go."

Loretta set Mitzy down and took the cup. Loretta held the cup to her nose and breathed in the sweet fragrance.

"Has Nate contacted you since he moved?" Tina asked.

"He moved? I wondered why he hadn't stopped by. Where did he go?"

"He got a job in New York." *He didn't tell his mom? Rude.*

"Well, he is a smart boy. I'm sorry to see him go, but I'm sure they are happy to have him there."

She dipped her fingers into her cup and let Mitzy lick the warm tea from them. "Where do you work?"

"I'm a nurse. I work at Mercy hospital."

"That's what I wanted to be. A nurse. Then I married Alvin. He was so sweet at first. We used to go dancing and stop for a drink. He did like to party."

She lit up a cigarette and blew out the smoke.

"I started my training and then I got pregnant with Nate. Then Alvin lost his job at the tire shop and things went to hell in a hand basket."

She took another drag on her cigarette.

Tina held on to every word.

"Sounds like you and Nate had a difficult life."

Loretta nodded.

It was actually a miracle that Nate had been able to become successful—to get through college and become a scientist. And now it made perfect sense as to why he would choose to live in that mansion—stark and clean.

"Loretta, would you take offense if I did a little cleaning for you? After you've been ill, I'm sure it's been hard to keep up."

"Of course not. I would be grateful."

Tina rose and Loretta put her legs on the couch. She picked up the remote and turned up the volume. Tina took the afghan from the chair and laid it over her.

Tina started in the kitchen. My word, what a mess. She wished she had brought some surgical gloves. She supposed antibacterial soap and water would kill anything she managed to touch.

She got the kitchen somewhat squared away and peeked in on Loretta. Her head was back and her mouth open, snoring softly.

Tina followed the hall, looking for a vacuum. She peeked into Loretta's room. Maybe she should start a load of laundry. She tugged on the sheets. How long had it been since they'd been washed? She threw them in and added some soap, emptying the container. She should offer to go to the store for her. Had Nate been taking care of all her needs?

She peeked into the other room and stood at the doorway. This must have been Nate's room. A single bed and small dresser still stood in the room. A poster of Einstein was tacked on the wall. Tina tried to imagine Nate as a little boy. Did he ever feel the love of his dad? Pictures of Nate hiding under the bed flooded her mind. Having met Alvin, she could imagine he could get a little rough.

She began to dust the long-neglected room. She hauled the

vacuum in, moving furniture and sucking up years of dust. Something stuck to the end of the wand and Tina lifted it up to examine. A photo. She pulled it away from the suction and stared at it. Nate and his dad sat on a hay bale with a large pumpkin on his lap. She felt a lump form in her throat and quickly tried to swallow it down. She wasn't going to let a memory trigger what she had lost.

She thought about texting Nate to tell him where she was but thought better of it. She should leave well enough alone.

She found a broom and swept cobwebs. She was hesitant to vacuum the living room. Loretta needed her sleep. Instead, she grabbed a wet rag and started dusting and wiping flat surfaces. When she finished, Loretta had opened her eyes.

"You're awake! I hope I didn't disturb you."

Loretta sat up and looked around the room her eyes wide.

"It's like my fairy godmother came!" She smiled. "Nate used to come over once a week and bring me groceries and Chinese food. Then we'd watch Jeopardy." She looked at Tina. "He's a good boy, you know."

Tina nodded. "I pray for both of you every day."

"We could use it. Nate shouldn't have had to go through a childhood like he had. His dad loved him. He just got addicted to those darn drugs and it turned him into something else."

"Has he ever been to rehab?" Tina asked.

"Rehab? I'm sure not."

"Do you think he would go?"

Loretta shrugged. "I don't know. It's pretty expensive, isn't it?"

"Probably. But maybe there's a way. He's going to kill himself the rate he's going."

"It's sad. I loved him so much. Still do. I told Nate he needs to forgive him." Loretta stroked Mitzy. "Maybe you can convince him of that."

Tina bit her lip. She didn't see that happening any time soon.

Chapter Forty-One

Tina spread a tarp on the floor and poured peach paint into a tray. She paused to pull her hair into a messy bun.

"I love this color for a background." Tina wrapped her hand around the handle of the roller and applied paint to the nursery wall.

"I knew you could choose the right one. I can't wait to see how your mural turns out. How about a tree? With birds. And a nest. And a window. I love that you're an artist. All I can do is imagine something, but you, girl can bring my dreams to life." Kaitlyn sighed.

She was dressed in some old comfy sweats, her t-shirt bulging over her baby bump. She picked up an edging brush, dipped it and began painting the corners.

"How's baby doing?" Tina said. "The ultrasound you sent was so cool! Have you decided on names yet?"

"It's great. I love being pregnant. When it moves, it's the most amazing thing. Luke loves when I put his hand on my tummy and he can feel his little person." She stroked her bulge. "Haven't settled on names. We're not going to find out the sex until it's born. I want to be surprised. But if it's a girl, you can bet we'll put Tina in there somewhere!" She grinned.

"Have you heard from Nate?" Kaitlyn asked.

Tina shook her head. "You'd be the first to know if I had."

"Yeah, but, work has been so busy and we haven't really talked for forever." Kaitlyn dipped her brush. "Are you doing okay? I mean, it's been a few months now since he left."

Tina nodded. Was she okay? The ache was still there and she still couldn't wrap her mind around why Nate had abandoned her. Things were going so well. Maybe if she hadn't tried to talk him into rehab for his dad he would have stayed. She must have really ticked him off. But still, would that have been an excuse to leave without saying goodbye? Did she mean so little to him?

"I guess so. I'm only volunteering at the foundation twice a month now instead of every week. It's not the same without Nate there. Dad turned Nate's office into a work room."

"But things are going alright with your dad, right?"

"Yes. I can't believe how much of a weight has lifted. He's so easy to talk to now."

Tina shrugged. "Funny how you can perceive things to be a certain way and a little dialogue can open the door to understanding."

Tina moved the pan to the next wall.

"Wish I'd have talked it out with him sooner."

"You had a lot of grieving to overcome. It's not easy." Kaitlyn picked up a damp rag and wiped a wayward drip. "What are you doing with your other days off now that you're not volunteering?"

"You're not going to believe it, but I started going over to Nate's mom's house and helping her out. Remember I was over there with Nate when his dad found her on the floor and I went with her in the ambulance?"

Kaitlyn nodded.

"I just felt like I should go check on her since Nate was gone. She's alright, I guess, but her house was a disaster."

"You probably cleaned it up, didn't you?" Kaitlyn smiled.

"Of course! You would have too. Probably like when you helped out grandpa William."

"Yeah, his house was pretty messy when I started. Did you know that he and Martha are dating? I wouldn't be surprised if they got married!" Kaitlyn let out a laugh.

"Two weddings in a year." And Tina had hoped the second wedding would be hers. Guess that dream washed down the tube.

"Has Nate called his mom? What if he called and you answered the phone? What would you do?"

What would she do?

"Maybe pretend I'm someone else. A maid. A neighbor. Awkward." Tina shrugged.

"I don't really know. I hope he'd be bold enough to do some explaining."

They finished the last wall. Tina poured the extra paint into the can and tapped on the lid.

"I'll go wash these brushes out and then I've got to get going. I'm having lunch with my dad."

"Wait, come here. Quick." Kaitlyn took Tina's hand and placed it on her belly. "Feel it?"

Tina eyes widened and her mouth opened in awe. She put her face close to it and said, "Hi baby, this is your Auntie Tina. I can't wait to meet you!" She wrapped her arms tightly around her best friend.

"You're gonna make the best mama ever!"

Tina met her dad for Thai food. They ordered Chicken Marsala and Chai tea. Posters of Thailand were plastered on the wall. A large carved elephant sat in front of the counter.

"Have *you* heard anything from Nate?" Tina stirred her drink and looked up at him.

"Nothing. I thought maybe he'd contact me to let me know how his new job was going. Or see how the foundation was holding up without him." Mark's lips formed a crooked grin. "You?"

"Nope. Nothing. I just don't get it, dad. Everything was going so well. Then boom, all of a sudden it's ended. I want to let him go, but I tell ya, it's really hard. I think about him all the time. Is he getting used to the fast pace? Has he got a good team? Have they reached a cure goal?" She stirred her rice and whispered, "Has he found another girlfriend?"

Mark put his hand on hers.

"Look at me."

Tina lifted her eyes.

"Nate was a really great guy. And you seemed like a perfect match. The way I see it you've got two choices." He held his finger up. "One, forget him. Two, pray about it. God's got his own timing for things. Maybe he'll come back. Maybe he won't. But I'm sure at some point you'll find peace and you'll know what to do."

"Option one isn't working for me. I guess I'll depend on option two. I could use a little peace." She took a bite. "I love you dad."

"You too, muffin."

Chapter Forty-Two

Nate donned his joggers and laced up his Nikes. He was oblivious to the clear blue sky shining above the skyscrapers. He didn't see the pink cherry blossoms blooming on the trees lining the sidewalk. He never noticed the sounds of the taxis, squeak of the bus wheels or rumble of the subway. His mind was focused on the dream he'd had. There hadn't been a lot to it, but the one clear picture was of Tina, her red hair sparkling in the sun and curls flowing down, her green eyes focused on him as she ran slo-mo across a meadow towards him.

He couldn't shake the picture from his mind. Had he really done the right thing? Leaving? It seemed like the only way. Because if you really loved someone, you'd keep them safe. You'd protect them from harm. And if he were the one who could cause harm, that meant he had to stay far, far away.

Still. He pictured her at home and wondered if she had just moved on. There would be no reason for her not to. But the thought of her with someone else…

He jogged in place at a crosswalk, waiting for the light to change.

He thought of Portland. He missed working at the foundation. He missed the calm of jogging on the trails with Tina and the centering effect they had had on him. He even missed the rain. But most of all he missed Tina. He had loved being there with her. Her smile. Little things but, he realized now, meaningful things.

Nate walked through the revolving door of Langone. The hospital was always busy. Patients and their families, volunteers, receptionists, and physicians. And researchers. It was a wonder how he could have worked here for six months, pass the same faces in the hall every day and no one ever greeted him or even given a nod. Maybe it didn't matter. He'd head to his locker, change, and do the one thing he was good at. Work on cures.

♥ ♥ ♥

Nate had jogged back to his apartment at the end of the day, chugged a glass of water and sat down on the couch. He rested his feet on the ottoman and stared aimlessly out the window and the pigeons flying and resting on the tall building ledges. He picked up his phone, the first time all day. It had been so busy—meetings, peer review of clinical trials, and sitting in on an interview of a new research candidate.

He scrolled through Instagram. When was the last time he'd done that? Spencer and his family on a hike. Kaitlyn with a profile of her baby bump. Tina. He set down his phone and stared out the window. His pulse quickened. He picked it back up and stared at the sun sparkling on her red hair, her green eyes intent on something ahead. How could this be the same picture as in his dream! It was as if she were looking directly into his soul. How could he ever think he was capable of hurting her?

His phone buzzed. Mercy Hospital. Could this be her?

"Hello."

"Mr. Bronson?"

"Yes, this is Nate Bronson."

"Hi, this is Evelyn. I'm a social worker at Mercy Hospital where your mom is admitted."

"What happened?" Nate placed his hand on his forehead.

"I'm afraid she had a stroke."

"She's okay, though, isn't she?"

Why didn't he know this? He knew he should have been calling her to check up on her, but something about being this far away had become out of sight, out of mind. A twinge of guilt ran through him.

"She has some paralysis. She's able to talk, however, so that's a good thing."

Nate put his phone on speaker and set it down. He started pacing the room.

She continued. "You are the only one listed for a contact. Could you come in tomorrow to talk?"

"I'm in New York." His mind kicked into gear thinking of plane reservations.

"Oh, I thought you were local. Well, is there anyone here we could consult? She needs someone to make accommodations for a live-in caregiver, or she needs to go into a nursing home before we can release her."

Nate sat down heavily on the couch.

"Alright. I'll have to make arrangements with my work and I'll try to get on a plane tomorrow. I'll let you know." He added her number to his contacts.

Langone hadn't exactly been happy about Nate's leaving so abruptly. They'd just have to deal with it. He needed to be there for his mom. He found Evelyn's office and sat down. He was anxious to see his mom but wanted to find out first what needed to be done.

A potted philodendron sat on a plant stand in the corner. Magazines littered the coffee table and a water cooler stood in the corner. He filled a cup with water and picked up a running magazine. He rolled his shoulders to lessen the tension and wished she would hurry and call him in.

"Mr. Bronson, Evelyn will see you now." A petite woman led him down the hall.

Evelyn stood and held out her hand. "Nate? Evelyn. Glad to meet you. Have a seat and we'll get started."

Nate nodded. "How was your flight? Thank you for coming so quickly. We love getting to know your mom, but she is anxious to get back to her little dog."

Nate couldn't imagine her without Mitzy.

"It was fine. Long."

"Here are some brochures listing different caregivers and nursing home options. Medicaid will cover some of them, but you'll have to look into them more thoroughly for yourself. Do you have anyone to help you make these decisions?"

Nate shook his head. Asking Alvin to help wasn't on his radar.

"Alright. Take a look at these and get back to me. The sooner the better. She can't live alone anymore."

Nate left and found the elevator to Loretta's room. She lay

in the bed, raised so she could see the television. The sheet outlined her frail body.

"It's the second L in the acronym LOL meaning 'how funny'."

"Loud," they both said at once, knowing Ken Jennings would be proud of them.

Loretta's jaw dropped as she looked at Nate.

"Son! You're here! Where have you been?" Loretta motioned with a limp hand. Nate kissed her on the top of her head.

"Hi mom, how are you?"

"I could be a lot better if you'd bring me some cigarettes," she said. Her voice was hoarse.

"Not gonna happen. Sorry. What's going on?"

Loretta tried to adjust herself in the bed to see him better.

"I guess I had a stroke. Can't move my hand too good. Been going to physical therapy, but it's not helping."

She held her twisted hand for him to see.

"Your legs work?"

"Not really. They put me in a wheelchair every time I have to go out. I need to get out of this place. They won't let me smoke and everyone's always poking around telling me what to do."

"I'm working on that mom. We have to find you a caregiver or you'll need to go into an elder care facility."

Nate wasn't sure how she was going to take this, but it had to be done.

"Listen, I've got to go and take care of some things. I'll come back later, okay?" He squeezed her good hand and left.

Chapter Forty-Three

Nate's steps were brisk as he walked down the hall. He hoped finding a caregiver would be easy. She wouldn't want to leave her trailer. Then again, a nursing facility would be in better shape than where she lived now. And then there was the issue of her dog. Would a facility take Mitzy? Fat chance. No, he was going to have to find a live-in.

He bought a coffee at a kiosk in the lobby and sat on a bench. He rubbed the back of his neck as he glanced through the brochures. This was not going to be easy. He made a few phone calls, writing down details on each brochure. He stood up, downed the last of his coffee and tossed the cup in the trash. Out of the corner of his eye, a streak of red hair.

"Tina?" Her back was turned to him. He hurried behind her as she strode down the hall.

"Tina!"

She turned. "Nate?"

Her jaw dropped and her face turned into a scowl. She crossed her arms, turned, and kept walking.

"Tina, wait."

He put his hand on her shoulder. She shrugged it off and took a few more steps.

"I need to talk to you." He couldn't let her just walk away.

"I have nothing to say to you."

"Please." He stepped in front of her.

"You abandoned me!" she snapped. "You didn't even say goodbye."

"I," he faltered. "I... that night. After you left in the ambulance," he looked down. "I had a fight with my dad."

"And?" Tina said flatly, her jaw tightened.

"I was furious. I was livid with him and I exploded."

Nate looked at his feet. "I hit him and pinned him down."

Tina started to walk away.

"Tina, don't you see? When I saw how angry I got, I had to leave. I was horrified at what I had done. I didn't even recognize myself. All I could think was that I could possibly hurt you. Leaving seemed like the only option."

"Hurt me? Hurt me? What have I ever done that would cause you to want to hurt me? What can you imagine me ever doing that would bring on such rage?"

Her face grew red and she looked ready to explode.

Memories of them together flooded Nate's mind. Good memories.

"Nate, why are you letting the pain of your past dictate the hope and promise of your future? Do you want to live alone for the rest of your life? Without anyone to help carry your burdens? I don't. And if that's what you want, you just head on back to New York where everyone loves and admires you. I don't really care."

She pivoted and walked away.

Nate stood, stunned. He needed to talk to someone. This whole thing was confusing. But who? Tina was who he had always confided in. Obviously, that wasn't going to happen. Spencer? He knew him but had never really opened up to him. No, that wouldn't work. Nate wouldn't want to interrupt his family time.

He looked at the time. He should go visit his mom again before he left. He stopped to read a sentence written on the hospital wall.

Show compassion and mercy to one another.

Was that a message for him? He tucked it in the back of his mind.

When he entered Loretta's room, an occupational therapist was showing her strategies for helping her eat. Holding utensils was difficult. It was hard seeing her like that. Each scoop of the fork laboriously lifted to her mouth.

"Hey mom." Nate sat in a chair opposite her bed. "Just wanted to check in on you again before I went..."

Before he went where? Where was he going to stay? His house was empty. No one had bought it yet. Maybe he could sleep there. But when he pictured himself sleeping on the floor, he thought better of it. He'd just get a hotel room.

"Nate, I'm glad you're here. We've got things to talk about."

She turned to the therapist.

"I'm through eating. I don't want any more."

She pushed away her tray. The therapist cleaned up and left.

"What's on your mind?"

"Your dad checked into a rehab. Can you believe that? I never thought I'd see the day," she said.

Nate's eyes shifted, taking it in. "Somewhere in Portland?"

"Yeah. He called me a while ago to tell me. He wanted to apologize. It nearly broke my heart." She placed her thin hand on her chest.

"Do you think it will do any good?" He hoped it would.

"He already sounded like it was doing him some good." Loretta reached for his hand. "Nate, you need to go see him. He needs you. You need to talk to him."

"I don't know mom. I don't think he'll want to see me."

Nate looked away, shame washing over him.

"Just go. Call tomorrow. You have to make an appointment."

"Well. Maybe I should go to your house and get it ready for you to come home." He pictured the mess. Probably moldy food in the fridge.

Loretta looked at her son. "Are you alright? You're awfully quiet."

"Mom, do you think I could turn out to be like dad? I mean, he was really cruel to me. To us. Could I become that person? Could I ever hurt the people I love?"

He felt a lump forming in his throat. Of course, he could. He had hurt Tina, hadn't he? Maybe not physically. But still.

"Nathan, your dad had a whole bunch of problems that you don't have. The only thing that's going to take away the hurt is to go talk to him. Open your heart. Let him in."

Nate's shoulders gave a slight shrug.

"I'm really tired now. You'll come see me tomorrow? And ask those nurses when I get out of this place. I want to go home." She closed her eyes.

He stood to go. He had a lot to think about. He could tell tomorrow was going to be an awfully long day.

Chapter Forty-Four

Tina couldn't get away fast enough. She took the stairs two at a time to her floor and charged into the staff room. Her fists were balled at her side as she stomped around the room. *Who does he think he is? Walk out on me and then one day pop in and expect me to have a rational conversation with him?* Adrenaline was still pumping through her.

"Tina? What's going on?" It was Kaitlyn. "I saw you rush past."

Tina fell into Kaitlyn's arms and began to sob.

"It's okay. Get it all out."

Tina sniffed and pulled back. "It's hard to get a good hug with that basketball between us. " She let out a little snort. Kaitlyn handed her a napkin.

"Sit down." Kaitlyn took a Magic cookie bar off a plate and handed it to Tina. "Here, there's nothing sugar and chocolate can't cure."

"Nate's here." Tina looked up. "He stopped me downstairs. I guess he's here for his mom."

"Nate? Really? What did he say?"

"Just seeing him brought out this rush of anger in me. I didn't realize it was all pent up. I just wanted to get away."

"Did he want to talk to you?"

"Yes. But I yelled at him." Her voice broke.

"You yelled? Little Miss-always-calm-girl yelled?" Kaitlyn's eyebrows raised.

"He said that night when we went to his mom's cuz she had a stroke? And I left in the ambulance. He said that he had a fight with his dad and pinned him to the ground."

Tina's hands shook.

"He said if he could get that mad, he was worried he could hurt me and so he thought the best thing to do was to leave and get as far away from me as possible."

"Woah." Kaitlyn sat down. "Do you think he wants to get back together with you?"

"I don't know. He definitely wanted to tell me why he left."

Tina's hands shook as she poured a cup of coffee.

"I think he's so confused about his relationship with his dad and the abuse that he's afraid he'll become his dad."

"Sounds like someone else I know—not the abuse, but being mixed up about a relationship with her dad..." Kaitlyn put her hand on Tina's and locked eyes.

"Before he left I told him he should try and have a talk with him, that it made all the difference for me and my dad. He didn't think that could ever happen."

"So, what are you going to do?" Kaitlyn finished her cookie and rubbed her belly.

Tina put her hands on her bent head. "I don't know. I still love him." She looked up. "Kaitlyn, I think I need you to pray for me. For him. For us."

Chapter Forty-Five

Nate wasn't sure what he expected, but it wasn't this. He had envisioned a building needing a good pressure wash, with peeling paint and a sidewalk you could stub your toe on. He parked his mom's Buick in front of an ordinary house with a pristine sidewalk bordered by box hedges. He wasn't sure if he should just walk in or ring the doorbell. He reached his finger towards the bell.

The door opened to a large, broad-shouldered man.

"Hi, can I help you?" His deep bass voice was soothing. He held his hand out to Nate. "Name's Roger. I'm the counselor here."

"I was hoping to visit my dad, Alvin Bronson."

"Oh, sure, let me get him. Come on in—have a seat."

He motioned towards a comfy couch.

Nate chose to stand. He wandered over to the picture window. A large grassy yard was fenced and hemmed in by rhododendrons and azaleas, both beginning to bloom pinks and reds. A white bench sat next to a koi pond. In the dining room was a large table surrounded by picture windows. Dancing flames from a gas fireplace gave the place a homey atmosphere and took the chill off the spring day.

"Nathan. You came!" Alvin reached up and patted Nate on the shoulder.

Nate involuntarily flinched.

"Dad."

It was all he could say. What do you say when the last time you saw someone you had knocked him on the ground?

"Come sit over here. I'll leave you to yourselves," Roger said and left.

Nate sat in the chair opposite the couch. The pendulum clock ticked. Blue Jays chirped outside the window. This was awkward. Was his dad going to say something? Or should he begin?

"Well? How is it?" he asked.

"It's been hard, son. I'm not gonna lie. Real hard. But I think I'm on the right side of things now."

Nate sat stiffly and looked at the painting on the wall—the silhouette of a person looking into a pond and seeing his reflection.

Alvin's face was shaved, scars, but no longer scabbed. His hair was buzz cut, and his fingers were no longer twitching, nor his foot continually tapping the floor. He was uncharacteristically calm.

"Look son, I don't know how to say this."

Alvin rested his arms on his knees and leaned forward.

"I want to tell you how sorry I am for all that I done to hurt you. Real sorry."

Nate nodded. About time. Nate crossed his arms and looked away.

"I ain't been the best father. Or husband. I admit it."

He swiped his mouth with the back of his hand.

"Look, I grew up with a dad that was just like me. When I

was your age, I thought I could be better than that. And well, I was, for a while. And then I lost my job and things went downhill from there. I couldn't pay no bills and I started drinking. And that led me to meth." Alvin ran his hand through his short hair.

Nate wanted to believe he was sorry. When Alvin looked at him, his guilt was palpable. But now, hearing Alvin talk about his past, it confirmed that he *could* turn out like his dad. It was generational, just like some of the syndrome genes passed down from one family member to another. Maybe Alvin was sorry, but Nate couldn't shake the idea that he could end up in a rehab someday, telling his son the same story.

"Meth is harsh. It takes control of you and you become incapable of living without the rush. When I began taking it, it made me all calm, or at least I thought I was, and I became oblivious to those things that were bringing me down. The reality is, I was not only bringing myself down, but the people I loved were being pulled down with me. This place has helped me see things clearly."

Alvin sat back, allowing time for Nate to respond.

"I'm not trying to make excuses for the way I treated you and your mom. That was wrong. I'm just want you to know the reason."

Was it possible for his dad to become a new person? He thought of Ricardo and Denzel. A bigger question plagued him. Was he able to let things go and forgive his dad and see him as a new person? Was Tina right when she had said that unforgiveness didn't hurt the person you hated, it held *you* captive?

"Do you remember that time when we went to the pumpkin patch? I was about five. You came on our field trip."

Nate glanced up at him.

Alvin stroked his chin. "Yeah, I think I do. You chose an enormous pumpkin. It was too big for you to carry."

"That is the only good memory I have of you."
Alvin jerked like he'd been sucker punched.

"The only one?" he whispered.

"The only one. When mom bought me a guitar, I hid it. You called me a sissy for wanting to play it. I was sure you'd take it and smash it. That guitar meant everything to me."

"I used to hide quaking under my bed when you were beating on mom and hoping against hope that you wouldn't find me. I had to hide the cigarette burns and bruises on my arms when I went to school so no one would call child services and put me in foster care. I was always worried about who would take care of mom if that happened. Cuz you sure as heck wouldn't."

Alvin's hands trembled. His hazel eyes were swimming in tears, his lips thin and brow furrowed. He shook his head and closed his eyes, wiping them with the sleeve covering the back of his hand.

Nate had waited all his life for this moment. For his dad to apologize. He had dreamt of pounding the reality into him. Alvin needed to realize the damage he had done to Nate and his mom. Nate straightened his shoulders.

Alvin fell to his knees at Nate's feet.

"Please Nathan, please forgive me. I can't even begin to tell you how sorry I am." His voice broke.

Nate slowly reached his hand out, hovering over his dad's shaking shoulder. It took all he could muster to place his hand in a symbol of forgiveness. Alvin looked up slowly and gave a slight nod. Nate patted him on the shoulder.

Nate let out the breath he hadn't known he was holding in.

"Are you two ready for some snacks? I just took a tray of fresh chocolate chip cookies out of the oven and I've got a fresh pot of coffee," Roger said.

Nate helped Alvin to his feet. "I don't know about you, but I could use something to sweeten the afternoon," Nate said.

"I'll go to my room and freshen up a bit, if you don't mind," Alvin said.

Roger motioned to a chair. "You okay?"

Nate took a cookie. "Yeah. I guess. Forgiving isn't easy, I'll say that."

"No, it is not. But hopefully this will be a new beginning. Healing takes time."

"It was hard growing up with him. How do I know I won't turn out like him?"

"Nate, your past is not an indication of your future. It's not contagious and it's not something passed down to you. What do you do for a living?"

"I'm a researcher. And I'm pretty good at it." Nate took another bite of his cookie.

"You seem confident. What else is going on in your life? You got a girl?"

Nate looked out the window. Did he want to open up about this? He stalled with a sip of coffee.

"I don't know. I had one. A really smart, beautiful red head. But that all changed."

"Do you want to tell me about it?" Roger stood. "Let's walk out to the pond."

The fresh air felt good on Nate's face.

"The last time I saw my dad, he had come to my house to tell me that he found my mom out cold on the floor. The only time he went to her house was to try to get money, so I didn't think he was telling the truth. Anyway, Tina was over for dinner and we ended up sending mom to the hospital with a small stroke. I was so angry at dad for not calling the ambulance himself that I hit him."

"How'd Tina take that?"

"She didn't know. She went in the ambulance with mom. The fight happened afterwards. Anyway, I couldn't believe that I hit him and how angry I was and all I could think was that I'd be like my dad— hurting her or worse, hurting a future child. So, I ran away to a job in New York."

"Do you love her?" Roger tossed some feed to the Koi.

Nate's chest swelled. Did he love her? More than anything he had ever loved in his life.

"Yes. Yes I do."

He glanced at the sliding glass door.

"And I know what I have to do."

He turned, adrenaline filling his veins.

"Can you tell my dad I left? And I'll check in with him later?"

Nate nodded at Roger and hurried to the door. He just hoped he wasn't too late.

Chapter Forty-Six

Nate jumped into his mom's ailing Buick. He stuck the key into the ignition, pushed the accelerator and listened as it turned over several times before the motor caught. He put the pedal to the metal. Flooring it took him to a breathtaking thirty-five mph. A guy could watch the grass grow it was so slow. He needed to get his Lambo out of storage. His fingers nervously tapped the large steering wheel.

He had to see Tina. He didn't care what it took, he had to win her back. He had thought about texting her but was afraid she would ignore it. He'd just go to her house. Wait, what day was it? He glanced at the dashboard to see the date and then wished again he was in his own car. He relived the days since he'd arrived in Portland. Thursday. That was her volunteer day. Maybe he should go to the foundation.

He replayed his conversation with Tina. What was it she had said? About letting the pain of your past dictate your future? That must have been the truth she had realized on the trip with her dad. In fact, talking to Roger brought him to the same conclusion. He didn't have to turn out like his dad.

He saw Tina's impassioned eyes when she had asked him if he wanted to live alone the rest of his life? No. He absolutely did not want to spend another minute without Tina. And if that meant giving up his job, that's what he would do. He could always get another job in Portland. Or anywhere Tina wanted to live for that matter. Her happiness was more important than his own.

Nate turned into the foundation parking lot. His heart sank when he didn't see her Fiat. He thought about going in. Maybe they would know where she was. But then he'd get caught up talking to Spencer and Mark and he didn't have time for that.

The Buick lumbered out and he headed towards Kaitlyn's. She had to know where Tina was.

Nate twisted his head, easing out the tension in his neck. He couldn't stop his fingers from tapping on the steering wheel. *Come on you old hunk of junk.* What was he going to say to her when he found her? Maybe she'd go on a walk with him. He'd apologize first. And tell her about seeing his dad. And make sure she knew he had taken her advice.

And tell her he loved her.

He parked in front of Kaitlyn's house and ran to the door. Kaitlyn answered. Her brown curly hair tumbled around her shoulders. A fitted knit top showcased her growing bump.

"Nate? What are you doing here? I thought you were in New York."

"I was. My mom had a stroke. I'm looking for Tina. Do you know where she is? I thought she would be at the foundation, but she's not."

"Did you text her?"

The corner of her lips tipped up. Was she enjoying his pain?

"No." Nate looked down. "I wasn't sure she'd respond."

"Why don't you come in. You can catch me up on what's going on in your life."

Kaitlyn opened the door wider and stepped aside.

"I don't want to be rude, but I need to see Tina. Do you know where she is or not?"

"Actually, I'm not sure. She goes to your mom's every other Thursday, but since your mom is still in the hospital, she wouldn't be there. Come on in."

Did he just hear her right? Why would Tina be going to his mom's house? If she had treated him like he'd done to her, he wouldn't think of doing something for her dad, even as much as he liked him.

Nate followed Kaitlyn into the kitchen where she poured him a cup of coffee and offered him a slice of freshly baked pumpkin bread. Kaitlyn took out her phone and spoke a message.

<Tina, where are you? I've got someone here who's dying to see you.>

She set her phone down.

"I lied Nate. When I said I thought you were in New York. Tina told me she saw you. She was pretty upset. What's the story? Out with it."

She checked her phone for a return message. Nothing.

"Did she tell you why I left?"

Nate stared at his treat. His coffee sat untouched, becoming tepid.

"Yeah, that you hit your dad and was afraid you'd turn into him. But really, Nate? Just taking off and abandoning her? That was rude. It was just plain cruel!"

Nate drew circles around salt that had spilled on the table.

"I was so scared. I thought that leaving was the most loving thing to do."

"So, you do love her."

"Was there ever any doubt?"

"Well yeah, when you left without a word."

Kaitlyn checked her phone again.

<Who? I'm just finishing grocery shopping. I'll come over when I'm done.>

Kaitlyn showed it to Nate. He breathed a sigh of relief. And then anxiety punched him again.

<Nate>

"I guess this will be the deciding factor. Either she'll come, or she'll hide."

Kaitlyn set her phone down.

"Listen, Bub. If you think you want to win her back, you're going to have to convince her you love her. And you have to move back here. She has to know that you'll sacrifice for her. That she's everything to you."

"I already thought about that. I can't expect her to leave her friends and her job. And she'd die without being here for you and your baby."

Kaitlyn patted her belly and leaned her head down towards it.

"You want your Auntie Tina here with you, don't you?"

A little chuckle escaped her lips.

"Tell me about your mom. Is she going to be okay?"

"She had a stroke. Her speech wasn't affected, thank goodness. But her hand and foot are paralyzed."

Nate was grateful to have been able to have the heart-to-heart with her.

"Tina has enjoyed getting to know Loretta. I'm sure you saw how she got her house all cleaned up. That was a chore."

"That was Tina?"

Nate pulled his head back, confused.

"I was shocked that it was so clean. I had wanted to get her a housekeeper, but she always refused."

"Well, Tina thinks your mom is just a doll. If you manage to get things worked out with her, I'm sure she'd be glad to have Loretta for a mother-in-law."

Kaitlyn winked.

Nate and Kaitlyn startled as the front door slammed open and Tina marched in.

Chapter Forty-Seven

Tina stomped in and leaned against the wall. Nate stood, arms limp looking at his feet.

"Well?" Tina crossed her arms. If looks could kill.

"I needed to see you, Tina. A lot has happened since I saw you at the hospital."

Nate put his hands in his pockets. There was an undertone of tension.

"I think you guys should go for a nice walk. Catch up. Find a place to watch the sunset. I think I'll go take a nap. Baby and I need to rest," Kaitlyn said and left.

Nate raised his eyebrows questioningly towards Tina. She gave an imperceptible nod and headed to the door.

Tina didn't notice that the spring air was comfortable. Or that the skies were a beautiful blue and slight breeze caught her hair. On any other day, she and Kaitlyn would have rejoiced in the longer days and hope for summer. But today, she was here with Nate. She longed to have the relationship they had six months ago. But if that were to happen, he had a lot of explaining to do. She took off at a fast clip.

"I did what you told me I should do," Nate began. "My dad checked into rehab and I went to see him."

He took her advice? Tina side-eyed him. She wasn't ready to give him the satisfaction of looking at her full on. He might stare into her eyes and that would undo her.

"I didn't expect the place to be like a house. It was really beautiful."

They moved to the side as a couple with a leashed box terrier passed them.

"Anyway, I was surprised. My dad was clean shaven and had a buzz cut. I've never seen him look so good. He wasn't even jittery like that night."

Tina hoped this was going to be a happily ever after story. She wasn't sure she could take it if it weren't.

"He," Nate faltered and swallowed. "He told me he was sorry. I wanted to believe him, but I told him what it was like growing up with him. I just didn't feel like him telling me he was sorry was enough. I'm ashamed to say it was a verbal attack."

Tina felt her shoulders relax.

"I guess I felt that way talking to my dad, at first," Tina said. "It's hard to open up and tell someone about the pain you endured. You're not sure you can trust them."

Nate nodded.

"True. He told me he had been doing alright until he lost his job and he started drinking and that led to meth. He told me my grandfather, who I never knew, had been the same way and all I could think was that I was right—it was possible for the same attributes to be passed down to me."

"A person always has a choice, Nate. You don't have to make the same bad choices that he made."

Nate's pace slowed.

"Tina," Nate stopped and faced her. "He fell to his knees

and begged me to forgive him. Then those words on the wall at Mercy blasted into my mind—you probably know which ones — *Show compassion and mercy*. And suddenly forgiving seemed an easy thing to do. It was like the wall crumbled. I'm not sure I can even adequately describe it."

"Zechariah 7:9."

Nate looked at her, eyebrows raised.

"It's the scripture—where that's found in the Bible."

Maybe God *had* answered her prayers. She hadn't imagined Him popping His word into Nate's mind. But hey, He was a big God, and nothing was impossible.

"It's going to take some time building a relationship," Tina said.

Not just with Alvin, but with her, if that was where he was going.

"I know. But I think I'm ready to work on that."

They crossed the street to the park. Two little girls sat on swings, their legs dangling as a teenager pushed them. A soccer team was practicing. Tina smiled, remembering when she and Kaitlyn had been on the team in first grade. She longed for those easy days.

Nate sat down on a bench. Tina joined him leaving space between them. She closed her eyes and let herself sink into the moment. She started to relax.

"Tina." Nate ran his hand through his hair. "I know I was a real jerk. Leaving like that. I thought I was doing the right thing."

He flicked his gaze at her.

"Nice that you can admit that you were a jerk. I'd say more like an idiot or an imbecile."

The corner of her mouth turned up.

"Tell me about your job."

Tina wasn't ready to let her heart enter that territory yet.

"It's been good. New York is fast paced. And noisy. Busses, taxis, subways. There were a group of guys on the sidewalk under my apartment blasting their music and singing karaoke at like three in the morning. It's crazy. But the people I work with are very focused and on top of the latest research. I've learned a lot. But…"

Tina glanced up at him. His brows knit together.

"But?"

"As hard as I tried to forget you," he added hesitantly, "I can't. Your face is always in my mind. Your laughter. The sparkle in your eyes." His eyes stared at the ground. "Tina, I'm sorry I hurt you. You didn't deserve that."

Tina found herself holding in her breath. They fell into a long silence. The sun was setting, and vibrant golden rays shone through the pink clouds.

"I was ready to follow you to New York. It would have made a lot of changes for me. Ones I wasn't sure that I wanted to make. But I would have followed you because I knew that you had accepted a prestigious position and fulfilled your dream." Tina said. She let out a long breath.

Nate reached for her hand.

"I love you Tina. And I don't want you to leave everything for me. I love my job. But you are more important to me than anything. A job is a job. It's not a relationship. It's not what I want to be married to."

Tina's fingers gripped his hand.

"And what *would* you like to be married to?"

She flashed an impish grin.

Nate turned toward her and cupped her face in his hands.

"It's not a what. It's a who."

He moved his thumbs to caress her lips.

Tina was overcome and laughed through her tears.

"Are you asking me to marry you?"

Nate slid his hands to the back of her neck and pulled her into a soft kiss. He pulled back and held her gaze.

"Yes. Yes I am."

He wiped a tear from her cheek with his thumb.

Tina's mind flew a million miles an hour. He would move back home for her? Had his house sold? Did he have to give up a lease in New York? He'd be here for his mom. That was good. And his dad. He'd have to find another job. Probably wouldn't be that hard, considering his prestigious award. Her dad would be okay with this, right? They'd have to start planning a wedding. Before Kaitlyn was due? Or after? Would she want to wear a bridesmaid's dress while pregnant? Maybe wait until her baby was old enough to be a ring bearer.

Nate looked at his watch.

"How long do I have to wait for an answer? Should I be nervous?"

"No. I mean yes. I mean no, you don't have to be nervous. And yes. Yes! I will marry you!"

She stood and pulled Nate to his feet. She clasped her hands around his shoulders and let her lips fall into his for a lingering kiss.

I do love him— the way he smells, the feel of his thick hair through my fingers, and the way the world feels brighter when he's near.

"I've missed you Nate Bronson."

Tina melted into his arms. Yeah. She could live every day of her life with his smile.

Chapter Forty-Eight

Kaitlyn lay on the couch, absorbed in a novel when Nate and Tina entered arm in arm.

"How's your book?" Nate asked.

Kaitlyn looked up and held up a finger.

"Hold on, I have to finish this page."

Nate melted in the smile Tina gave him. He sat down in the armchair, pulled Tina onto his lap and waited.

"Did you two have a nice walk?" Kaitlyn waggled her eyebrows.

"Actually, yes. We got a few things worked out," Tina said.

Luke came in through the back door wearing coveralls covered in paint smears and sawdust.

"Nate. Tina. When did you get here?"

He walked over to Kaitlyn and gave her a quick kiss. What was it about Luke that made him so gentle? So self-assured? Nate wanted to be more like that.

"Just now. What have you been up to?"

Tina moved to the floor where she leaned against Nate's chair between his sprawled-out legs. Nate ran his fingers through her hair, loving the fragrance.

"I've been in the shop—working on a cradle."

He looked at Kaitlyn, a broad smile filling his face.

"Luke learned to carve. You should see it! It's a work of art."

Kaitlyn sat up.

"Wait, I thought you were in New York. Are you here for a visit?" Luke asked.

Nate squeezed Tina's shoulders. "My mom had a stroke. The hospital called and they wouldn't send her home until I found a caregiver for her."

Luke stroked his chin. "I might be able to find someone for you. Healthy Kids works with refugees and a lot of them are skilled and looking for work."

"Really? That would be an answer to prayer."

Nate couldn't believe he just said that—an answer to prayer? He was sounding more like Tina every day.

"So," Tina looked at Kaitlyn. "Nate asked me to marry him," she said nonchalantly. "Does he meet with your approval?"

Nate held his breath. This was a make it or break it moment. If Kaitlyn didn't approve, he was toast.

Kaitlyn squealed and looked at Luke. Then skipped over to Tina and held her hands out to pull her up. They fell into an excited embrace. Kaitlyn held her at arm's length.

"I assume you said yes!"

Watching them brought a warmth to Nate he didn't know he had. How could he have thought of leaving this behind? Their friendship was unique. He hoped he could develop that same intimacy with Tina. Not to take Kaitlyn's place. He could never, would never take her place. No. He just wanted that type of relationship. To have Tina as his best friend for the rest of his life.

Kaitlyn turned to Nate and held up her *mom* finger.

"You need to know, mister, that if you should *ever* hurt my friend again, you will be banished from the kingdom."

Nate put his hand on his heart, his face serious.

"Repeat after me," Kaitlyn said. "I, Nate."

"I, Nate."

"Do solemnly swear."

"Do solemnly swear."

"To *never* ever say an unkind word, cause distress or harm Tina in any way ever again."

Nate couldn't help but let out a chuckle and repeated after her. He gazed at Tina.

Tina smirked.

"And I will provide Kaitlyn with brownies whenever her little heart desires."

Nate raised an eyebrow.

"What? I was collateral damage in this whole mess." Kaitlyn's hand went to her hip.

Nate grimaced.

"And I will provide Kaitlyn with brownies whenever her little heart desires."

That was a big ask, but one which he was determined to succeed at. He couldn't live through being responsible for breaking their hearts again.

Nate followed Tina to the shop where he left the old Buick to be serviced. He knew his mom wasn't going to ever drive it again, but at least it would be ready for the caregiver. He jumped into Tina's Fiat and they drove by his house. She pulled into the driveway and he phoned the realtor, asking him to take the house off the market. Together they lifted the sign off the hook and placed it in the garage.

"This is okay, isn't it?" Nate's eyebrows met. "Or would you rather I sold it and we picked something out together?"

It struck him that he was not going to be alone anymore. Decisions should be decided upon jointly.

Tina put her hands on her hips and looked over the house.

"I guess I could get used to it. That is if you'd let me paint the walls— white isn't my personal favorite. And it's big enough for game nights. That's a plus."

"I'll do whatever you want, babe." Nate grinned.

They drove towards the hospital. Nate's shoulders tightened when he passed the emergency entrance, memories flashing through his mind of that horrible night. He gave his head a shake. A lot had happened since that night. This was the start of a new beginning. He needed to look forward, not back.

Loretta was sitting up in the bed when they entered her room.

"Hey mom, how are you doing?"

"Nate. And Tina?" She lifted her eyebrows in surprise.

"Come in. Sit down." She pushed the remote towards Nate. He took the cue and turned down the TV.

"Hi Loretta. We have some good news for you."

Loretta looked up expectantly.

"You should get to go home in a few days. My friend Luke has someone to care for you when you go home." Tina took Loretta's hand.

"I don't need no one to take care of me. I can get by just fine by myself." Tina looked at Nate.

"Mom, you can't hardly walk and your hand…"

Loretta pursed her lips and glared at him.

"They won't let you go home unless you have someone with you. Nate can't be there for you all the time. And if you fell, you could break a hip and that would spell disaster." Tina patted her hand.

"Mom let's give it a try. If you don't sync with this person, we'll get someone else."

Nate knew she was stuck in her ways but hadn't expected this response. He changed the subject.

"Ready to hear some real exciting news?"

"It can't be better than going home, now, could it?"

Nate looked at Tina.

"I've asked Tina to marry me." His lips formed a huge smile. It seemed like that was happening a lot.

"Well now, ain't that something. Tina's a nice girl, son. You made a good choice." She nodded at Nate. "You be good to her, now. I won't put up with you hurting her."

"I'll keep him in line, don't you worry," Tina said.

"There's something else I want to tell you. I went to see dad in rehab." Loretta shifted to sit up straighter. "We had a good talk. I wanted to thank you for encouraging me to do that."

"That's good. Real good. I'm proud of you."

Nate let out the breath he had been holding.

"And as soon as I'm able to move back, I'm going to work on our relationship."

There were so many reasons to return home. Life seemed to be falling into place.

Nate set out plates and silverware. They were expecting Mark to show up at Tina's for dinner. He couldn't deny that he was feeling nervous. It wasn't like he didn't get along with Mark. But he *had* ditched his daughter. He wasn't sure what facing Papa Bear would be like.

Nate came up from behind and wrapped his arms around Tina, clasping his nervous hands on her waist as she stirred the bubbling gravy on the stove. Tina leaned her head back against him and he kissed the top of her head.

"Did you talk to your boss yet?"

"No. My flight is on Sunday. I'll go back and tell her on Monday and see what it takes to get out of my lease."

"How do you think she'll react?" Nate released her and leaned against the counter, his legs crossed at the ankles.

"Probably won't be happy. But a guy's gotta do what he's gotta do. I've already started scouting out jobs in Portland."

Tina opened the oven and checked the roast.

"Smells good in here. Wish I were staying for dinner, but Daniel and I have a date," Miya said and opened the front door. "Oh, hi Mark." She stood aside and let him in. "Later." She wiggled her fingers and stepped out.

"Nate? Are you here on vacation? I wasn't expecting to see you." Mark held his hand out. They shook and he patted Nate on the shoulder.

"I had to come back for my mom. She's in the hospital with a stroke." Nate looked at Tina. "And I needed to mend some fences."

Mark raised an eyebrow.

"Hi daddy." Tina gave him a bear hug.

"What's cooking? Smells good."

Tina set the roast on the table and poured the gravy in a small pitcher.

"Your mom would be so proud of you, Tina. " Mark turned to Nate. "How's that job going? Learning a lot?"

"Yes. It's been great. Those researchers are the best in the nation." Nate caught Tina's eye and held it. "I'll be looking for a new job however."

"You will? Was it grant funded?" Mark dug into his twice baked potato.

"No. But, well, I asked your daughter if she'd marry me. That is if you approve." Nate sucked in his lips.

"And I said yes, dad!" Tina beamed.

"And you're moving back? Why that's wonderful." He held out his hand. "Welcome to the family, son."

Marrying Tina would be amazing enough on its own. But Nate could see that Tina came with a package deal. Her dad and close friends would become his as well. He would be surrounded by those who would help him on this journey called life. It would be a road he no longer traveled alone.

Epilogue

Two Years Later

Tina ran the vacuum over the living room floor. She had finished the bedrooms, mopped the kitchen floor and tidied up. She stopped to sweep a stray lock of hair out of her face and locked it in place with a hairpin.

Ultimately, Tina realized that her worth was not found in her relationship to others, but in who God sees her as— beautiful, whole and worthy of His love and redemption.

Kaitlyn would be arriving in an hour to help get ready for Bible study. The study had been Nate's idea. Who would have guessed? Being surrounded by Spencer and Luke and Tina's friends, Nate had realized that the something different he saw in them was something he longed for.

Tina puffed up the pillows on the comfy couch. Nate had kept his stark pristine white couch, but Tina had insisted on a comfy, snuggle-under-a-quilt-and-read-a-book couch as well. The red upholstery contrasted with the deep teal focus wall she had painted. And Nate's colorful painting blended in perfectly.

Taking a feather duster, she brushed around their wedding photo sitting on the mantle above the gas fireplace. She picked it up. Her dad had dug around in the closet and found her mom's wedding dress, carefully preserved in layers of tissue in a sealed tub.

When Kaitlyn had watched Tina try it on, she squealed with delight at the perfect fit. Off the shoulder neckline and crisp seams down the bodice flattered her figure at the waist. It then transformed with slight pleats into a soft ball gown skirt that floated with every step down the aisle.

She had removed her mom's locket, the first time since she had died and allowed Nate to replace it with a silver locket of his own—his photo on one side and her mom's on the other.

The whole wedding had been magical.

Nate's pinstriped tux and flashy red tie, so out of character for his serious nature, had made her smile. Little Claire had toddled her way down the aisle tossing rose petals. She had stopped halfway down, bouncing up and down to the music, to the amusement of all.

Her dad had walked her down the aisle, arm in arm. His warmth encouraged her, completed her.

The highlight was when, after Nate had said how much he cherished her and she had vowed her lifelong love to him, he kissed her, and the whole front of the church instantly lit up, twinkling with hundreds of tiny white Christmas lights.

Tina gazed at her ring and smiled. She had just set the photo down when she heard a quick knock and the front door opened.

"We're here!" Kaitlyn held Claire, her little legs wrapped around her mom's waist. Tina took the diaper bag as Claire wiggled her way to the floor.

She ran directly to Chuck's cage and started to open the door.

"Claire Kristina! Stop! Remember, no hands."

Tina interjected, "Chuck doesn't like it when you get too close."

Claire obediently sat down, eyes glued to the chinchilla.

"I got out the ingredients for the cheesecake. The cream cheese is already softened."

Tina led Kaitlyn to the kitchen where bowls, utensils and the springform pan sat waiting.

"How was your day?" Tina asked.

"Full, as usual. I picked Claire up from the sitter after work. I think she's getting a new tooth. She was a little cranky. Anyway, Luke will be here soon. He had to finish up a few things at work." Kaitlyn unwrapped the cream cheese and put it in the bowl along with eggs and sugar.

Claire heard the sound of the mixer and came running. "Up!" she held out her hands and Tina set her on the counter. "I help."

"Yes, you can, sweet pea." Tina touched her nose with her finger.

"How's Nate's job going?"

"He's loving it. He seems to have learned a whole lot in his short time in New York and says his research buddies appreciate what he's brought to the table. I think he'd love any job where he could find a solution."

Kaitlyn handed the spatula to Claire to lick the remains after she poured it into the pan.

The oven bell dinged and she set it on the rack. Tina handed Kaitlyn a wet washrag to wipe Claire's little hands and set her on the floor.

The door opened. "Hey honey, I'm home." Nate came in, slipped off his shoes and gave Tina a kiss.

"I'm sorry I'm a little late. I stopped by mom's to check on her." He shook his head. "I still can't believe that she let my dad move back in with her. I tell you, he's a changed man."

Tina smiled. "Starting to believe in miracles, are you?"

Nate nodded. "Sure am."

Claire ran over to him and jumped up and down.

"Unka Nate! Up!"

Nate laughed as he picked her up and swung her around till she wiggled down giggling.

Luke walked in with a bag of chips and dip.

"Hey Claire, Nate got you all wound up, didn't he? Come give daddy a hug."

She ran over and wrapped her arms around him.

"The others should be here shortly."

Tina stepped back and watched. She was surrounded by all the people she loved. Living life. Living their faith. A living hope.

Afterword

I hope you enjoyed Book 2 of the Mercy Series.
Watch for Book 3

The Way to My Heart

Chapter 1

Peter Gunderson's fingers held the top of his locker door, unable to let go. His eyes searched the empty space one last time. He removed the Yoda sticker from the door and latched it shut. A grin crept up as *that log had a child* snuck into his mind.

The We'll-Miss-You sign, colored in by Kaitlyn McCarthy and Tina Halverson was taped to the wall. He couldn't help but smile as his eyes slid over the various items he'd been so familiar with the last three years— stethoscopes, blood pressure cuffs, IV poles, syringes. All symbols of times of caring. Times of pranks. Peter swallowed the lump in his throat.

Daniel Wright pulled him close, his elbow crooked around Peter's neck.

"Stay out of trouble!"

He released him. *Like he was going to get into any trouble now without the Invincibles.*

He pulled off his name tag and key card and laid them next to his vocera on the desk.

"You know they'll always take you back. You know, like if you change your mind," Kaitlyn said.

Peter thought back to the many mistakes he had made in the past three years. *Nah, taking me back was never gonna happen.*

He shrugged on his Carhart jacket over his scrubs that Kaitlyn's mom had made for him, covered in John Deere tractors, and started down the hall.

"Game night at my house Tuesday," Tina called.

He turned and gave her a slight nod, knowing that that part of his life was behind him.

♥ ♥ ♥

Outside he looked up one last time at the lighted Mercy Hospital sign, placed his helmet on his head and hopped on his motorcycle. He started his old friend and sped away.

He needed to get home to his mom. Her fibromyalgia was preventing her from the passions of her life, and he wasn't going to let anything interfere with being there for her. This time.

He sped down I-5 thankful that it wasn't raining and not much traffic. What could he have done for her, really, when their house burned? He had been finishing his final studies for the NCLEX and there was no way he could leave. Well, now he'd make up for it. She'd see.

AFTERWORD

─── ♥ ♥ ───

Olivia Olsen hopped off her 4-wheeler and dusted off her jeans. She scanned the field.

"Evelyn?"

"Over here!" Her hair was covered with a straw hat, and she held pruners in gloved hands. Olivia strode over to her. "I could use some help. These dahlias need to be deadheaded."

Olivia breathed in the fragrant blooms, snagged a pair of pruners from the shed and started clipping. She reached high above her head to the fading pinks and yellows. She gazed across the long rows of breathtaking beauty.

Evelyn had such talent with things that grew. And everyone in the valley knew it too. They came from miles around for photo shoots and to buy her beautiful blooms and produce. Gunderson Farms had even been listed online as one of the top growers.

Evelyn looked up. "Why are the chickens squawking? Seems like they're all riled up."

Olivia turned to look where chickens were scattered everywhere. A loose pig was running through them, with the border collie, Ruby, on his heels.

"Oh no! I'll go see what I can do."

She set down her clippers and ran toward the wayward animal. She gave a whistle, and Ruby crouched down. The pig stopped, put his head down to snuffle in the grass. Olivia walked quietly towards him, but as soon as he looked up, he took off again, followed by Ruby, crouching down to herd the wayward pig.

"Ruby, you're worthless when it comes to pigs!"

AFTERWORD

Jake rounded the corner. "Hey, what's going on? Here, let me help you!"

He ran towards them. Olivia walked slowly towards the back of the pig which had stopped again. He snorted as his nose grubbed in the grass. Olivia gave a lunge and grabbed its hind leg, skidding along behind him. Jake strode over.

"Here, I've got him."

Olivia gave him a scalding look that would cause a ripe cornstalk to instantly shrivel. It was enough to make him hold up his hands in surrender.

Peter pulled up and parked in the driveway. He removed his helmet and replaced it with a ball cap. The smell of fresh cut hay caught him. In the distance, he could see his father on the John Deere slowly making his way in circles, the mower leaving cut golden alfalfa laying strewn behind it.

He remembered sitting on that tractor on his dad's lap, learning the ways of the machine.

"You start the engine like this," his dad would say. "Be careful not to...."

He was allowed to choose the music in the glassed-in cab—Raffi or sometimes KidSongs. They would change the words and sing

Bumping up and down in our big green tractor, till our work is done.

The tractor would hum its way through the fields.

Peter had been glad there had been a commotion and no one had looked up as he approached. He could surprise his mom this way. He scanned the flower field and saw his mom's sunhat. It took only a few

Olivia. Right where he would expect her to be— in the middle of some pandemonium. He watched the pig scenario. Ruby squatting on the ground, black ears back and eyes eager. Olivia grabbing the pig's hind leg as it squealed to high heaven.

Jake jumping in to save the damsel. Olivia giving him that look. Jake holding up both hands in surrender, frowning and shaking his head.

Peter crossed his arms and let out a chuckle. Oh, that girl could be feisty. And obviously, Jake didn't know her like he did. Stepping in to help a woman who could manage herself? Well, that was downright suicide.

He turned back to the flower field and searched for his mom. Seeing her standing between two rows of red and purple mums, he snuck up behind her and put his arms around her waist. She jumped and turned.

"Peter! What are you doing here?"

She grabbed hold of his forearms. "Taking a day off?"

"Hi mama." He grinned. "More than a day off. I quit my job today and am going to stay here and help you and dad out."

She waved her hand like she was swatting flies. "You quit your job? Why in the world would you do that? Nursing is a good job!"

"Yeah, I know. The patients will be better off without me. It's really not my jam. I wasn't really cut out for it anyway. I'd be better off being here with you guys taking some of the load off."

He moved his hands to her shoulders, holding her eyes.

"And you and I both know that your health isn't that great. I want to be here to help you do as much as you can, so you're not overwhelmed."

"Does Ross know you're here?"

Peter squinched up his nose, making his eyes wrinkle.

"Okay—so obviously you and your dad have been scheming. Well, judging by the sun, it must be getting close to dinner time. Let's go see what can wrestle up."

About the Author

Jan Johnson has been writing since fourth grade when she wrote and her dad published The Little Red Man, a space story. That was back in the day when we were all sure aliens lived on Mars.

Jan lives on a sheep farm in Brownsmead, Oregon a mile from the Columbia River with her husband Ed. Don't mistake living on a farm as meaning she likes animals. Well, she actually does— from a distance.

She's passionate about building relationships, meeting new people and hearing their stories. You know what they say—Love God, Love people.

When she isn't writing, starting something new, or podcasting, she catches up with her ten children who are scattered hither and yon.

Connect with me at www.jan-johnson.com

facebook.com/janreajohnson
instagram.com/janreajohnson

CPSIA information can be obtained
at www.ICGtesting.com
Printed in the USA
JSHW080926280523
42285JS00002B/4